Praise for *The End of the World is Flat*

'In between punching the air and shouting "yes!", I laughed so hard
I nearly fell in my cauldron. A masterpiece'
Julie Bindel

'A bracingly sharp satire on the sleep of reason and the tyranny of
twaddle. Simon Edge reveals how extraordinary delusions have the
power to captivate us – until, one by one, we start coming to our
senses'
Francis Wheen

'Without mercy, this merry romp punctures the idiocy that would
turn language and good sense upside down and try to divide us all
into either true believers or bigots. It's a frightening reminder of
what happens when we reject the power of dialogue'
Simon Fanshawe

'A highly-entertaining satire about ideology, social media
manipulation, and lobbying fiefdoms that have overstayed their
welcome. This is *Animal Farm* for the era of gender lunacy, with
jokes – and, right now, we all need a laugh'
Jane Harris

'This book is very, very funny. It's also way too convincing as a
horror story – Simon Edge writes a completely believable account
of how this kind of ideology could seep into great institutions. And
possibly, in another form, did'
Gillian Philip

'A satire that skewers the insanity of gender-identity ideology with
the wit and brilliance of a modern-day Swift'
Helen Joyce

Simon Edge read philosophy at Cambridge and was editor of the revered London paper *Capital Gay* before becoming a gossip columnist on the *Evening Standard* and then, for many years, a feature writer on the *Daily Express*. He is the author of four previous novels. He was married to Ezio Alessandroni, who died of cancer in 2017. He lives in Suffolk.

THE END
OF THE
WORLD
IS
FLAT

SIMON EDGE

Lightning Books

Published in 2021
by Lightning Books Ltd
Imprint of Eye Books Ltd
29A Barrow Street
Much Wenlock
Shropshire
TF13 6EN

www.lightning-books.com

Cover by Ifan Bates
Typeset in Bembo, 18th Century and Helvetica Neue

British Library Cataloguing in Publication Data
A catalogue record for this book is available from the British Library.

Printed by CPI Group (UK) Ltd, Croydon CR0 4YY

ISBN: 9781785632402

A time is coming when men will go mad,
and when they see someone who is not mad,
they will attack him, saying,
'You are mad; you are not like us'
St Anthony the Great

For Allison, Gillian, Julie, Marion, Maya and Rachel.
Heretical globularists all

PART ONE

The admiral knelt before the crucifix that he'd attached to the bulkhead of his cabin and began to pray.

'Lord God Almighty, send me a fair wind, I beseech you, that our little fleet may voyage safely across the Ocean Sea and claim the bounty of the Indies for your glory, and for that of your noble servants, their Catholic majesties. Put courage in the hearts of the men of our three ships, for I know they lack it. Watch over us as we plot a course that no man has ever sailed.'

And help me prove wrong that sneering, self-regarding sack of hot air they call the Bishop of Avila, he wanted to add, but his eminence no doubt also had the ear of the Lord. If the admiral asked God to choose between them, he was in danger of emerging the loser. Better not to mention the bishop. Success would speak for itself when the time came.

Despite his success in persuading the Queen of Spain to back his voyage, his own humiliation before the learned council, five years earlier, still rankled.

As the promoter of an adventurous scheme that turned so much popular wisdom on its head, he had long grown used to ridicule. He expected urchins to tap their temples as he passed them in the street, mocking him: the famous madman who believed the earth was round. But he had hoped for better from the professors and the elders of the Church who gathered at the Dominican convent in Salamanca to hear his case and report back to their majesties.

Their attitude to him was downright childish. He could see them frowning and nudging each other – 'what did he say?' – in a pantomime display of not understanding his Spanish. His Genoese accent was strong, he knew that, and his grammar admittedly chaotic, but he had spent his adult life making himself understood to Spaniards, from the lowest cabin boy to Queen Isabella herself. If they could understand him, so could these greybeard professors and shaven-headed monks. They did it for effect, to knock his confidence. They followed his Spanish only too well when he started challenging their beloved superstitions. At that point, they brought out their whole arsenal of arguments.

'Are you seriously asking us to believe there's a part of the world where everything is inverted?' scoffed a professor of mathematics from Cordoba. 'Where the trees grow downwards and the rain falls up?'

In vain did he try to explain Aristotle's concept of gravity, that an object would always fall to the earth. These wise men did not want to hear such things from a rough, ignorant sailor.

More objections followed. 'Even if you could sail down

over the horizon to India, surely the gradient would be too steep for you to sail back up again?' That was a friar, one of their hosts.

'These countries on the bottom of the world – where are they mentioned in the Bible?' croaked the elderly Archdeacon of Leon, his finger trembling as he pointed it accusingly at their petitioner. 'If they're inhabited by men, those men cannot be descended from Adam. And that, sir, is heresy!'

All the while, the man of the sea attempted to maintain his dignity, but it was difficult, particularly as he watched the face of the bishop, the arbiter of the council, who would relay its verdict to their majesties. Avila made no secret of his scorn, hear-hearing louder, nodding more vigorously than anyone. At the mention of heresy, his eyes shone with the light of the Inquisition.

Years of delay ensued. The navigator was forced to trail around Spain after their majesties, watching the bishop, his nemesis, drip ignorant warnings into the queen's ear: the scheme was vain and impossible; her majesty should do what the King of Portugal had done and send the Genoese rogue packing; it would degrade the dignity of the crown to lavish honours on a stranger with no name or reputation.

No name? Cristobal Colón was a decent enough moniker. It wasn't quite the one he was born with, but he had made it more Spanish so that it tripped more easily off their majesties' tongues. And now, at last, he had a splendid title to go with it. Grand Admiral of the Ocean Sea, no less, even before they had cast off or sailed a single league across that water. Because, in the end, the queen had ignored the Bishop of Avila and his council, and said yes to Colón. She had given him three ships and her blessing. The western route to the Indies was his to secure, to justify her faith in him.

Light was beginning to enter his cabin through the thick panes of glass at the stern. It was time to give the order. The admiral made the sign of the cross, heaved himself to his feet – after so many years of waiting, he was an old man of forty-two, with stiff knees to prove it – and strode out onto the deck. The captain of the *Santa Maria* awaited his nod, which the signal officer would relay to the captains of the *Pinta* and the *Niña*.

Let the adventure commence.

1

From her doorway, Mel Winterbourne watched Shane, her deputy, with interest. He was waiting impatiently next to the printer, shifting from one foot to the other and grabbing each page as soon as it appeared, virtually pulling the paper from the rollers, rather than letting it drop into the output tray. Mel had worked in an office environment long enough to spot a colleague printing documents on the sly.

She'd been trying to wean herself off teasing him, but he presented too easy a target. She set off for a casual walk around the office. Focused on his task, he didn't notice her sidle up behind him. A few inches from his ear, she said softly: 'Printing out your CV, Shane?'

His entire body jerked with shock as he spun to face her, the blood rushing to his cheeks. He was half a head shorter than Mel, stocky, with cropped hair and a full Victorian beard.

'No,' he said. He grabbed the papers he'd printed so far and clutched them to his barrel chest. 'It's just…erm…a report.'

'Honestly, it doesn't bother me either way,' she said. 'There's no law against applying for jobs.'

'But I'm not app—'

She turned away, brushing off his denial, so he couldn't see how much amusement her ambush had given her. She wished she could see him squirm, but she'd have to make to do with the mental picture.

Mel meant what she said: she wouldn't have the slightest objection if he looked for another job. No reflection on his abilities: Shane Foxley was the perfect deputy – competent but unthreatening. Rather, the simple truth was that, if he found another job, she'd feel less guilty about her plan to shut the whole place down.

The same went for the whole team, presently hunched over mobiles or tapping quietly at keyboards. When she was their age, office life was all personal phone calls and yacking; this generation was so much more earnest and diligent. She really did wish them well, and it pained her to have to let them all go.

They would hate her for it, of course, but she'd never cared about popularity, and in the end they'd all be fine. In its twenty-year life, the Orange Peel Foundation had set a benchmark for effective single-issue campaigning, and other employers would fight over its staff. They would all get a decent severance package, too. That was the least Mel could do for them.

There were three dozen of them now, what with the part-timers and the job-sharers. It was a far cry from the one-woman operation she'd set up in her thirties, as a sideline from her day-job as a journalist.

At the time, she'd been deputy travel editor of the *Sunday Standard*. It would have been a wonderful gig, if only her boss hadn't grabbed all the plum trips for himself, leaving Mel to run the desk during his frequent absences. She spent all her time chasing copy, writing headlines and proof-reading spreads, while he swanked around the world's flashiest hotels. In the normal run, she'd have expected to inherit his job eventually, but he told anyone who'd listen that he wasn't going anywhere.

Then she had her big idea.

She got it from an item in the news pages of her own paper. Two English backpackers had gone missing during a trek across Australia and were initially feared dead. The drama dominated the UK front pages for the best part of a week, as an anxious nation feared the worst. Then the couple turned up safe and well. Asked at a press conference how they'd got so badly lost, the male of the pair explained that Australia was much bigger than it looked in an atlas. The duo promptly became a global laughing stock. Australia's Prime Minister was widely reported as saying: 'Couldn't the stupid Poms have looked at a bloody map?'

Without wishing to be a kill-joy, Mel could see their point. The ridiculed Brits had made a previous trip across Alaska, which looked as big as Australia on the traditional map of the world, but in reality was only a fifth of the size. They had indeed looked at a bloody map. That was the problem.

At the press conference, nobody mentioned the sixteenth-century Flemish cartographer Gerardus Mercator, but Mel knew enough about the history of map-making to identify his role in the story. The travellers' confusion derived from

Mercator's solution to the age-old problem of how to represent a spherical earth on a flat sheet of paper. He chose to treat the planet as if it were a cylinder, not a globe, so that lines of longitude which actually intersected at the poles became parallel. Displayed on every schoolroom wall, the Mercator projection made Greenland the size of South America, when it was really no bigger than Mexico. If the stupid Poms had tried to walk from Baffin Bay to the Greenland Sea, they might have been pleasantly surprised.

The projection's greatest absurdity was to make Antarctica look bigger than all the other continents put together. To divert attention from this unfortunate distortion, maps were often printed with most of Antarctica chopped off, so that the equator came two-thirds of the way down the page, rather than bisecting the map at its mid-point. That reinforced the sense, already entrenched in global power relations, that the northern hemisphere was more important than the south.

This much Mel had known already, but she began to read further into the subject, looking at why an alternative had never emerged.

Mercator's map had endured for nearly five centuries, she learned, because sailors liked it: the projection distorted areas and distances, but navigators could rely on it to send them in the right direction. That was what mattered most when you were trying not to get shipwrecked.

Nevertheless, many other cartographers had proposed solutions of their own. Mel learned to distinguish 'conic', 'cylindrical' and 'azimuthal' approaches, and to tell the difference between 'interrupted' and 'uninterrupted' projections. She came to understand that each rival map always had its own merit – representing shape, direction, distance or size accurately

– but none could ever get all those elements right. It wasn't that nobody had managed it yet; it was a mathematical impossibility, because there was no way the surface of a sphere would be rendered accurately in two dimensions.

But one approach, to Mel's eyes, came pretty close.

In an 'interrupted' projection, the surface of the globe was effectively unwrapped and laid out flat. The result was an accurate representation of the surface area and shape of the planet, but it didn't fit neatly into a rectangle, so it looked peculiar at first sight. The best-known example of this approach was nicknamed the 'orange-peel' projection, because it resembled the skin of an orange, carefully removed in one piece and then flattened out.

It was next to useless for sailors, because the interruptions in the map – the voids in the orange peel – were deliberately arranged to cut through oceans rather than land masses. For anyone else, it presented every country accurately and had the further merit of never letting the viewer forget the earth was a sphere, not a rectangle.

With the story of the lost Poms still in the news, Mel went to see her editor. She told him she wanted to tell the history of map projection from Ptolemy, the Greek mathematician who first described the problem in detail, to Mercator and beyond, with examples of why these abstruse cartographical arguments mattered.

The editor, a forty-a-day man who lived in dread of each week's sales figures, laughed in her face. 'I've been in this business a long time,' he wheezed, 'and I can tell you this: the word carto-sodding-graphical doesn't sell papers.'

Mel could see his point, and she kicked herself for messing up her pitch, but she refused to back down. 'Trust me, it doesn't need to be dull,' she insisted. 'Will you let me write it anyway? I'll do it on spec, entirely in my own time. Just give me a chance to show you how interesting I can make it.'

Armed with his grudging go-ahead, she pulled out all the stops to construct the feature. She persuaded Sir Beowulf Fitch, the aristocratic, chilblained polar explorer who happened to be an old family friend, to give her a quote. That, in turn, helped coax a contribution from Teddy Skillett, the heart-throb adventurer then hacking through the Amazon rainforest on BBC2. Both told her Mercator was more trouble than he was worth and should have been binned a couple of centuries ago.

She struck further gold when she secured a response from Cora Odell, the telegenic professor of geography famous for delivering a racy series of Reith lectures. 'Everyone agrees that Mercator needs updating,' Odell said, 'but squabbling map-makers haven't been able to unite around a suitable replacement.'

Finally, Mel quoted a primary-school headteacher from Hampshire – it was actually Rachel, one of her closest friends from university – who said people would always picture the world as they'd been taught to see it as kids, which was why it mattered to show it accurately from the outset. She added that she'd love the opportunity to teach a class about an orange-peel map: it conveyed a tricky concept in a fun way that children would love.

The celebrity names won Mel's editor over, but her diligent approach seemed to impress him too. For their part, the newspaper's designers made a good job of the layout, using vintage maps, seafaring portraits and a nice shot of an orange being peeled to create an appetising spread.

The subsequent postbag demonstrated that the subject had struck a chord. The *Standard* liked to put its name to crusades on a range of issues, from the legalisation of cannabis to courtesy titles for the same-sex partners of peers, and alongside them it unveiled the Orange Peel Campaign. Fitch and Skillett had already endorsed the call for the orange-peel projection to be taught in primary schools. The eponymous hosts of the kids' TV show *Zak 'n' Jack on da Box* now joined them, along with Dame Daphne Aduba, the iconic former presenter of *Play School*.

With Rachel's help, Mel prepared a lesson plan to introduce the orange-peel concept to youngsters. After a lot of fiddly work with a pair of sewing scissors, she managed to cut out a single piece of orange-coloured felt that could be wrapped around a globe, with no gaps or overlaps, and then spread on a flat surface. Rachel loved it, as did her colleagues who tested it in the classrooms. They all said Mel ought to get the continents printed on the felt and sell these shapes as an educational resource.

This took time and energy, but Mel discovered she enjoyed it far more than commissioning travel articles. A friend of her father's encouraged her to set up a charity, showing her how to apply for start-up funding. The procedure was daunting at first, but the advice and guidance were good, and within a year she was able to cast off from the *Standard* and pay herself a small salary as director and sole employee of the Orange Peel Foundation.

She worked twelve-hour days, but the rewards were great, as she persuaded first primary schools and then whole education authorities of the merits of her case. Rachel was right: demand for the orange-peel maps was strong. The resulting income meant Mel was able to employ staff: just one part-time assistant at first, who then became full-time, followed by a second colleague, and so on.

As the foundation grew, secondary schools asked for their own resource packs. Mel was in constant demand as a speaker, patiently explaining her own solution to the Mercator problem to everyone from WI groups to committees of MPs. She and her staff talked regularly to the media while also lobbying the publishers of maps and atlases. They engaged in international outreach too, re-peeling the orange to centre whichever country they planned to target.

As the charity matured, it developed a kitemark scheme called the Zest Badge, which proved to be an idea of genius. Every business and public body that wanted to show off its progressive, modern credentials could do so by demonstrating, for a small fee, that it was Orange Peel-compliant. It cost those participants peanuts relative to their turnover, but for the charity itself, the fees amounted to a handsome income.

Mel's proudest moment came, after fifteen years, when she went to Buckingham Palace to receive the MBE. As her guests, she took her parents, who treasured the video of the occasion. She was one of the few recipients of the honour ever to be invested by Prince Philip, and her own treasured memory was the Duke saying to her, with the merest flicker of a wink: 'I hear we gave you this for drawing maps on oranges.'

Much more recently, she had been summoned to meet a different kind of royalty: the leadership of Google in Silicon Valley, whom she'd spent years lobbying for a more modern approach to the digital maps on billions of mobile phones.

She appreciated that Google maps were meant for scrolling, in which context the odd-shaped voids in the orange peel would make no sense. Nonetheless, it was absurd that the world's most influential corporation continued to respect Mercator's distorted country sizes. The idea was to persuade them to consider using some other, more accurate projection.

At the suggestion of Xandra Cloudesley, her board chair, she invited Shane to go with her. 'No offence,' Xandra had said, 'but he's closer to their generation. You never know when a millennial might come in handy.'

Mel wasn't happy to be lumbered with Shane, but she was glad of the moral support, as well as one significant piece of input. On their way into the Googleplex, they passed a life-sized effigy of a T-Rex skeleton, which Shane had read was meant to be a reminder to all the company's staff of what happened to dinosaurs.

'Tell them Mercator is the T-Rex in this story,' he suggested.

It was a good idea, and she worked the line into her presentation. It seemed to work. The t-shirted executives responded appreciatively to her address. Some of them had already done enough homework to acknowledge that a problem existed. The meeting ended with a commitment on Google's part to commission a study into an alternative way of presenting their maps.

As they emerged from the building, Mel and Shane gaped

at each other in gleeful disbelief. Mel even allowed herself to be high-fived.

There was a downside, though. She knew, as they flew back across the Atlantic, that this was the beginning of the end. Once the Google study was under way, there would be little left for Orange Peel to do. She'd long believed it would be better to go out riding high on success, like the charity equivalent of *Fawlty Towers*, than to carry on for the sake of it, inventing new problems just to keep everyone employed. That would be fundamentally dishonest.

Even if it meant abolishing her own job, the most satisfying and authentic thing any campaigner could ever say was surely, 'My work here is done.'

That was the subject of her meeting with the trustees this afternoon.

The original big names – the Fitches, Skilletts and Adubas – were long gone, making way for a less starry but harder-headed board: City types who knew the ways of the world and were prepared to offer their professional expertise and wisdom in return for philanthropic cachet. At their helm was Xandra, founder and CEO of Hippo PR (because hippos were always depicted as smiley, lovable creatures, even though they were the most dangerous animals on earth). She exuded loud, camp fun but left no doubt that crossing her would be insanity. Mel had observed that tacit rule and had always found Xandra to be a supportive chair.

Mel's phone rang. It was the main reception desk downstairs, letting her know Ms Cloudesley was on her way up to the boardroom.

'Thanks,' she said, picking up the single hard copy of her

report on the dissolution of Orange Peel, which she'd printed out at home for confidentiality. That was a tip Shane ought to learn.

The boardroom was on the top floor of the building they shared with two smaller NGOs, an environmental consultancy, a graphic design studio and a teeth-whitening clinic, whose staff flashed dead-eyed smiles that smacked more of salesmanship than affability.

To her surprise, Shane stood waiting at the elevator doors, a brown A4 envelope in his hand. He was still looking shifty, trying to avoid her eye. It was her own fault: she must make more effort not to goad him. She assumed he was going out to post his secret letter and was surprised when he joined her going up.

'What floor?' she said, her hand hovering over the buttons.

'Same as you. Xandra asked me to come,' he added, seeing her raise her eyebrows. He looked at his watch, then started brushing lint off his lapel.

'Did she?' Mel shrugged as if it were no skin off her nose, but she was irritated. If Shane was in the room, how was she meant to make her confidential presentation on winding up the foundation? That was the main item on the agenda. What the hell was Xandra thinking?

The lift pinged as they reached the top floor. Maybe Mel could have a quiet word before the meeting started.

But Xandra was already in place at the head of the boardroom table. She inclined a cheek to be air-kissed. Her cheeks were her most striking feature. Her first face-lift had been subtle, taking years off her without looking obviously artificial, but the slope since then had been slippery: she'd had her nose narrowed, her lips widened and her cheeks filled, and the latest procedure had left her skin shinily taut over two improbable apple-mounds. Even though Mel knew to expect them, they shocked her every time she saw them. On these occasions, she always had a flash of worry that she'd say 'face' or 'nose' at some inappropriate moment, because those were the words in her head. Please let her not do it today, in front of Shane.

Three other people sat at the table. Damon Burch, on Xandra's left, was a merchant banker in his late thirties who took his board duties seriously, in what Mel assumed was a bid to keep himself human; if so, it was working. Next to him was Geena Holland, an old friend of Xandra's and a partner at one of the big accountancy firms. Geena had never given up smoking; she had a throaty cackle but was also a tough operator. Opposite Xandra at the bottom of the table was Cyrus Benjamin, a tech entrepreneur of around Damon's age who claimed to have become a millionaire at the age of twelve after launching a start-up in his bedroom. Mel had never entirely believed this, and the story had been entertainingly debunked in a recent best-selling account of the dot-com boom, but Cyrus had his uses. He'd played a valuable role in setting up their meeting in California. The only missing board member was Miranda Zappel, a corporate lawyer who had a habit of sending apologies.

'Miranda won't be joining us today, which means we're all here,' said Xandra, when Mel and Shane had taken their seats. 'I hope you don't mind my asking Shane to join us, Mel?'

She knew Xandra didn't care if she minded or not, but there was no point in showing her annoyance. 'Of course not. Why would I? Although Shane won't have seen the report I've sent you all, in which I set out my proposals going forward.'

'Going backward, I'd have said,' said Xandra. She glanced theatrically around the table, and Geena obliged with a smoky chuckle. 'It's hardly a vision for the future, is it?'

Blood rushed to Mel's face. It was going to be that kind of meeting, was it? 'We're a charity founded with specific objectives,' she said. 'We've achieved them more comprehensively than we ever dreamed possible. What are we supposed to do? Pretend we haven't achieved them, so we can carry on paying ourselves nice salaries?' This was much harder with Shane listening. She'd planned to find a better moment to break the news. 'As I say in my proposal, we've set the bar for successful single-issue campaigning. The name Orange Peel is now synonymous with smart, effective lobbying. I'm proud of that and I'll be even more proud if we can also make it synonymous with knowing when to leave the stage in a dignified way.'

'I'm afraid I'm not really a growing-old-gracefully kind of girl,' said Xandra. She held out her hand, and Shane leaned across the table to pass her the envelope he'd been carrying. She opened it and pulled out several copies of a stapled document. 'I certainly don't believe in turning my back on success. We've built something wonderful here and we're not shutting it down if we can help it. Not on my watch.' She slid one copy across to Mel, handing the others to Damon to pass round. 'This is another version of the future, which I asked Shane to write. Do have a glance at it. It contains an interesting proposal, made by one of Cyrus's Silicon Valley friends. Shane went to see him while the pair of you were in California, didn't you, Shane?'

He nodded awkwardly, not lifting his eyes from the notepad in front of him. He seemed as uncomfortable as Mel, but that didn't excuse him. Clearly, they'd been conspiring against her. Except perhaps Damon. Mel hoped she hadn't completely misjudged the banker with a soul.

She picked up the top sheet, which bore the heading:

Orange Peel Foundation
A new direction: programme for expansion

She raised an eyebrow. 'Expansion? I've nothing against expansion in principle. I'm the one, as I hope I don't need to remind you, who grew this organisation from nothing to where we are today. But what kind of new direction? We're not like a manufacturer, where you can simply come up with a new product line. We've expanded the orange-peel concept all over the world. Our work is literally done.'

'Actually Shane has discovered an unexpected but bold new route for the next stage of Orange Peel's journey,' said Xandra. 'Perhaps you'd like to explain it yourself, Shane?'

Shane looked like it was the last thing in the world he wanted to do, but no one refused Xandra. He cleared his throat. 'As Xandra says, while we were in California I had a meeting with Joey Talavera, thanks to Cyrus, who—'

'*The* Joey Talavera?' said Mel, failing to hide her incredulity.

Talavera had made his fortune with the Zype video-conferencing app, but he'd made his name by marrying a member of the Vardashian family. He was now the worldwide media's favourite handsome billionaire, with a fondness for cameo guest-spots in sitcoms. He was also keen on conspiracy theories: thanks to a recent Netflix documentary that he'd financed and fronted, forty percent of Americans, plus a worrying proportion of the rest of the world, believed the moon landings were fake.

Shane nodded. 'The one and only.'

If they'd been alone, Mel would have asked why the hell he'd done this without telling her. In front of the board, that wasn't an option. With the possible exception of Damon, she was clearly the only one in the room to be unaware of the meeting. Drawing attention to her ignorance would only rub in her own humiliation.

'And what did the one and only Joey Talavera have to say?'

'It turns out he's a massive admirer of Orange Peel. He's followed everything we've done and is hugely impressed. It was very flattering. For all of us.'

Mel forced herself to smile. 'I'm sure.'

'Anyway,' Shane continued, 'he was keen to talk to us because he has a cause of his own, something he's passionate about, and he thinks we're the people who can sell it to the rest of the world.'

'A cause? Please tell me it's not the moon landings.' Mel looked around the table for support, but nobody met her eye.

'Maybe it's better if you just look at the document,' said Shane, fidgeting with a strand of his beard. 'You'll find the key section on page three.'

Mel flicked to the third sheet, where she saw a paragraph headed 'the Talavera campaign'. Her eyes widened as she started to read. At the end of the section, she burst out laughing and felt a sudden surge of relief. 'This is a joke, isn't it?' The whole thing was clearly an elaborate prank at her expense, designed perhaps as some kind of tribute to her success.

'It's not a joke, Mel.' Xandra's face might have lost much of its capacity to show expression, but there was no mistaking her seriousness.

Mel looked around the table again, her relief draining away as quickly as it had come. 'You're not actually expecting me to sign up to this nonsense? It flies in the face of everything we've ever stood for. There's no way I'd let Orange Peel trash its own legacy like this. How could you ever think I'd stand by and allow my foundation to sell its soul?'

'I don't, Mel,' said Xandra. 'None of us do. That's why, when Joey Talavera reached out to Cyrus, we asked Shane to take the meeting. We knew you'd refuse to contemplate it, because that's the way you're made. Your sense of principle is admirable. But you have to know that we, as a board, are of one mind on this: we're not prepared to put our staff on the street and dismantle this wonderful organisation that we've all had a hand in building. So I'm afraid, if you're certain you're unable to go down this route, we'll need your immediate resignation.'

Mel was struggling to breathe. Her mouth had gone dry, her head throbbed and she thought she might pass out. She looked at Damon, but his eyes were fixed on his own copy of Shane's document. They really were all in this together.

Xandra held out her hand for Mel's copy of the Talavera document and tucked it back into her folder. 'Of course it will be an entirely amicable parting of the ways, with no public mention of any disagreement. You can work a respectable notice period, so none of the staff need know. You've had a long and brilliant run, and nobody would expect you to stay forever. I'm sure you've got one more big job in you. Go off and do that, with our blessing. Obviously we'll need you to sign this confidentiality agreement, otherwise it might be tricky for us to give you the reference you'd need.' She slid another set of printed papers across the table. 'But I'm sure that won't be a problem, will it?'

Mel blinked. Xandra was offering her a pen.

'It's all right. I've got my own.' She was conscious of speaking in a dazed whisper. This was deeply degrading, but what other option did she have? To make a scene and insist on staying in the job that she was planning to abolish anyway? She had clearly lost the support of the treacherous Shane and there was no point in appealing to the rest of her staff, even if they had the power to support her: once they knew they were all doomed under her leadership, they would back Shane's coup. She tried to focus on the new paperwork.

'The terms are very generous, as you can see,' Xandra was saying. 'The severance comes with Joey Talavera's compliments.'

The figure Mel found herself looking at wasn't so much generous as colossal. She wasn't a greedy person, and a fortunate start in life had left her with few material wants, but this was a staggering sum. She felt sick at the prospect of agreeing to the deal, but her staff would keep their jobs, she'd have a large lump sum to invest, and the world would just have to make what it could of Orange Peel's lurch into the realm of insanity. What other choice did she have?

'Where do you want me to sign?' she said softly.

Shane, who was clearly familiar with the document already, indicated the place with a stubby, nail-bitten finger.

There was one consolation, she thought, as she scrawled her name. The charity she'd built from scratch might shed its own integrity and become a laughing stock, but it would never persuade the public to sign up to Talavera's deranged scheme. That was the craziest thing she'd ever seen, and not even an outfit as slick and smart as Orange Peel had a cat in hell's chance of selling it.

2

Shane wasn't proud of being a snake. It didn't come easily to him. He tried to console himself with that thought whenever he felt guilty. It didn't always work, so a better strategy was to remind himself of all the times Mel had belittled, patronised or undermined him.

She wasn't a shouter, far from it: she was probably the most even-tempered person in the whole office. She expressed disapproval in a much more subtle way, with a tight little frown, like the shadow of a passing cloud, and then it was gone. She kept any real annoyance to herself, which seemed an admirable quality at first, but then became unnerving.

No one – certainly not her deputy – was allowed into her confidence. Her remarkable level of self-assurance came, no doubt, from a public-school education and an effortlessly top-drawer background: as Shane knew from idle googling, her father was Sir David Winterbourne, former permanent secretary at the Home Office, and her maternal grandmother was the detective novelist Henrietta Maxwell-Wyckes, an early rival of Agatha Christie's. It gave her an innate sense of superiority that revealed itself in any number of small ways. For example, Mel knew all about Shane's home life, having met his husband Craig several times, but Shane had no idea if Mel had a partner. She said 'we' occasionally but, if he fished for more detail, she clammed up. Perhaps there was a select inner circle permitted to know such information, but he – educated at an East Lancashire comprehensive – was clearly not a member.

She looked down on him even when she praised him. When he first got the job, she introduced him to visitors as 'my clever young deputy', which he heard initially as a compliment, but she continued to say it without let-up when he'd been there two or three years, and it began to irritate. No CEO would talk proudly about their 'clever deputy': that would highlight an obvious threat. But a 'clever *young* deputy' was no threat. She might as well be patting the head of a child.

At other times she'd refer to 'you young people', with a wave of the hand that grouped Shane with the rest of the staff. It masqueraded as self-effacement, lampooning her own middle age, but it also emphasised the gulf between herself and everyone else. It came up with anything related to IT. 'You young people are so good with all this modern technology,' she'd say, and it was true that her own abilities were woeful. But she created the impression that knowing your way around a computer was for little people, while she conserved her energy for higher matters.

When they discussed it at home, Craig said Shane was too

sensitive, hearing slights that weren't intended. But Shane knew Mel didn't really think he was clever. One time, he talked about their aim for some target or other going awry, which was one of those words he'd mainly seen written down, and it came out as 'oary' instead of 'a-rye'. On another occasion, he made the mistake of pronouncing 'hyperbole' as 'hyper-bowl'. Mel wouldn't let either of them go. Months after the initial faux pas, she was still finding ways of working those words into conversation so she could mispronounce them.

'It's just bantz,' said Craig, trying to make him feel better.

'Trust me, Mel doesn't do bantz.'

He was certain of this. Knockabout teasing involved a degree of back and forth, whereas Mel's jokes were all private, marked by lip-twitches and eye-rolls, which she seemed to assume everyone else was too dim to notice. She thought it particularly hilarious that Craig was an occasional churchgoer and that Shane sometimes went along too.

'How was your weekend?' she'd twitch on Monday morning. 'Anything racy in the sermon?'

Shane would smile through gritted teeth.

With any other travelling companion, he'd have been excited beyond words at the prospect of a two-day trip to Silicon Valley, but it filled him with dread. An hour within the walls of one of the world's most powerful brands was an immense privilege, but all he could picture was the time he'd have to endure in Mel's company.

When Cyrus texted out of the blue, about a week before their departure, asking to get together for a drink, and then told Shane that, while he was in San Francisco, he should attend a meeting so hush-hush that not even Mel knew about it, he was surprised and flattered. Discovering that the appointment was with Joey Talavera, more glamorous than any Google executive, restored the thrill he ought to have been feeling all along. He agreed without question, and only later fell to wondering why Talavera wanted to see him. Cyrus had nothing to offer in that regard. It would become clear in good time, was all he'd say.

The flights turned out to be more bearable than anticipated. Although they'd booked economy, someone at British Airways – or perhaps it was Google, or even Talavera – seemed to be smiling on them, and the check-in clerk upgraded them to business. This was a first for Shane, who gorged on savoury pastries and cocktail sandwiches in the business lounge, and stocked up on free copies of *The Economist* and *The Times* for the flight.

'There's no need, you know,' said Mel. 'You'll get all that, and more, on board.'

No doubt she was right but he carried on anyway, taking pictures of the buffet and his Bloody Mary to send to Craig. He knew it was sad to be so impressed, and he should probably pretend he came to places like this all the time, but what the hell? As his husband was never slow to point out, you could take the boy out of Ormskirk, but you couldn't take Ormskirk out of the boy. 'It's all FREE!!' he texted excitedly.

On the plane, they had wide seats with massive leg-room, plus more cocktails and restaurant-quality food on china plates. It was a relief not to be jammed elbow to elbow with Mel, as they would have been behind the curtain. Even better, she took a sleeping pill immediately after her meal, burying herself under a blanket and an eyeshade for the rest of the flight.

Shane wanted to stay awake to watch as many movies as possible, but the Bloody Mary in the lounge, the welcome-aboard champagne and the wine with dinner defeated him, and he too slept most of the way. He occasionally woke to take note of where they were on the flight path – although San Francisco was well south of London, their route took them over Greenland and the Canadian Arctic – then dozed off again.

To be in San Francisco was a dream come true, even with Mel as a companion, and it was beyond amazing to see Silicon Valley and to go inside the Googleplex. He was pleased that Mel took his advice seriously when he suggested a line about dinosaurs for her presentation. She seemed incredibly nervous, a side of her he'd never seen, and he feared her pitch might be a disaster. But in the end, she knocked it out of the park, and the response of the Google execs was way better than either of them had hoped. When their Uber delivered them back to their hotel, Mel stood cocktails in the bar to celebrate. For once, she chose to be convivial, with a fund of indiscreet stories about Xandra, Geena and various other Orange Peel grandees. She nudged her anecdotes along with her eyebrows, inviting him to fill in any blanks with his imagination. It was shameless innuendo, all under cover of complete deniability: she didn't explicitly tell him that Sir Beowulf and Dame Daphne once had a torrid affair while married to other people; she merely allowed him to think it. The tales made Shane laugh and he wondered if Craig was right, and he'd been too harsh on her.

She reverted to type, however, when he tried to turn the conversation to the future of the foundation.

'People will say we've done everything you set out to do. We need to show that isn't true, otherwise…'

'Otherwise we'll have to close?'

'Well, yes. So we'll have to, erm, come up with a diversification strategy as a matter of urgency, don't you think?'

'Leave that to me,' she said with a self-contained little smile, signalling to a waiter for the bill.

A few moments earlier, in their shared moment of triumph, he'd been tempted to confide in her about his appointment the following day with Joey Talavera. It felt wrong to leave her out. Whatever game Cyrus was playing, didn't Shane owe his primary loyalty to Mel?

But now that she'd put him back in his place, he was relieved not to have said anything. She didn't deserve to be included.

Officially, the pair of them were free all next day, before leaving for London in the evening. Shane's appointment with Talavera was at ten in the morning, and he'd been fretting about how to slip away without Mel's knowledge. In the event, there was a message waiting for her at breakfast from the hotel manager, offering a range of complimentary treatments in the spa. This gift was hers for the taking at nine-thirty, which was precisely when Shane had been told to expect Talavera's car.

'The invitation seems to be for me only,' she said. 'I'm sure a young man like you can find something to amuse you in this city for the morning, can't you? Go and check out the Castro. I'm sure Craig won't mind. Or perhaps Grace Cathedral is more up your street?' There it was again, the mocking twitch of the lips. He must have been mad to think about telling her where he was really going. 'We'll need to leave for the airport at about four o'clock,' she added, slipping back into boss mode. 'Can you make sure you're here by three?'

Not sure whether to be impressed or unnerved by the skill with which Talavera seemed to be stage-managing their trip, he promised he'd be back in good time.

At nine-thirty a leather-upholstered Tesla duly picked him up, driven by a glassed-off Hispanic chauffeur who was as silent as the vehicle. They drove back the way he and Mel had travelled the previous day, down the peninsula towards Silicon Valley. As they reached the town of Palo Alto, they turned up into the hills. The rolling landscape seemed rural, with vineyards on the slopes; only the cameras and elaborate security gates at the entrance of each property offered any clue that this was the super-rich equivalent of a suburb, where every house was a sprawling estate.

Eventually, they turned in at one of these entrances. Two redwood trees stood sentinel on each side of the driveway. Without any prompting from the driver, the gates rolled silently apart to admit them, then slid closed behind them. Clearly, they were being watched by unseen eyes.

Ahead lay a sweeping drive composed of bricks in a herringbone pattern. A young Latino gardener, sweeping the bricks, stood aside. He touched the brim of his hat as they passed; the chauffeur, obviously superior in the hierarchy, didn't even nod.

The drive wound between two vine-clad hills, then rounded a corner to reveal a cluster of buildings nestling in the valley bowl. At their centre rose a tower, stuccoed in salmon pink, with arched windows beneath a terracotta-tiled roof. To the right of the tower ran a similarly stuccoed colonnade, beneath another tiled roof, leading to a set of garages, all with arched entrances and the same rustic-rendered walls. To its left stood the house itself, with a colonnaded porch at ground level and rows of arched windows on the floor above. The whole place had the air of a monastery in Italy or Spain – if monasteries had fleets of Teslas parked in their garages.

The chauffeur murmured into his phone as he got out of the car and opened the door for Shane.

'Mr Talavera will see you in the cabana, sir. Follow me.'

Shane's disappointment at not going inside the mansion evaporated as they proceeded along the herringbone path into another colonnade and then out on the other side of the house. Laid out before them was a manicured box garden through which ran a series of narrow, gurgling canals, each lined in swimming-pool blue. These channels fed an infinity pool, with a putting green beyond.

'This way, sir.' It was his guide's polite but firm way of telling him to stop gawping.

Shane could not resist asking, as he caught up: 'Is Krystal also at home?'

'Mrs Talavera is at the main residence, sir.'

Hearing reproach in the correction, he immediately regretted his over-familiarity, but this was also remarkable news. 'You mean…this isn't the main residence?'

The chauffeur smiled in a way that made Shane feel smaller than usual. 'No, sir. Mr Talavera only uses this home when he needs to visit his company office in Menlo Park.'

'Right.' A pied à terre. Silly of him not to realise.

The driver pointed to a single-storey building beneath a clump of trees, finished in the same stucco and tiles as the rest of the estate. 'You'll find Mr Talavera over there. He's expecting you.' Before Shane could reply, he turned and retreated towards the house.

Left on his own, Shane was suddenly weak with nerves. How did you approach a billionaire whose face had been on the cover of *Time* and *Vanity Fair*? He still had no idea why he'd been summoned. What had Cyrus told Talavera about him? What was the guy expecting? And how could he possibly live up to it?

His host's voice interrupted his thoughts. 'Hey dude. Come on down here. Don't be shy.'

The figure beckoning to him was taller than he'd expected. Most people were tall to Shane but, in his limited experience, celebrities tended to be smaller than you thought. Joey Talavera was a hulking exception.

He wore a baby-pink polo shirt that merely emphasised his masculinity. Its sleeves struggled to contain his bronzed biceps, and the mane of dark hair cascading over his collar gave him a leonine grandeur. Shane struggled to process the injustice of it all. He could accept an old, fat and jowly billionaire or, if necessary, a young and nerdy one; but to have the body of a tennis ace and the looks of a Calvin Klein model was a sign that life's lottery had been rigged.

This godlike figure extended a massive hand. 'Great to meet you, Shane. Thanks for making the time. Sorry to have you haul your ass down here, but I figured you might get a kick outta seeing the place.'

'Definitely. It's amazing.'

'Thanks, dude. Glad you like it. The yard here is modelled on the Alhambra in Granada, Spain. Do you know it? No? My family was originally from Andalusia, many centuries ago, and this whole place is inspired by traditional Spanish architecture. Take a seat, man. What can I get you to drink? Spring water?'

Shane tried to say that spring water would be fine but his voice cracked and it came out as an inarticulate mumble. He told himself to get a grip.

His host pulled a bottle out of a fridge in the cabana, along with a plate of ready-cut lemon wedges. 'Ice? Yes? I wasn't sure. I know you guys don't have ice cubes over in Europe, do you?'

'Erm, we do actually, but...' He tailed off. It was easier not to argue.

Passing him a glass of water full of ice, Talavera dropped into a wicker chair and sat facing Shane, his nut-brown thighs splaying wide as his cargo shorts rode up his legs. Shane felt at once overdressed in his long trousers and button-down white shirt, and deeply relieved not to have exposed his own pale spindles.

'How are things at the Orange Peel Foundation?' said his host. 'You know, I'm a great admirer of what you all do.'

'Cyrus told me. It's very flattering.'

'Cyrus! I love that guy! How's he doing?'

'Good, I think. He sends his regards.'

'Back at him. All the way.'

'As for how things are going, the answer is brilliant, as of yesterday. We had an amazing meeting at Google.'

'Yeah, I had a hunch it might be. So your work's all done now, right?'

'I wouldn't quite go as far as—'

'Don't worry, I get it. These are strategic matters and you can't talk about them with outsiders.'

'Well, you're a friend of Cyrus, so you're not a complete outsider. It's just that—'

'Look, dude, I'm here to help. That's why I had you come out here. I mean, you've been wondering, right?'

Shane nodded.

'Let me show you something.' Talavera picked up his phone and started scrolling.

Shane leaned closer, assuming he was meant to look at the phone screen, but his host pressed a button on the table beside him and a widescreen TV slid up from a slot behind a miniature box hedge. The screen, shining bright despite the sunlight, showed a picture synched from Talavera's phone: a circular plan of the globe viewed from directly above the North Pole, framed by two stylised olive branches.

'You know what that is?'

'Sure,' said Shane. 'It's the logo of the United Nations.'

'Correct. Now look what happens if I do this' – he flipped to another version of the emblem, from which the olive fronds had been removed – 'and lay it alongside this one.'

The stripped-down UN logo sat next to a rougher, hand-drawn image, showing the continents in black and the surrounding oceans in a circle of white.

As he studied the two images, Shane saw that the layout of the continents, with the northern hemisphere towards the centre and the southern hemisphere around the edges, was strikingly similar.

'Describe what you see,' said Talavera.

Shane had no idea where this was going, but it seemed important to assert his know-how. 'Erm, I see two azimuthal projections, both centred on the North Pole. At first sight, you might mistake them for aerial views of the earth from directly above the Pole, but they're not. If they were, you'd only see the northern hemisphere, but in both these images you can see South America, southern Africa and Australasia arranged around the outer parts. That means they're both theoretical projections.' His host didn't react, so he continued: 'I don't know if you're familiar with that word "azimuthal"? Most people aren't. It's basically a cartographical term to describe the kind of projection that shows the globe as a circle, with concentric rings rippling out from one particular point. In this case, that point is the North Pole, so the concentric rings correlate roughly to lines of latitude, which would be shown as horizontals on a standard Mercator map.'

As he spoke, he had the feeling he was losing Talavera, who

now leaned over to him, his bronzed knees all but touching Shane's trousered ones. His eyes shone.

'Dude, wake up! There is no mistake, because these *are* aerial views. You're looking at the evidence. The map on the right was drawn by Samuel Birley Rowbotham of Stockport, England, who also went by the name Parallax, and was a warrior for truth at a lonely time in history. He was mocked for his views, but when all the countries of the world came together to form a united body, in the aftermath of World War Two, just look what they chose as their logo!'

He stopped expectantly.

Shane stared at the two images, feeling a drip of cold sweat trace its way down his ribcage. 'I'm sorry, I'm not really—'

'Let me help you out. Parallax was the leading zetetic thinker of the nineteenth century. You see, you're not the only one that can use fancy words. This one means a free-thinker, someone who refuses to believe what they're told to believe just because everyone else swallows it. Parallax rejected globularist dogma and he spent his whole life trying to tell people the truth, in lectures all over England. He drew the map on the right with his own hand. His audiences believed him but the establishment refused to take him seriously. They still tell the same lies to this day, but the scales are falling from more and more people's eyes. And this here is the clue that's been hiding in plain sight all along. Without telling anyone what they were doing, the UN adopted Parallax's map as their logo. They added some more circles and changed the colours but otherwise it's identical. And the Parallax drawing is the truest representation of the world.'

Shane crossed his legs and frowned in concentration, cursing Cyrus for sending him to this lunatic and trying desperately to think of a polite way to respond.

'That's why I invited you over,' Talavera continued. 'You guys have done an amazing job of changing the way people picture the world we live in. You've just won the support of Google, which is awesome, but now it's time to finish the job and tell the whole truth. Doesn't that give you a head-rush, my friend? Together, we're gonna help billions of people see the truth their ancestors sensed all along. The earth is flat, man, and it's time to come clean about it.'

3

Shane sat in the rear of the Tesla, staring out at the entrances to palatial estates. He was no longer awe-struck. Shell-shocked was more the size of it. Grateful not to have to make small-talk with the monosyllabic driver behind his pane of glass, he attempted to process what had just happened.

For two hours he'd listened, bound by his obligations as a guest as well as deference to one of the richest and most influential people on the planet, while Talavera expounded his certainties.

According to Joey, the earth was as flat as a vinyl disc, which would be completely obvious to Shane if he visited the Talaveras at their ranch in the Mojave desert (as Mrs Talavera, the former Krystal Vardashian, was keen he should do). This understanding was shared by every human who ever lived, until foolishness and deception intervened. Equally clear since the dawn of time was the understanding that the sun and the moon tracked the course of the equator, which ran halfway between the North Pole and the ice wall that ringed the earth's outer edge. The consensus was shattered by Copernicus, with his contrarian theory that the planets rotated around the sun, and Galileo, who faked experimental results to support the 'Copernicious' – Talavera was proud of that word – theory. For their idea to make sense, the earth had to be globular, which meant people on the bottom walked with their heels above their heads. Enter Isaac Newton, whose theory of gravity was designed to explain away this absurdity.

'But it was only a theory, dude! It's an idea, a suggestion, not some kinda iron law, the way we're taught in school. And it's dumb. The theory says the sun's gravitational pull keeps all the planets in the "solar system"' – his air quotes expressed his scorn – 'in their respective orbits. Suppose for a moment the solar system actually exists. This force called gravity keeps the moon rotating around the earth. So when the moon comes between the earth and the sun, why doesn't the sun steal the moon away from the earth? That's what it should do, because it can hold much larger planets than earth in its orbit over much great distances. The truth is, there's no such thing as the solar system, and there's no such thing as gravity either. Objects only fall because they're heavier than air.'

'But, erm, isn't the point of the theory that the earth exerts a greater gravitational pull on the moon than the sun does because it's so much closer?' ventured Shane. 'That's why gravitational force is pulling us into these chairs not towards the sun.'

The eyes blazed even brighter. 'Come on, dude! You're falling for the hoax. Because that's what it was, and that's why this great country of ours was founded: to fight back against it.'

'But…surely Christopher Columbus believed the earth was spherical? That was the whole reason he came here, no?'

'Columbus? I'm not talking about that faker – who, by the way, never set foot in North America. I mean George Washington. You didn't know our first president was a flat-earth believer? I'm not surprised. They covered it up. But that's why he broke with England, to get away from Copernicious superstition.'

And so the bizarre history lesson continued. Tens of thousands of settlers had turned their backs on Europe to get away from the globular beliefs to which their whole continent was in thrall. One of Washington's greatest successors, Franklin D. Roosevelt, was also a true believer; the Yalta conference between FDR, Stalin and Winston Churchill was designed to usher in a new age of truth, under the umbrella of the fledgling United Nations. That was why the UN chose the flat-earth map as its emblem – only FDR died before the spinning-ball hoax could be exposed. His successors chose instead to take the illusion to a whole new level.

This was, of course, the fake space programme, a multi-billion-dollar piece of stagecraft which would enrich the contractors who created the illusion. The moon landing was fictitious, scripted by no less a figure than Arthur C. Clarke, and filmed in Arizona. 'It's a place called Meteor Crater and I can take you there, dude. It'll blow your mind. You can see all the exact formations from the "moonwalk" shots.' More scornful air quotes.

Some flat-earthers had begged Neil Armstrong and Buzz

Aldrin to come clean about the hoax for years, but Talavera believed in the astronauts' sincerity: they were brainwashed, using highly sophisticated Cold War techniques, to think they really were travelling through space and walking on the moon. The real conspiracy was much higher up. Kennedy and Khrushchev held a summit where the Soviets let the US keep the film rights for the moon hoax as long as they were allowed to stay in Cuba.

'Of course the heads of the TV networks were all in on it, and the movie studios too. And Howard Hughes was involved, against his will. That's why he disappeared from view: they kidnapped him and plundered his companies to fund it all. They deliberately made him lose his mind to keep him quiet. I've gotta hand it to them, the whole thing was genius. Because if you say to anyone the moon landings were fake, they tell you, "No, man, I saw the whole thing on TV." I mean, it's hilarious, right? The entire world saw the Stark family massacred at a wedding in *Game of Thrones*, but then the whole cast showed up alive and well at the Emmys. 'Cos it's TV, right? It's make-believe. I saw Leo DiCaprio drown in *Titanic*, like, six or seven times, yet the guy was sat right there, where you're sitting now, only last week. 'Cos that's how the movies work. I saw it on TV! Give me a break.'

Uncomfortable as he was, listening to his host's diatribe, Shane was dreading the moment it ended, when he'd have to say something in reply.

'So?' said Joey, as that moment duly arrived. 'Whaddaya think?'

'Erm, in the sense of...? Well, there's certainly a lot of food for thought in what you say. It's all fascinating, but I'd need to do some reading of my own. You know, to look at the sources for some of this information. The plans at the Yalta summit, for example. Is there documentation?'

'Dude, it's the greatest hoax the world has ever seen. You think they wrote it down?'

'No, but if President Roosevelt had decided to end the, erm, deception, he'd have told his officials, no? Or written it in his diary?'

'You think they didn't mop up all that stuff after he passed? If it existed, they destroyed it. Shredded, burnt, all gone. Same with Kennedy/Khrushchev, before you ask. We're not dealing with amateurs here.'

'No, I can see that.'

'Listen, dude. Take all the time you need. I don't need a decision right now. Sleep on it. Talk to Cy. Take a whole week if you want. I'll give you my assistant's cell, so you can reach me directly.'

'When you say "decision"…?'

'Whether Orange Peel's in or out. It's time to tell the world the truth, my friend.'

This was every bit as bad as he'd feared. 'You know I'm only the number two, right? I'd have to speak to my CEO, Mel Winterbourne.' He'd never been so happy to assert his juniority.

Talavera made a 'whatever' face. 'Don't worry about Mel. We can square things with her.'

'Really?' What was going on here? How much of this did Cyrus already know? And was Xandra in on it too? Shane clutched at another straw. 'One thing I don't understand, though…'

'Hit me.'

'Well, Mr Talavera…'

'Joey.'

'Well, erm, Joey…you're not just one of the richest men in the world, you're also amazingly influential. Your face is everywhere. Why do you need a charity like ours to help you spread the word? Surely you can do it far more effectively on your own? Like, a massive PR campaign with you fronting it, and your wife, of course…'

'Which everyone would dismiss as the ravings of a crazy billionaire and his dumb celebrity wife. Don't get me wrong: Krystal is one of the smartest people I've ever met, but that's the way it is. If you have beauty, people think you can't have brains. No, dude, you guys have something that money can't buy. Two things, in fact: credibility and integrity.'

Whereupon he undermined his own statement by writing down the amount for which he proposed to buy the credibility and integrity of the Orange Peel Foundation. Ironically, given Joey's contempt for star-gazers such as Copernicus and Galileo, it was astronomical.

The Tesla had rejoined the Central Freeway, following the signs for the Golden Gate Bridge.

Shane's instinct was to call Craig there and then, to share every crazy detail, but he didn't trust the driver's glass screen, even if he spoke softly. What if the back of the car were mic'd up and the guy could hear every word? In ordinary circumstances, that thought would be paranoid, but billionaires had their own normal and this one had spent the past two hours demonstrating his own special level of batshittery.

In any case, Shane's priority ought to be letting the board know what had happened. They'd sent him on this covert mission and they no doubt had high hopes for its outcome. He'd have to break the news that Talavera was off his rocker.

He started writing a text. 'Hi Cyrus. I'm on my way back from Joey's. A very strange morning. Would be good to talk it through with you. Don't get your hopes up though.' He was about to add 'because the guy's totally cray-cray', but he reminded himself that Cyrus and Talavera were friends, so he ought to tread carefully.

Barely a minute after he'd pressed send, his phone rang.

Shane answered in a whisper. 'Hey Cyrus. I can't really talk right now.'

The voice crackled in his ear. 'You're with Mel?'

'Erm, no, not that. Still in the car, on the way back to the hotel.'

'And you're not alone in the car? Got it.'

'Yeah, that's kind of it.'

'Give me a shout when you're free to talk.'

'Will do. It should be in about twenty minutes.' He dropped his voice further. 'Like I say, I really wouldn't get your hopes up though.'

'Ha! He gave you the full flat-earth routine, did he? Did it freak you out? I can imagine. Still, it's the future, and the future is bright for those who see it coming, right? Talk to you later.'

He rang off, leaving Shane open-mouthed. Today was getting worse and worse: Cyrus had clearly known about Talavera's proposition all along and it hadn't put him off. Was everyone in the world going nuts?

A Hispanic voice interrupted his thoughts. 'Are you feeling unwell, sir? Would you like me to increase the ventilation or stop the car?'

Shane realised he must have been groaning. The driver was thinking of his upholstery.

'No, don't worry. I'm good. Thank you, though.'

He struggled to compose himself for the rest of the journey.

Back in his room, he steeled himself to speak once more to Cyrus, who picked up at the first ring.

'Hi Shane. Can you chat freely now?'

'Yes, I'm on my own now. Unless the room is wired.'

'What? Why would it be?'

'Just because… No, don't worry. This place is beginning to get to me, that's all.'

'It's lucky you're coming home then, isn't it? So, go on. Tell me how you got on with Joey. Did he lay out the full case?'

'Yes, you could say that. You've heard it all too, then?'

'Maybe not all of it. I don't know the guy that well, to be honest. But I'm aware of the gist.'

That was a relief, at least, to hear they weren't close friends. 'I got the full presentation. He's very passionate.'

'I can imagine. I don't need to hear the details now. But did he say what he wants Orange Peel to do?'

'Yes, he did. I expect you know already.'

'And did he mention any financials?'

'Oh yes. He was very specific about those.'

'How much?'

Shane told him.

Cyrus whistled, then said: 'Look, I know this is all a bit of a stretch for you. Trust me, it's the same for all of us. But we need to be open-minded and pragmatic about our future, otherwise we won't have one. That's certainly Xandra's view. And we're relying on you to think outside the box. That's why we asked you to go to Joey's place, rather than Mel. You haven't mentioned anything to her?'

'No, not a word. You told me not to.'

'Good man. Listen, have a good flight, buddy. I'll see you when you're back.'

Shane lay on the bed and closed his eyes. He no longer had any inclination to call Craig. What might have been a funny story suddenly seemed much less droll.

He could see what was happening. The board had decided to freeze Mel out and now favoured Shane instead, which would be flattering if their motive weren't so obvious: they knew Mel would tell them where to stick their pragmatism, whereas they were relying on him to be a soft touch. He yearned to show them how wrong they were. He hoped he'd be brave enough.

He must have dozed off, because the next thing he knew, he was being woken by a loud knocking. It took him a moment to remember where he was. The knocking grew impatient.

'Coming,' he shouted, looking at his watch. It was three o'clock, the time Mel had told him to get back. He could see her through the peep-hole.

'You've been asleep,' she said when he opened up. It was a statement not a question. 'I should save it for the flight. I'm just checking you're packed and ready to leave.'

'I will be. Have we booked an Uber?'

'Yes, "we" have. It'll be here in an hour.'

'Awesome. I'll meet you in reception at four.'

He closed the door and stumbled into the bathroom to splash water on his face. He realised he was starving: he hadn't eaten since breakfast. He picked up his room phone and ordered a club sandwich, then clicked the TV on as he set about packing his bag.

The CNN newscasters were taking turns, almost line by line, to bark through the stories of the day, on a screen framed by weather and stock-market graphics, with ticker-tape headlines running along the bottom. It all seemed so frenetic: the news lines declaimed so urgently, the clips of talking-head commentators cutting from one to the next with barely time to get started. The producers seemed terrified the viewers would get bored if they had to look at the same face for more than three seconds. The station had twenty-four hours of this to fill, then rolling on into the next day. No wonder so many Americans were wired and agitated all the time.

Bombarded by ever-changing voices and images, he didn't pay much attention to the news stories: arguments over an agriculture bill in Congress; heavy flooding in Louisiana; a supermarket shooting in New Mexico.

The next item, however, made him pay attention.

'In the city of Quincy, Massachusetts, protestors today tore down a statue of Christopher Columbus,' began the female anchor.

Her male counterpart picked up: 'Witnesses say about two hundred people gathered downtown before marching to the statue, which they pulled down with ropes. The statue broke up when it was toppled. The protestors then tossed the pieces into the harbour.'

His colleague continued: 'Columbus has long been a controversial figure for his treatment of the indigenous communities he encountered in the Caribbean. Statues have been toppled or removed in many cities.'

As she spoke, the screen showed pictures of cheering protestors, wearing black bandanas over white faces.

Shane expected some kind of outraged response to follow from conservative opponents, but none came. In this deeply divided country, where culture wars had become a way of life, there seemed to be a rare consensus. Columbus might have given his name to cities, counties, parks, plazas and highways across the US, as well as a movie studio, an air-force base and the federal district containing the nation's capital, but that nation seemed to agree it was time to wash its hands of the guy.

To think that, for generations of schoolchildren, Columbus personified the idea that the earth was a globe. Unbidden, a thought entered Shane's mind. He wished it hadn't, because he could sense it was the start of something and he had a suspicion it might prove hard to dislodge.

If the Lord God Almighty was planning on granting his prayer to put courage in the hearts of his men, the admiral wished He would get on with it. Any more trembling from the crew and the timbers of the ship would start to vibrate.

The fear did not just infect the *Santa Maria*. The same affliction beset all three ships, at all levels, from cook to captain. In fact, the admiral suspected that the masters of the other two vessels were deliberately whipping up the fear, for their own ends.

Just three days out of Palos, Martín Alonso Pinzón, who commanded the *Pinta*, raised a distress flag, obliging the *Santa Maria* to lay up alongside to investigate. 'We can't steer,' he called across the water, when they were close enough to hear. 'The rudder has come away from the sternpost. We're powerless to set a course.'

The admiral scented sabotage. Back in Spain, the *Pinta*'s owner had not bothered to hide his distress as the ship was pressed into royal service. No doubt he imagined his precious caravel sailing off the edge of the world. Accordingly, the admiral suspected the difficulties with the rudder were planned in advance. It was surely no accident that the trouble began as the fleet approached the Canary Islands, where they were due to stop to restock provisions and fresh water. The admiral knew what they expected him to do: impatient to press on, they hoped he would commandeer a replacement vessel, leaving the *Pinta* behind, and Martín Alonso could no doubt count on a fat reward for his treachery. Unfortunately for him, the admiral had no intention of chartering a new ship. Instead, after making a temporary fix with ropes, he ordered the men to fashion a new rudder from stiff oak on Gran Canaria, making the *Pinta* sea-worthy again. Poor Martín Alonso had to pretend he was pleased.

If only he could have used the same stout oak to stiffen the spines of the crew. Setting sail once more, they passed the island of Tenerife, whose peak belched smoke and spat fire. Few of the men had seen or even heard tell of a volcano in action, so the sight transfixed them. Even those who had witnessed an eruption before took it as a dread portent.

The admiral had his own fears, but not of falling off the edge of the world. The vision that cost him sleep at night was of mutiny. He was under no illusions about his vulnerability: if enough of them decided to revolt, he was lost. They would be hanged for it if they returned to Spain, but they might see that as a risk worth taking, such was their terror of the voyage. He would rest easier once they lost sight of land. If they could no longer see their own world, it might exert less of a pull on their hearts.

Finally, the last of the Canaries disappeared from view, but there was no change in the mood on board. The weather-bronzed faces of the crew were pale with trepidation.

'What's the matter with them all? Is it really such terror of the unknown that grips them?' the admiral asked De La Cosa, his captain on the *Santa Maria*.

'In their eyes, we've taken leave of the world. Not just the part they know, but the whole of it. Everything they hold dear is behind us. Ahead lies only peril and the abyss.'

'Nonsense, man. Ahead lies bounty: gold, spices, silks. Their hearts should brim with joy to think of the treasures that await us when we round the world and arrive at Cathay and the island of Japan, whose very beaches gleam with ingots and precious stones.'

'Those wondrous places may exist, but the men don't believe it's possible to round the world, as you put it, so they will never see these riches.'

The admiral looked him in the eye. 'And you? Do you believe you're about to sail your own ship off the end of the world?'

'Of course not. I trust completely in your judgement and your skill at reading the sea and the stars.'

De La Cosa's words sounded brave but his moment of hesitation gave him away. He was as terrified as the men.

The admiral realised he was wasting his breath and had no chance of persuading any of them. He had no option but to push them on and wait for them to see the wisdom of his venture with their own eyes, once they reached the Indies. Then they would thank him well enough.

4

On the flight home they were upgraded again. This time Shane took less delight in the pampering and the freebies, as Mel was quick to notice. 'You're getting blasé about it now you're a business-class veteran,' she twitched.

'Yeah, maybe you're right,' he said, humouring her. It was either that, or tell her the real reason, namely that he'd been knocked for six by a clandestine meeting a few hours earlier.

To do so would be a blatant disregard of his instructions from Cyrus, but he'd been considering it all afternoon. He thought about it in the Uber on the way to the airport, and again as they waited in the lounge. If he came clean, matters would be much simpler. Mel would be horrified at the board's intentions, as well as their treachery in plotting behind her back, and she'd refuse to countenance any association with Joey.

But then what? Xandra and Cyrus would either admit defeat and allow Mel to wind the foundation up, as Shane suspected she had in mind, or they'd find someone else to implement Talavera's crazy project. That person wouldn't be Shane, who'd already have shown his disloyalty by blabbing. Either way, he'd be out of a job.

He'd been through that possibility too, ever since their meeting at Google. If Orange Peel wound itself up on a high, he'd be very employable. By contrast, losing his job after defying the board would tarnish his record. He'd get a reference from Mel, but not from Xandra or the others, because he'd be a whistleblower. That might sound heroic, but it would make him a terrible prospect as a hire.

It was all right for Mel, who had a family home in Kensington, a 'little house' of her own in South London (as she persisted in calling her million-plus place on Clapham Common) and a cottage in the Dordogne. At her age, she'd have paid off any mortgages and no doubt, like all boomers, she had a fat pension saved up. By contrast, Shane and Craig had just taken out a massive loan to buy a first-floor conversion flat in Zone 4 and were stretched to the limit. As a junior doctor, Craig would earn decent money if he survived the first ten gruelling years or so and fulfilled his ambition to become an orthopaedic consultant. For the moment, he toiled as a house officer, on the bottom rung of the training ladder, and Shane paid the lion's share of the mortgage. He couldn't ignore that responsibility.

And yet... Could he really sell his soul? Because that was the alternative. Shouldn't he put conscience before self-interest?

He came closest to telling her as they waited for their flight to be called.

'You didn't tell me what you got up to this morning while I was at the spa,' she said, discarding her copy of *Newsweek*.

He took a deep breath. 'Actually I had quite a bizarre experience. I've been meaning to tell you about it.'

Sipping at her Chardonnay, she glanced at the departure screen, where their flight was still marked 'Wait in Lounge'. 'Oh dear. Did you meet a leather man in the Castro? Or a hippie in the Haight?'

There it came again, that self-satisfied smirk. She couldn't resist being snide.

She looked expectant, waiting for him to elaborate, but his resolve had vanished. Why should he trust her with his confidence, jeopardising his entire future, when all she ever did was patronise him?

'This is the pre-boarding announcement for British Airways flight 286 to London Heathrow,' interrupted the loudspeaker. 'We invite those with small children, and any passengers requiring special assistance, to begin boarding at this time.'

And with that, not only was the moment gone, but so was Mel's curiosity about where he had spent the morning.

Once airborne, they sat in their respective headphone bubbles watching movies over dinner, then settled down to sleep when the cabin lights went down. A couple of glasses of wine helped knock Shane out.

He dreamed he was at a billionaire's ranch in the desert, looking out over a wilderness as flat as a vinyl album. His host was not Joey Talavera but a surprisingly sculpted Cyrus, clad in just a sarong, holding court by the pool. Shane wanted to see inside the ranch but, when they went indoors, he was on the set of a game show, being ushered into the hot seat in front of a cheering audience. Cyrus had disappeared, replaced by a tiny figure with the skin of her face pulled back so tight that she could barely blink. At first Shane took her for Anne Robinson, about to make him the weakest link, but he realised it was Xandra, low-cut and top-heavy. He got it into his head that he was meant to answer questions about Christopher Columbus, but she had other ideas.

'Shane, I have some choices for you,' she said. 'Here's the first one. Your brother Darryl is in prison. You can either get him out or bank ten thousand pounds. Which is it to be?'

Shane did indeed have a ne'er-do-well brother Darryl. He was sorry, if not totally surprised, to hear he was in prison, but surely the sentence would be up soon enough? 'Bank ten thousand pounds!' he shouted, and the audience cheered as a totaliser lit up and a triumphant jingle played.

'Next life choice. Your mother Wendy has cancer. Will you save her life or take fifty thousand pounds?'

Again, his dream-brain thought this was a cinch. His mother was the most selfless person he knew and she would want him to enjoy the money. 'I'll take fifty thousand!' he cried, to more ecstatic cheering and an even louder fanfare.

'Your husband Craig is set upon by masked attackers. Will you fight them off or take one hundred thousand pounds?'

He was terrible at fighting, so what was the point of them both being hurt, when he could pay off so much of the mortgage in one go? The programme-makers were counting on him to go for the sentimental option, but he was made of stronger stuff. 'I'll take one hundred thousand pounds, Xandra!'

The audience roared as balloons and confetti fell from the ceiling, and now he was being escorted to a celebration press conference. But there were no journalists to be seen. Instead, they entered a stark, bare room where his parents, brother and Craig stood waiting, disgust and contempt on their faces.

'How could you betray us all, you greedy little toe-rag?' demanded his father.

Suddenly Shane saw what he'd done.

'I didn't mean to. I don't know what I was thinking. I'll give the money back. Don't hate me, please. Forgive me.'

It was no good. They all turned their backs on him. Darryl put his arm around Craig, which he'd never done in real life. Shane sank to his knees, begging them not to disown him, but they seemed not to hear. No wonder: although his mouth was open, no sound would come out, even when he strained every muscle…

He woke with a start, sweating under his airline blanket. It had all been so vivid, he must have cried out. But quiet reigned in the cabin. The only sounds were the low roar of the ventilation and the breathing of his sleeping neighbours.

He was trembling with the trauma of his dream, although its details were already sketchy. He tried to recall them, then decided that forgetting was probably for the best.

Uprighting his seat, he tapped his digital screen to check the progress of the flight. The map showed the same route as their outbound flight and put them somewhere over northeastern Canada. What would Talavera make of this course around the top of the world, he wondered. No doubt it would all form part of the great conspiracy: the pilot and co-pilot in the know, viewing the world from their own vantage point as a giant, flat dinner plate, while the fake route map hoodwinked the 'sheeple' passengers.

That wouldn't work, though, even for a nut-job like Joey. In daylight, any passenger in a window seat could look down at the ice-caps and see that the map was broadly accurate.

That set him wondering what route Parallax would expect them to take. Talavera had airdropped the graphic onto Shane's phone. He opened his photo album and clicked onto the Victorian drawing of the flat, circular world. The British Isles were easily spotted, directly below the North Pole. The Americas were to the left, misshapen from this perspective, with the southern continent wider than it was long, and the northern one flipped around by ninety degrees, so that New York formed its bottom-most point and Seattle stood at the top. Nevertheless, it was easy to locate San Francisco and draw a straight line by eye to London.

He blinked in surprise. The direct route on the Parallax map crossed Nevada, Idaho and Montana into Canada, and traversed Manitoba and the Hudson Bay to overfly Baffin Island, the Davis Strait and Greenland. It then skirted the eastern flank of Iceland before entering UK airspace at the northwestern tip of Scotland, roughly following the course of the M6 and the M1 to Heathrow. In other words, the route over a flat earth was virtually identical to the one they were flying.

The discovery unsettled him. Until now, he'd assumed there must be any number of simple ways to demonstrate the idiocy of flat-earth beliefs. Pointing a plane in a particular direction in order to see where it ended up would have featured high on that list. On this present flight, however, that experiment wouldn't change a single mind. The same course worked for both theories.

How many other killer arguments fell down so easily? Once people began to doubt what they'd always been told, how hard would it be to settle the question one way or the other?

Just like the toppling of the Columbus statue, it was food for thought.

There were three messages on his phone when they landed. The first was from Craig, who'd managed to do a swap with a colleague to get a night off that evening, a rare event for someone who worked eighty-hour weeks. He suggested they meet for a pizza in Soho.

'I'm going to be on call till five, so text me with a time and a place and I'll see you there. Looking forward to hearing all about your trip. See you later.'

The second was even more of a surprise.

'Shane? It's Xandra. You're probably still in the air, so you'll get this when you land. Cyrus tells me you had an interesting time with Joey Talavera. He probably horrified you, didn't he? Don't worry, we've all been there. Metaphorically, I mean. You're the only one who's visited him at home, you lucky devil. Anyway, we should have a chat about all this, you and I. Discreetly, obviously. I mean without…well, you know what I mean, I hope. Also, there's someone I want you to go and see. He's an utter eccentric, borderline bonkers, if I'm honest, but he's an absolute genius and enormously influential. I'm going to—'

She was cut off as she ran out of time. Shane played the third message.

'These damn things never give you long enough,' resumed Xandra. 'Can't you change your settings or something?

As I was saying, I'm making you an appointment with a fascinating person who I think will give us a lot of guidance. His name's Robinson White. You won't have heard of him because he keeps an incredibly low profile. He's a kind of lobbyist, specialising in getting impossible causes into the mainstream, not by persuasion but by…well, you'll find out. I'm going to suggest you meet him in a couple of days' time. That should give you a chance to catch your breath. This thing's going to run out again, isn't it? I'll text you the details when I've…'

Sure enough, it ran out again. She seemed to have decided she'd made her point and didn't come back for a third attempt.

It took him nearly two hours to get home. He and Mel caught the Piccadilly Line together, crawling stop by stop through the West London suburbs as far as Green Park, where they each changed onto a different line. At London Bridge, Shane missed his above-ground train by seconds and had to wait twenty minutes for the next one. No one ever visited shabby, down-at-heel Plumstead unless they lived there. Although the place was slowly growing on him, he couldn't help noticing it would have taken him less time to get from Heathrow to Birmingham.

Going out again was the last thing he wanted to do, but Craig had clearly gone to great trouble to arrange the time off and Shane couldn't let him down – particularly at a time when he badly needed his husband on his side. It was clear that Xandra and Cyrus wanted him to take up the Talavera cause. He needed to be able to discuss it properly with the person he trusted most.

He booked a table at a place in Greek Street, then had

an hour and a half before he needed to leave the flat again: enough time to have a shower and drink some strong coffee, but not much else.

When he set out, he was at least going in the opposite direction to the rush-hour flow, and he got a seat on a half-empty train all the way into town. That created a topsy-turvy sense, which was somehow appropriate. It was only nine o'clock in the morning, California time, but he hadn't fully acclimatised while he was there, and now his body clock didn't know where the hell it was meant to be. On top of that, his whole life had been pulled inside out by the meeting with Joey.

Just past Greenwich, a text pinged in from Xandra. 'I've fixed your appointment with Robinson White. Day after tomorrow, 1pm. 120 Pardoner House, London Bridge. He wants to give you lunch.'

'Awesome, thanks,' he texted back, wishing he meant it.

He'd started on a bottle of red wine and demolished most of the bread sticks by the time his husband arrived. Craig had developed dark shadows under his eyes that prematurely aged him, and his skin looked pale and spotty, the consequence of too much on-call junk food, but his curls and his grin were as boyish as ever. The sight of him made Shane feel calmer.

'It's so good to see you.'

'You too. Hey, don't get emotional. What's up?'

'Sorry. Nothing. Well, there is something but… You first. How are things?'

'How are they ever? Since I last saw you, I've held the hand of one, two, three…no, four dying patients in the middle of the night. I've been publicly bollocked by two different consultants for someone else's mistakes. I messed up a cannula. I had a patient fall out of bed and none of us knew how to work the hoist. And I've drunk three gallons of cold, weak coffee. So nothing special. All completely par for the course.'

'Poor you. I wish there was something I could do or say to help.' His own worries, with their sun-kissed, billionaire-acres backdrop, seemed indulgent in comparison.

'I know you do, but there isn't. I wanted to be a doctor, and this is how it is. It always has been and it always will be. I either suck it up or wimp out. For the moment I choose to suck, however much it sucks too.' He managed a weak grin. 'See what I did there? Now come on, tell me about your trip. How was Google? Was it amazing?'

'Let's order first. I'm starving.'

They chose their pizzas – capricciosa for Shane, quattro formaggi for Craig – then Shane began his story. It would have been tactless to dwell too much on the luxuries that came with their upgrade, so he focused on the ups and downs of travelling with Mel and their triumph at Google, followed by their awkward conversation over drinks.

'And the next day, of course, I had my appointment with Joey Talavera.'

Their food had arrived, with more wine, and Craig was stuffing a folded slice of pizza into his mouth. 'Sorry, I'd completely forgotten about that,' he said. 'How was his place? Was it incredible?'

'Massive. Brand new, I think, but built to look like an ancient Spanish hacienda. The kind with its own infinity pool and golf course, obviously.'

'And was Krystal there?'

'No, she was at their main house.'

'This wasn't his main house?'

'Duh! Actually that's what I said too. This was just his pied à terre, apparently, for when he's working at the office.'

'Shame you couldn't meet her. But what was he like? And why did he want to see you?'

'He was hot. Super, super hot. Even more in the flesh than he is in pictures. He was wearing these shorts that made his legs look like trees. I was sweating anyway because it was, like, California. But the thighs didn't help.'

'Okaaay. While I was on the ward, drowning in piss and vomit.'

'Sorry.'

'Go on, anyway. Why did he want to see you?'

Shane faltered. This had to be done but it was so difficult. He dropped his voice. 'He's a deranged flat-earther and he wants that to become Orange Peel's mission.'

'Yeah, yeah, very good. What did he really want?'

'I'm serious. That's exactly what he wanted.'

Craig's eyes widened. 'No! Seriously? That's hilarious! But why was he asking you? Why not Mel?'

'Because they knew Mel would tell them to shove it. They're not so sure about me.'

'When you say "they"…?'

'Xandra, Cyrus, Joey. They're all in on it.'

'Xandra and Cyrus are up for it? Wow. Like, really, wow!'

'I know, right? It's because Joey's prepared to pay. I've seen the figure he's offering. It's, like, silly money.'

'And if you say no?'

'I reckon they'll boot me out, same as they're going to boot Mel out.'

'No!'

'They haven't said that in so many words, but it's pretty clear that's what's going on, if you join the dots.'

'Does Mel know?'

'I don't think she has a clue. If she does, she's hiding it well.'

'Wow.'

'So you said.'

'What else can I say?'

'You could start by telling me what the hell I'm going to do.'

Craig pushed his half-eaten pizza aside. 'What do you want to do?'

'I want it all to go away. I want to rewind the last three days, back to when I'd never heard of Parallax and his stupid map, and to—'

'Para- who?'

'A Victorian nutter. Real name, Samuel Birley Rowbotham. People like Joey worship him as the founding father of the flat-earth movement. I won't bore you with the details.'

'It sounds like you've been reading up.'

'A little bit, on my way into town. I've got no choice. Xandra's booked me an appointment with some shadowy lobbyist who's going to tell me what Orange Peel needs to do. He specialises in making people believe the impossible, apparently.'

'That'll be interesting.'

'Yeah, right.'

'No, I mean it. The dark arts and all that? It'll be interesting to see how they work.'

'Do you want to take my place?'

'No thanks. I've got a prior engagement with a colostomy

bag and a bucket of sick.'

'Do you really think I should go?'

'Yes, I do.' Craig's voice was heavy with wine and lack of sleep. 'Look, we all have to put up with stupid stuff at work. In my case, it's getting bollocked by a bastard consultant who's too busy playing golf and coining it from private patients to know who does what on his ward. In yours, maybe you just have to pretend you believe some medieval nonsense.'

'Not just that. They think it's the greatest conspiracy ever hatched and they've rumbled it.'

'Now you're talking. It sounds exciting. And very post-truth. Zeitgeisty. Weird that Joey Talavera would go for all that, though. I mean, the guy's a self-made billionaire. He's meant to be a genius. How come he's into the world's stupidest conspiracy theory?'

'Your guess is as good as mine. I suppose even the brightest people are allowed to have their blind spots. And he lives in such a bubble, it must be very easy to get completely detached from reality. He's got the whole world bowing down before him, telling him how brilliant he is. Maybe the critical faculties that most people need, just to get through life, end up atrophying with lack of use.'

'Maybe.'

'So you wouldn't leave me?'

'Definitely not.' Craig grinned. 'As long as I get the odd trip to the Talavera mansion. And lunch with Krystal, of course.'

Shane managed a smile back. 'I guess that's a possibility.'

'There you go. No leaving will be necessary. Seriously, don't worry about it. It's good that you have integrity, but you also have more than half a mortgage to pay. I'm the do-gooder in this family and you're the main bread-winner, remember?

Until I make consultant, anyway.'

'If you say so.'

'I do recommend one thing, though.'

'What's that?'

'Keep records. Maybe a diary. Just in case it all goes pear-shaped and Xandra tries to blame you. Any notes you take now will be your insurance policy.'

5

Shane stared up at the tower block. The sign beside the door said Pardoner House, but was this really the place? A London Bridge address for an ultra-powerful practitioner of the dark arts suggested premises in the new business quarter around the Shard. Instead, Google had led Shane in the opposite direction from Borough Market and the South Bank, and across Jamaica Road, which marked the clear boundary between riverside affluence and its less glamorous South London hinterland.

Pardoner House was one of a cluster of towers named after characters from *The Canterbury Tales*. There was also a Prioress, a Knight and a Wife of Bath House, although the references would have gone over Shane's head without the sign marked 'Chaucer Estate'. Each tower was clad in a newish, silvery overcoat to mask the original brick or concrete beneath. The paintwork was in decent condition and the patch of garden separating each building looked recently tended, so it might well be a good place to live. He'd simply not expected to find Robinson White on a council estate.

He keyed number 120 into the intercom, still not certain he was in the right place. If the voice that answered was frail, elderly or bewildered, he had his apology ready.

He didn't need it.

'Hello?' boomed the reply, in an accent more suited to the Henley Regatta than North Bermondsey.

'It's, erm, Shane Foxley. I think you're exp—'

'Top floor.' The door gave a soft clunk, indicating it was open.

A Millwall fan had been at work with a marker pen on the lift walls, and the carriage itself reeked of weed. Refurbishment didn't seem to have reached this far: an ancient mechanism groaned as the car slowly ascended. Getting out on the twelfth floor, and finding himself on a bare, tiled landing, Shane felt suddenly light-headed. He pressed a thumb and forefinger to his temples, trying to blink the wooziness away.

A door opposite him flew open and a voice familiar from the intercom bellowed: 'Feeling a little high after your ride in the lift? Don't worry, you're not the first and you won't be the last. They don't call it Jamaica Road for nothing. Do come in. Robinson White. Call me Robbie or Robinson but not Robin, if you don't mind. I hate that.'

The man waiting for him on the threshold, hand extended in greeting, looked about sixty. His balding head was shaved completely clean, and he sported a salt-and-pepper goatee. In stark contrast to Shane's own formal suit, he wore a baggy white vest, exposing a fresh-looking tribal tattoo on his left shoulder, and Adidas jogging bottoms. He wiped his face with a towel.

'Excuse the sweats. I've been on the rowing machine. Give me two ticks and I'll change. Go on through and make yourself at home.'

White disappeared up a flight of stairs to the upper part of what was evidently a duplex penthouse. Shane found himself in a book-lined hallway, with volumes from floor to ceiling. On the few patches of available wall hung pictures in ornate gilt frames: a still life, a horse's head, a Madonna and child. They belonged to a wholly different world to the austere landing outside and the potent lift.

The only doorway opened straight ahead into a massive drawing room, far larger than Shane would ever have expected, with immense windows looking down onto Tower Bridge and beyond towards the Shard and the London Eye. Characters in TV dramas enjoyed this kind of view, but he'd never met a real person living against such a backdrop.

Remarkably, the spectacular panorama wasn't the most extraordinary aspect of the room. That distinction belonged to the furniture, which looked more suited to a chateau than a council flat. Delicate armchairs, with oval backs upholstered in pink silk and gilded legs tapering to the tiniest of pointed feet, stood about a low round table with a marble top and a frieze of Grecian hunters chasing around the rim. A brass pendulum clock in a glass case ticked away on top of a rosewood console table whose legs were carved as ram's heads, with feet of hooves. In another explosion of gilding, an ornate mirror on the wall opposite the window reflected the incongruous view. Beside it, a winged lion took flight on a slab of stone or plaster, while a side table bore a large clay bottle with a narrow neck and handles at each shoulder. Shane crouched to examine the faded scene of javelin-throwers and wrestlers painted on the side.

'You're admiring my amphora, I see. It's late Minoan, we think. About three thousand years old.'

The owner of this object was now wearing skin-tight jeans with a black leather shirt hanging open over his rowing vest. In his own grey suit, Shane felt painfully overdressed. To think he'd worn his most adventurous tie, imagining it would create a splash.

'You mean it's a replica of a three-thousand-year-old vase?'

'Replica? Wash your mouth out, young man! If it's a fake, the chap who sold it me is going to get his legs broken. No, most of the stuff in here is real enough. The pots are largely Greek and Etruscan, with just the odd Egyptian piece here and there. The furniture is mainly Louis Quinze, with a smattering of Seize. Do you know furniture? You're very young; your interest will grow. As it happens, there is the odd piece of discreet fakery on the walls. Of the three Canalettos over there' − Shane noticed them for the first time − 'only one is real. As a bit of fun, I often ask visitors if they can spot which is which. Most can't.'

Shane approached the three neat riverscapes, with their perfect detail of eighteenth-century Greenwich, and peered closer to examine them. 'That one?' he suggested, although he could see no real difference between any of them.

White shook his head. 'It's not, curiously enough.'

'That one, then?'

'That would be telling. You only get one guess.'

Shane was still trying to take everything in. 'You have an amazing collection. Is it, erm, secure? I mean, I don't want to be rude but—'

'Is it safe to keep priceless paintings and antiquities in a Bermondsey council block? More than you'd think, as a matter of fact. Any serious thieves hunt for this kind of stuff in Knightsbridge, not here. And I have a certain kind of informal insurance in place that works better than any conventional policy. I've been here a long time, and I make it my business to get on well with the people who matter in this neighbourhood. I won't go into grubby detail, but I look after them and they look after me. The upshot is that no one would dare.'

'I see.' Shane was at a loss for what else to say. 'And how did you, erm… I mean, what brought you to this, erm…'

'Why am I living on a council estate? Because it suits me. It's home. A very long time ago, I inherited the tenancy on this flat from a close friend who died, and then I bought it, thanks to dear Mrs Thatcher, God rest her soul. My neighbours did the same, but when they wanted to cash in their investment, they found they couldn't sell it. No bank would give a mortgage on a twelfth-floor council flat, however magnificent the view. At that point, I stepped in with a cash offer that suited all parties, and now I have not one, but two twelfth-floor, duplex flats. The place became rather more airy once I removed a wall or two. The planning department wouldn't like it, but it's structurally sound, so no one need ever tell them, need they?' He raised a challenging eyebrow. 'Now, do come through to the dining room. I've done a rack of lamb with redcurrant sauce. I hope that suits you?'

'Amazing. It's very kind of you.'

Although smaller, the dining room was almost as ornate as the drawing room, with a view downriver to the towers of

Canary Wharf.

'Excuse the shocking lack of table linen, but I prefer informality at lunchtime.'

'Erm, yes. Of course.'

Shane had brought a bottle of Californian Shiraz from Costcutter, thinking he was splashing out by spending £6.99. It now seemed pitifully unworthy and he was grateful when his host spirited the bottle away without glancing at the label.

'I've got a rather nice claret that I think you'll like,' White said, bustling back from the kitchen with a tureen of vegetables, some warm plates and a decanter.

'Can I help you with anything?'

'You sit tight, look pretty and admire the view. I'll be with you in two ticks. I thought you could tell me about yourself over lunch and then we'll get down to brass tacks, as it were.'

Shane attempted to oblige as he ate, answering as best he could a series of questions about his own background, as well as Orange Peel's work and Mel's management style. He normally prided himself on his discretion, but now he heard himself edging towards and then lurching across that line. Perhaps it was the opulence that made him so eager to please; that, or the constant refilling of his glass.

'So,' said his host eventually, when he'd taken their plates and decanted another bottle to accompany some cheese, 'shall we turn to the matter at hand? If I'm not mistaken, you have an advantageous but difficult proposition to sell.'

Shane nodded. 'Do you need me to explain the background?'

'I don't. Xandra has seen to that with admirable frankness. Fear not, I am under no illusions about the – how can I put it? – eccentricity of the enterprise, and I'm aware of its extreme desirability from a vulgar, bottom-line perspective. But I'm more interested, for the moment, in how you personally feel about the whole thing.'

'Can I be honest?'

'I'd be offended if you were anything else.' White topped up Shane's glass with the newly decanted wine. 'I promise you, nothing you say to me here will go beyond these walls.'

Shane sighed. 'Well, I'm coming round to the idea that I have to do this. To suck it up, as my husband puts it. But the truth is, it makes me queasy just to think about it.'

'Because it offends your sense of morality to try and foist this nonsense on an unsuspecting public? Or because you haven't a clue where to start and you're terrified you'll mess it up, leading to personal ridicule and shame?'

It was a good question. Amid his general distaste, Shane hadn't thought hard enough to draw the distinction. 'A bit of both, I guess.'

'There is one consolation. If you're utterly ridiculed, you won't be doing anything immoral, by your own definition, because there's no danger of anyone believing you.'

'I suppose so. I'm not sure that's much of a consolation, though.'

'Good. I mentioned it by way of a thought-experiment, and your answer is revealing. It indicates that your greater concern is to do this properly: to succeed in the enterprise and not to be made to look a fool. Is that fair?'

Put like that, it made sense. He shrugged tentative assent.

'In that case,' continued White, 'we need to think of a strategy, don't we? And to do that, you're going to have to forget everything you think you know about lobbying.'

'Really?'

'Really. Trust me, this is what paid for my Canaletto. The

real one.'

There was no arguing with that. 'So…in what sense, forget everything I think I know?'

White smiled at him. Shane attempted to hold his gaze, but it was disconcerting. He reached instead for his glass.

His host continued: 'The Orange Peel Foundation persuaded the world to stop using a certain map projection, in favour of a different one that Mel regarded as more suitable. True or false?'

'True.'

'Tell me how you did it. In summary. What was your strategy?'

Shane considered for a moment. 'A lot of it was before my time, obviously, but Mel started by defining the problem. Deciding what was wrong with the existing way of doing things, then collecting examples and case studies to prove it. She also needed an alternative that would do the job better. Once she had that, she enlisted the help of various celebrity ambassadors and went out to talk to opinion-formers in the media. That was roughly the point where I came in. Together we got the message across, as we persuaded more and more people of the sense of our arguments.'

'Persuaded people of what?'

'The sense of our arguments,' Shane repeated, puzzled.

'Indeed. Are you beginning to see the problem? Your strategy is perfect when you have a sound case. But what if you don't? What if' – White speared a piece of stilton on his knife and waved it in the air between them – 'your task was to convince the world the moon is made of blue cheese?'

'Seriously?'

'Seriously. Give it a try.'

Shane tried to focus. 'I'd aim to gather the supporting arguments.'

'Such as?'

'I've no idea. I'd need to ask the client.'

'And if your client is as mad as a box of frogs? Come on, you're a bright lad. Think of some.'

Shane puffed out his cheeks. 'I suppose they're all negative. Burden-of-proof stuff. How do we know it's *not* made of cheese? The only people in a position to know one way or the other are Neil Armstrong, Buzz Aldrin and NASA. So we could insert some doubt.'

'Good. Although that's the easy part. The doubt exists already, because millions of people already believe the moon landings are a hoax – mainly thanks to our friend Joey Talavera, as it happens – so you're pushing at an open door. You can get as far as a position of uncertainty without too much difficulty. However, if that's all you do, you haven't fulfilled your brief. You need people to believe it really is made of cheese, otherwise you don't get paid. How are you going to do that?'

'I'd, erm…' Shane was not enjoying this game. He threw his hands up. 'Tell me the answer. What would you do?'

White leaned back, closing his eyes in concentration. 'What would I do?' he muttered, frowning and tick-tocking his head from side to side as if engaging in silent dialogue with himself. Suddenly his eyes burst open and he lurched back towards Shane, jabbing his finger. 'I'll tell you what I'd do. I'd find a couple of researchers, one a chemist, the other an astrophysicist, and I'd set them to work in a tame institution. The chemist would look at the composition of cheese. It primarily depends on casein, if I'm not mistaken, which in turn contains carbon, hydrogen, nitrogen, oxygen, phosphorus and perhaps some sulphur. That's just off the top of my head, so don't quote me. There's also calcium in it, of course, which is found in all kinds of rocks, isn't it? That will be useful. Meanwhile, the astrophysicist investigates every conceivable aspect of space dust. At some stage, there's bound to be some chemical crossover, some common properties, because everything ultimately is made of the same kind of stuff, no? Eventually, both the chemist and the astrophysicist will publish something learned-looking, which may or may not be scientifically interesting, but that's not the point. The operation will come into its own when we tip off some scientifically illiterate journalist – which accounts for about ninety-five percent of them, so they won't be hard to find – and encourage them to compare the two papers. The journalist will tentatively show it to their news editor, suggesting that it might, on a slow news day, suggest the moon is made of cheese, which of course the news editor loves, picturing the banner headline. At that point, we commission another astrophysicist to drill deeper into the possibility of major calcium deposits somewhere on the moon. Little by little, the idea begins to take root that there are a surprising number of common elements between the moon and cheese. That's simply a rough plan for starters, but how does it sound?'

Shane wasn't convinced. 'Would anyone believe it? It sounds like a bit of a laugh, something from the *National Enquirer* or the *Sunday Sport*, but not the kind of thing anyone intelligent would believe.'

'Who's talking about intelligent people? We're in the business of exploiting the gullible, those many millions of our fellow citizens without critical faculties. You can make them believe anything you like, if you put your mind to it. What it really depends on is obfuscation, spin and stealthy groundwork, with some guiding principles. One: use the press for your own ends but avoid media scrutiny. Two: control your own narrative. And three: do everything you can under the radar. Oh, and four: where possible, hitch your cause onto a more popular one, letting other people do the hard work for you.'

'Like the moon landings conspiracy, you mean?'

'Exactly. You see, you're getting the hang of it. If you can amplify the doubt that anyone ever went to the moon, which means the rock samples they supposedly collected are fake, you have a freer hand for your own speculation. Speaking of cheese, do have some more of this stilton before I finish it.'

Shane shook his head, whereupon his host skewered what was left, put it on a cracker and demolished it, grunting happily.

'So, to get back to my actual brief, your advice would be to commission some research?'

White was still chewing. 'Exactly. Get the ball rolling. Find some niche areas where someone can write some gobbledegook. Claptrap disguised behind long words. The language is important. If nobody understands a word of it, it's much harder to shoot down.'

The prospect was daunting. 'I understand what you're saying, but…'

'But what?'

'I honestly wouldn't know where to begin.'

'Nonsense. You're an expert on cartographical projections and their history, which means you have a strong grasp of a niche discipline and you have easy access to any number of poverty-stricken would-be academics who are itching to be taken seriously. You also, if I may return to that vulgar bottom line once more, have access to what I assume will be a colossal budget. You may not realise this, because you're still a young man finding his way in the world, and you think everything is going to be fair, but life isn't remotely fair. The greatest unfairness of all is that being obscenely rich gets you whatever you want.'

Shane remembered what he'd said to Joey Talavera three days ago. *You're a multi-billionaire, why don't you just pay someone to make this happen?* Now he could see how it worked.

'I can see the cogs whirring,' said White. 'Care to tell me what you're thinking?'

'I'm…I don't know. I suppose I'm beginning to understand the nature of the transaction.'

'Good. That will make everything simpler all round. Now, there's one final element of strategy I haven't mentioned yet, and it's the most important one.'

Shane had belatedly pulled out a pen and paper and was scribbling notes. 'Tell me.'

'A key ingredient to a successful campaign is passion. You need to bring people with you by stirring their emotions.'

Shane stopped writing. 'I thought the whole point was to do this under the radar?'

'Most of it, but not all. You certainly don't want to let everyone know your end-game. But remember, I also said you must control the narrative, and that narrative will require public buy-in. Now, what's the basic rule that every populist has always known, from Julius Caesar to Adolf Hitler?'

'You're saying my role model is Hitler?'

'Bad example. From Caesar to…I don't know…that chap who wants to take us out of the European Union.'

'Nigel Farage?'

'That's the one. What's his trademark approach?'

'I suppose…whipping up resentment.'

'Exactly. Populists understand that going negative is easier and more effective than being positive. Ask people what they're in favour of, and they take a while to answer. Ask them what they're against and they'll tell you immediately. Ask them *who* they're against, and they'll tell you even faster. People love to have an enemy. If they don't have one, they need to be given one. Thus, if your ultimate goal is to turn people against the idea that the earth is a globe – to make the very word 'globe' unacceptable – then you need to associate that idea with something or someone they already hate. You don't need to know who or what that is immediately, but it's worth bearing—'

'But I do!' said Shane. His ethical objections were fading, now that he saw the task as an intellectual challenge. 'I half-knew it already, but now you've put it so clearly, it's really obvious.' He was aware he was slurring as he raised his glass. 'I know exactly who the focus of our hate could be. If there was ever a figure in history who could turn people into flat-earthers in the twenty-first century, it's got to be him.'

White raised his own glass too. 'I'm delighted to hear it. So who are we drinking to?'

'To Christopher Columbus, of course!'

The youngest cabin boy on the *Santa Maria*, who had the keenest eyes, spotted it first. 'Look there,' he shouted, pointing down into the sea, as the admiral and De La Cosa came to join him at the starboard gunwale.

The older men saw nothing at first, but then the admiral spied it too. 'It looks like some kind of reed.'

Two weeks earlier there had been a false alarm when they found themselves in a great expanse of weed floating on the surface. It must surely have been ripped from land close by, the admiral reasoned. When no land appeared, he was forced to conclude the vegetation was some marine phenomenon, thriving on the sea as abundantly as it might on a rock in their own climes. The disappointment hit everyone hard, and they blamed him for it. No one said a word to his face, of course, but he saw the resentment in their faces.

This was different. A lone strand, it floated free, rather than grew there, and it was green, therefore fresh, so could not have travelled far. He would be vindicated shortly, he was certain of that; perhaps this was the day.

Within minutes there was a commotion on the *Pinta* too. As the ship's signals soon afterwards revealed, the crew had spotted a reed of their own, as well as a stick that looked hand-carved. A little later, the crew of the *Niña* also spied a piece of cane, while a flock of seabirds above their heads served as further confirmation that land was near.

The mood, at last, dared to lighten.

It was only two days since full moon, so the night sky was clear. The admiral took his watch on the sterncastle, straining his eyes to examine every inch of the dark horizon.

Two hours before midnight, his vigilance paid off, as he glimpsed a distant, twinkling light. Now it was there, now it was gone. Was it his imagination? He had stared so long, perhaps he was mistaken. He could not afford to raise his men's hopes again, only to shatter them.

'Captain!' he called.

De La Cosa appeared at his shoulder.

'Do you see? On the horizon, port side. Follow my finger. It's so uncertain a thing, I'm not confident to declare it definitely land, for fear of creating a false hope. Unless you also…?'

'I do see something. It's like a little wax candle bobbing up and down.'

This second opinion was all the encouragement the admiral needed. He issued an order to be passed around the whole fleet. 'Keep a sharp look out from now on. He who raises the first cry on sight of land will receive a silk doublet and an annuity of ten thousand maravedis a year.'

Ninety pairs of eyes attached themselves to that horizon. Ten thousand maravedis a year was a handsome reward. No man on any of the three vessels slept.

After four hours, their wait was over.

'Land!' came the cry from high aloft the nimble little *Pinta*, racing on ahead as usual. Moments later, the boom of her cannon sounded, to confirm the lookout's sighting.

The admiral muttered a prayer of thanks to the Lord who had guided them to safety. 'Furl the sails,' he ordered. 'We can't approach in the dark. We'll lay to until dawn.'

By daylight, it was clear the land in question was a small island, barely three miles long, and not the mainland of Cathay. The discovery disappointed every man of the fleet, but the admiral told himself there was no need for despond. The islet was unlikely to be a lonely rock in the middle of the ocean. It was more probably part of some chain off the coast of the great continent. All would become clearer once they went ashore.

He put together a landing party from the *Santa Maria*: a handful of trusted officers; Escobedo, the royal secretary sent by their majesties to confer official status on the expedition; and Torres, the converted Jew, who was fluent in the Hebrew and Arabic tongues and would serve as an interpreter with the people of the Great Khan, the ruler of these bounteous lands. In case of trouble, the admiral also selected a small band of sailors armed with swords and hackbutts. Together, this group of around fifteen men boarded the flagship's longboat and pulled for the shore, while similar parties also set out from the *Pinta* and the *Niña*.

The water was a clear, pale blue, with luminescent rock

below the surface and schools of bright fish darting in and out of little caves within it. The three boats headed for a cove with sand as white as snow. Behind it grew a forest of a lusher green than any they had seen in Europe. They had surely found paradise on earth.

From their anchorage offshore, they had not been able to discern whether the island was inhabited. But as they drew closer, they saw a crowd of about two dozen willowy, colourfully dressed figures awaiting them on the shore.

'Guns at the ready,' said the admiral softly. 'They're bound to be armed and they may be hostile.'

When they came nearer still, however, they could see that these people were not just unarmed, but naked. What had looked like bright clothing was actually paint on their bodies. They all seemed to be young men, with no womenfolk to be seen. Their hair was dark and coarse, worn in a low fringe at the front and short at the back, save for a long hank, like a tail. Their skin was tawny, similar to that of the Canary Islanders, and their bodies were strong and virile, in the manner of Grecian statues.

Several of their number now waded into the surf to pull the longboats onto the sand.

'Come on, Torres,' said the admiral as he stepped from the prow of the boat and landed heavily on the beach. 'Speak to them.'

Facing the islanders, the *converso* smiled broadly and bowed low. '*As-salaam aleikum.*'

The naked men smiled, nodded and whispered among themselves, but none returned his greeting.

'*Anahnu musafaroon min balad baid. Anahnu musihioon. Nati bism malak wa malakat isbania wa nuqadim tahayaatana ila al-*

khan al-azeem.'

They stared blankly at him.

'Tell them we come in peace and we bring greetings from the King and Queen of Spain to their Great Khan.'

'That's what I've just told them, sir. They don't seem to understand.'

'Try it in another tongue, then. Go on, man. What are you waiting for? Try it in Arabic.'

'That was Arabic, sir.'

'Well, do it in something you haven't tried. Say it in your Jewish tongue.'

Torres cleared his throat and tried again, but it was clear there was no common language between them. The islanders nodded and smiled, and the Europeans bowed low, so they communicated after a fashion. One of the Indians, as the admiral resolved to call these people, brought a tame bird with azure and yellow plumage, which chattered away in a voice that sounded almost human. This, it seemed, was a gift. In return, the admiral offered hawk's bells and glass beads. All the while he looked out for evidence of the gold they had come to find, but there was none on display, not even on the body of the man who seemed to be the local chief. No amount of sign language could elicit the information the admiral really wanted: how far away were the Chinese coast and the island of Japan, and where was the Great Khan's capital?

After a while, he noticed that they began to repeat phrases that were said to them: 'Island of Chapan', 'Great Khan', 'Where is the gold?'. This did not signify any kind of comprehension, sadly; they were so eager to please, they mimicked whatever was said to them. But that was a positive discovery: it surely meant they would make excellent servants. They also had no observable religion, and were therefore ripe for conversion to Christianity. Another excellent circumstance.

The visitors held a short ceremony in which their majesties' standard was unfurled and the admiral declared, with Escobedo as witness: 'I hereby take possession of this island for the King and Queen of Spain.'

'King and Queen of Spain,' repeated a voice at the admiral's shoulder.

Thinking it was an Indian, he turned to acknowledge this encouraging comment, but was astonished to find that the words had come from the tame bird. It seemed to have learned Spanish in less than an hour. Destiny was surely on their side.

He summoned his first officer.

'Sir?'

'Choose six of these men as captives to take back to the king and queen, then we'll make ready to depart. Make sure you pick the strongest of them. We don't want them dead before they reach Castile.'

6

Now that he had Craig's blessing, plus Robinson White on hand as his mentor, Shane was running out of reasons not to sign up to Operation Talavera.

Xandra and Cyrus made it abundantly clear, via their calls, texts and emails, what they wanted him to do, and his residual resistance crumbled. In the days and weeks after getting back from California, he knuckled down to writing the report Xandra had commissioned on the way forward for Orange Peel. Whenever any moral qualms assailed him, he pushed them away by thinking how impressive it would be to become a CEO at just thirty-one. He also thought – because Xandra hadn't neglected to mention it – of the salary.

He dreaded the board meeting at which the flat-earth fait accompli, in the shape of his own report, was to be presented to Mel. He didn't think of himself as a duplicitous or nasty person, but there'd be no escaping his own back-stabbing role.

In the event, he dealt with it much like the rest of the board, by not looking Mel in the eye. Feeling thoroughly sick afterwards, he fell back on recalling all those times she'd put him down.

'I know it's hard,' said Xandra, seeing his miserable expression after Mel had left the room. 'Putting your personal feelings aside to make the right business decision is a difficult thing to do, if you're a decent person. Now you've done it once, you'll find it gets easier. Think of it as a rite of passage.'

Didn't they say the same of murder? It didn't make Shane feel any happier.

The following day, he thought it best to work from home, to avoid any awkward confrontations. It was cowardly, but it also meant he could have long conversations with White in complete privacy.

'As I suggested when you came to lunch, you need to start with academia,' his new guru boomed over an encrypted video call on Zype (because he didn't trust normal phone calls). Dressed in what looked like full leathers and a muir cap, he wandered around his flat as he talked. His face bounced in and out of view as he flung himself into this chair or that sofa, only sporadically remembering to point the phone in the right direction. 'The research projects we have in mind will take some time to complete, so we need to get them up and running as soon as possible. Don't forget that universities are wonderful places to sow the seeds for some long-term havoc without anyone noticing you're doing it.'

Shane could see the logic of that, but panic engulfed him. All this was so easy to say, but where the hell was he meant to find the pliant researchers to work on these subversive projects? And how was he supposed to insert their studies into existing academic programmes?

'You start with the money,' said White. 'We need a dirty great pot of it. Fortunately that's not a problem for our Californian benefactor, although we probably ought to cover the trail so it can't be traced back to him. Not that there's any reason he shouldn't use his billions to fund scholarly inquiry for the benefit of humanity. It's just that the name Talavera is such catnip for the media, it risks drawing unwanted attention to our little enterprise, and we can't have that, particularly at this early stage.'

'So we need to set up some kind of front?'

'Let's not use such a sinister word. I prefer 'charitable foundation'. Something with a nice, bland name that gives nothing at all away.'

'Not the Centre for Flat Earth Studies, then?' Shane managed a wry smile, to show he was joking.

'No indeed. Tell me: what's your middle name?'

'Peter. Why?'

'And the name of your first pet?'

'Amber. But if you're trying to hack my bank account—'

'The Peter Amber Institute. It has a nice ring to it, don't you think? Yes, I think that will do very nicely. We ought to incorporate it in California, for simplicity. I have a lawyer chum over there who can register something discreetly, ready for Joey to drop some cash in. While he's doing that, we'll start recruiting researchers. That's where you come in.'

'I thought I might,' said Shane. 'I've got a number of questions, though. For a start, how much should we tell them? I mean, it's not like we can just say, come and help us prove the earth is flat, is it?'

'No indeed, it very much isn't. Subtlety is the name of the game. Fortunately, it's also my specialist subject. We need to establish our own research needs and then approach suitable candidates accordingly, without having to, er…'

'Reveal they're in the pay of a flat-earth nutter?'

'To be too transparent about our end-game, is how I'd have put it.'

'So we don't just make a general appeal for research proposals? That's what I was worrying about. I couldn't see how we'd phrase it.'

'No, indeed. It's the beauty of having billionaire funding. All we need to do is tap some impoverished young academics from the right disciplines on the shoulder and tell them we have some work we'd like them to do. They'll be so overjoyed, they'll say yes like a shot. If they ever wonder what their research is for and why we're paying for it, mark my words, they'll be far too canny to do so out loud.'

'So who's going to do the tapping? You or me?'

'We'll need a director. A young, penniless PhD graduate, I suggest. Someone with 'Dr' in front of their name will give our institute an air of authority. Luckily, there are hundreds of them about, all wondering how the hell they're going to make a living. If I see to the formalities of setting up the foundation, making it untraceable to Joey, why don't you trawl for some likely candidates? Draw up a shortlist of three or four. How does that sound?'

Shane felt his heart thumping. Where was he meant to trawl? He had no idea where to start. However, a voice in his head told him he was meant to be the boss now, so he ought at least to present like one.

'Sure, no problem,' he said, hoping that sounded more

convincing to Robbie than it did to his own ears.

'It's a ghastly cliché, but this is one time where a willingness to think outside the box really is compulsory. May I offer a tip?'

Robbie was no fool: he understood how badly out of his depth Shane felt.

'Please do.'

'The internet is a big place, so it may not be obvious where to begin. If I were doing this, I'd start on Twitter. That's the ultimate forum for the peddling of ideas, from the banal to the brilliant to the barking mad. The painfully uneducated rub shoulders with the world's most cultivated brains. We don't necessarily want the greatest genius in the world, but we do want someone smart with time on their hands. If they're on social media all day, chances are they have more free time than they want. Offer them a proper job and they'll be over the moon.'

'Sounds like a plan. Thanks.'

When they ended their call, Shane made himself a pot of tea and logged on to Twitter.

He began by searching on 'flat earth', not in any great expectation of finding what he wanted, but simply to see what it would turn up. The search yielded plenty of results, and not everyone tweeting on the subject was a conspiracy-theorist whack job. Unfortunately, all the sane people using the term did so in a derogatory way, throwing it as a taunt at anyone with unscientific views. True believers were more scarce and, to judge by their output, few of them had left school with a single qualification, let alone finished a doctorate. If Shane wanted to find intellectuals who might be sympathetic to flat-earth ideas, this wasn't the way.

As he considered what to do next, he remembered that

Talavera had used a fancy word for his own ideas. Something beginning with 'z'…zelenic…zametic…zoretic? A quick Google search showed that none of those existed. The Victorian flat-earthers had used the word to describe their studies, Joey said. In that case, it should feature in a history of the flat-earth movement. Shane went to Wikipedia. A familiar name jumped off the page as he scrolled down: Samuel Birley Rowbotham, aka Parallax. And there, sure enough, was his book, *Zetetic Astronomy: Earth Not a Globe*. Zetetic, according to the online Collins Dictionary, came from the Greek zētētikos, from zēteō to seek, and it meant 'proceeding by inquiry; investigating'. The flat-earthers seemed to have co-opted it to denote their own brand of free thought – in which 'free' meant free from fact, logic, observation or intelligence.

Shane took a deep breath and told himself not to be so sniffy. He had a job to do and a roof to keep over their heads, and he should approach the task in the same spirit as Robbie: as a challenge. It was up to him to relaunch the field of zeteticism so it was no longer the sole preserve of fruit-loops.

This was no small undertaking, as he realised when he typed 'zetetic' into the Twitter search bar. It was popular in profile names, especially in the US: @ThatZeteticGuy, @YoZetetic and @Zetetic_Egghead and so on. Several of them seemed harmless enough because they tweeted on mainstream topics – a retweet of a Kanye West meme, a picture of a sunset, chatter about Senate races that Shane knew nothing about – but the same could not be said for the user @ZeteticTimes, whose eponymous blog asked when the masses would wake up and see through the falsehoods imposed on them by the Orion Reptilian Empire and its human stooges. The blogposts were festooned with hashtags that spoke volumes: *#lizard,*

#fake, #toxic, #vatican, #pope… Also frequently mentioned was 'the fabricated cosmos industry (commonly referred to as "modern science")'. This chimed closely with some of Joey's theories, but the account served as a cautionary tale. If Shane wanted to change billions of minds, @ZeteticTimes wasn't the model to follow.

He persevered a little longer, experimenting with 'cartography', 'Copernicus' and 'globularism', but none of those got him anywhere: the results were either too bland or too crazy. He was clearly on the wrong track, which reassured him in one sense, at least: Robinson White wasn't infallible.

His confidence boosted by that thought, he realised it was up to him to show his own initiative. After brewing more tea, he kicked his feet up onto the sofa to think it through.

He reminded himself that he was trying to foist an insane view on an unsuspecting world in such a way that the world didn't notice the insanity. It was, by any reckoning, massively ambitious. The project would only succeed if it were run by smart people of the highest calibre. Smart, sane people. Flat-earthers who were already converts to Joey's world-view were, by definition, insane.

It followed, therefore, that the director of the Peter Amber Institute shouldn't be a flat-earther. The point of the institute was to create academic building-blocks that would give intellectual credibility to ideas currently held only by the ill-educated and the gullible. Its director ought to have a genuine passion for the areas of study in which they were going to work. Shane should therefore start by defining what those areas should be.

To prove the moon was made of cheese, Robbie had argued they needed to commission research projects from chemists and astrophysicists. What were the equivalent areas of study for flat-earthery? Taking a swig of tea, Shane grabbed a pen and notepad and started scribbling. To his surprise and relief, the ideas flowed and, ten minutes later, he had a list. It needed tidying up but, for something off the top of his head, it wasn't bad.

1. The othering of the South: how the arbitrary division of the world into hemispheres furthers structural racism
2. Cartography and the patriarchy: charting women's voices in the history of map projection
3. Columbus reassessed: the role of racism in cartographical myth-making
4. Creation myths and the understanding of science among the indigenous [fill in their ethnic name here] people of the Caribbean
5. The azimuthal myth: the semiotics of the United Nations logo
6. Alternatives to gravity: how Newtonian physics defined perceptions of the world for three centuries
7. In the quantum era, how can we be certain we know anything about the world around us?
8. How is mass consciousness influenced by theoretical hegemony?
9. Information, power and illusion
10. Perception and reality: how to make a mass hoax stick

No doubt any genuine academic would tell him these were more like student essay topics than titles of research projects.

Nevertheless, as an outline for areas of study, it did the job, suggesting a programme that would chip away at received wisdom without sounding more pretentious or absurd than any of the other stuff that came out of university humanities departments. It was more than adequate as a starting point for the future director of the institute.

More importantly, it revealed the key disciplines. Psychology, philosophy and history featured as much as physics and geography. What sort of person would be excited by that list? Male, probably, despite the nod to feminism. Young, but that was a given for a recent PhD graduate. What would they read for pleasure? Sci-fi, definitely. High-end classics: Asimov, Philip K. Dick. What would they watch on TV or at the cinema? *Inception, Lost, The Matrix*, obviously, and maybe *Black Mirror*... And *The Truman Show*. They'd see the idea of living life on a stage set as a genuine social experiment and want to know if it could be pulled off in real life. In fact...

He keyed 'academic research on the truman show' into Google. A second later his screen was flooded with links to papers: *The Truman Show* as a symptom of this or an argument for that. This was surely his candidate pool! Now he simply had to check them all out and find someone suitable. For the first time since taking this project on, he felt energised. He might actually be capable of doing this.

By the end of the afternoon, he'd found just the person. Dr S.Y. Rao was a doctoral graduate of the University of Calcutta whose thesis, a study of epistemology in the digital era, examined the influences of Descartes, Russell and Foucault on the work of a Californian philosopher called Professor Jared Baker. This would have gone right over Shane's head if it hadn't also borne the title 'How do we know we're not all in *The Truman Show* already?'.

This was clearly designed to be eye-catching, but its author could scarcely have imagined how much it would excite Shane. The biographical detail he harvested from Facebook, Instagram and LinkedIn confirmed the candidate's suitability – as well as the accuracy of his own profiling. Asimov got a name-check, as did *Inception* (plus Arthur C. Clarke and *Misfits*). The only divergence was that Dr Sonali Yashwant Rao – with her long, luxuriant hair parted in the centre and red bindi on her forehead – was definitely female.

'She sounds ideal,' White agreed, when Shane called to tell him of his discovery. 'Perfect in every way. On paper, at any rate – and that's all we've got to go on. You've done a great job. Mark my words, you're going to be much better at all this than you expect.'

Shane basked in the compliment. He sensed that effusive flattery came easily to Robbie, but it made a refreshing change from years of put-downs and snarks from Mel.

'Awesome. I'm glad you approve. I'll drop her an email.'

'Actually, I wouldn't do that. Let's find a more arm's-length way. We can make her sign a confidentiality clause, but it will be safer if she doesn't know she's working for Orange Peel. That way, if things hot up further down the line, she won't land us, or herself, in the soup. We can do it all through a third party. Cyrus is our man, I'd say.'

'Point taken on being discreet, but is Cyrus a good idea? It's a matter of public record that he's on the Orange Peel board.'

'Yes, but he's involved with other organisations too, so the connection won't be obvious unless you're looking for it, which your Dr Rao won't be.'

So they agreed that Cyrus would message their sole candidate to tell her the good news: she'd been headhunted as the inaugural director of the Peter Amber Institute of Palo Alto, California.

'No way!' she screamed, as Cyrus related it to Shane afterwards. 'That's so totally awesome. Palo Alto as in Stanford? I don't believe it. Honestly, I'm truly humbled.'

Cyrus hadn't explicitly said the institute was part of Stanford University; he'd merely chosen not to disabuse her.

The only snag, she said, when she'd finished her whoops and OMGs, was that she had a husband and a small son. Would they also get visas to live in the US?

Cyrus explained that the fledgling institute didn't yet have premises, so it *might* be possible for Dr Rao to take on the role without having to leave India. Once he'd assured her that her salary would be paid at US rather than Indian rates, any disappointment at not living the Californian dream evaporated.

Once she'd signed the paperwork, Dr Rao set about turning Shane's rough-and-ready list into a fully commissioned research programme. At Cyrus' direction, all the institute's work was saved to a Google Drive folder which Shane could discreetly access to monitor progress. He took a secret delight in seeing how each of his one-sentence topics, tossed so hurriedly onto the page of his notebook, developed into a structured outline running to three or four pages. He had no idea whether these outlines, couched in academic jargon, would make sense to anyone who could decode the gobbledegook, but that made them all the better. As Robbie had stressed from the outset, obscurity and mystification were their allies in this game. Clarity was the last thing they needed.

Among the many unfamiliar terms Dr Rao used, one stood out: Bakerian. Shane took this to refer to the Professor Jared Baker whom she had cited so often in her thesis. Google revealed that Baker was a professor of applied hermeneutics at Berkeley, and a wide array of links related to his academic career. For Shane, who hadn't a clue what applied hermeneutics was, these sources meant little. He found himself glazing over after a few lines and made a mental note to ask Robbie; he'd come to accept that White knew everything worth knowing and was often much better at explaining it than the internet.

His faith was rewarded the next time they spoke.

'Jared Baker is a very big deal in certain quarters,' his mentor boomed on a video call from his balcony, where he was wearing aviator shades in the spring sunshine. 'As I understand it, he's a bit of a lightweight. He's no Heidegger or Sartre, that's for sure. But he's been extremely adept at selling himself to a certain generation of humanities students and to make phenomenology the height of fashion across lots of other disciplines.'

'Wait, back up. What's phenomenology?'

'What's phenomenology?' White sounded surprised that anyone should need to ask. 'It's the study of appearances as opposed to things. Enlightenment philosophers like Descartes divided the world into a consciousness that perceived things and the things it perceived. Phenomenologists say you can't do that: all you have to go on is perception, so the only thing you can reliably talk about is appearance. That's a boon for people trying to argue away inconvenient phenomena. It's a way of saying they don't really exist. Baker specialises in appalling psychobabble. He won the academic equivalent of a

Golden Raspberry for his bad writing, if memory serves. But he has a gift for convincing the easily impressed that he's the bee's knees. Why do you ask about him?'

'Rao says "Bakerian" all the time. It's in virtually every paragraph. She loves him. If we want to make our ideas seem cutting-edge, I reckon we just need to say they're inspired by the great man.'

'That's a very good point. Nothing is too mad for the phenomenological world-view, and a generation of humanities students worship the ground he walks on. Yes, I do believe we've got our guru. All we need now is a good enemy for the haters, and we'll be in business.'

'We've got our enemy. Didn't we agree it was Christopher Columbus?'

'Oh yes, certainly him. But I was thinking of a living figure rather than a historical one. That will be so much more effective. A suitable candidate will emerge soon enough, you'll see. For the moment, Baker was an excellent spot on your part. What did I tell you? You're going to be good at all this.'

7

Craig could barely remember what it was like not to be exhausted. On the twelve-hour shifts around which his life now revolved, mistakes didn't just entail bollockings; they could also kill patients. He channelled every drop of energy into functioning while he was at work, trying to get through the day or night without some fatal cock-up. As a result, he had nothing sensible left for the world beyond the hospital gates.

That was his excuse for the terrible advice that, he now saw, he'd given his husband.

Swapping shifts to welcome Shane back from California was a major hassle, but he'd been determined to make the effort. Looking back, he could see he was assuaging his guilt for spending so much time at work. Not that Shane ever complained; his job at Orange Peel was demanding too, and he also stayed late. He fully deserved the perk of a trip to San Francisco, complete with jammy upgrade to business class. Craig was pleased that at least one of them had the chance to live the high life.

In making a fuss over Shane's return, he'd reckoned without his own frazzled state. The first glass of wine at the Soho pizzeria went straight to his head. By the second, it was an effort to talk without slurring, as his tongue thickened in his mouth. He really did want to hear about Google HQ, but he clean forgot about the bonus part of the trip, when Shane was whisked off to meet a celebrity billionaire at his private mansion. His third glass of wine was definitely a mistake, and he'd switched to babbling autopilot by the time they reached Joey Talavera's crazy proposition for Orange Peel. He dimly remembered Shane asked his blessing to accept the commission, but he wasn't in any fit state to give it. Not in any responsible way, with proper consideration for the consequences.

If there was any logic to the way his tired, drunken brain had operated that evening, the key factor was money. They'd both taken such pride in moving into their own flat: no longer servicing some rip-off landlord's mortgage debt, but paying off a loan of their own. With it came alarming adult responsibilities, however, and they were each daunted by that twenty-five-year term, which stretched further into the future than either of them could properly imagine. Shane was the higher earner, and the prospect of his income disappearing if Mel wound up Orange Peel, as she apparently intended, terrified Craig. That was his excuse.

The realisation that he'd green-lit something ridiculous, and potentially catastrophic, only hit him a couple of days later. Strap-hanging on the train as he came home from the hospital, he replayed the conversation in his head and saw with sudden clarity how stupid he'd been. Aside from the ethics of trying to hoodwink the world into some medieval delusion, Shane was playing a fool's game that would end in tears or derision — most likely both — and would surely cost him his job in the end anyway. Yes, the money was attractive, and he could take the cash for as long as Talavera offered it, banking as much as possible before Orange Peel was laughed into oblivion. But at what cost to his reputation and career prospects?

As the train pulled into Plumstead, Craig resolved to say all this before it was too late. But when he reached the flat, his husband was bubbling over with excitement about his boozy lunch with Robinson White, wanting to relate every detail. He'd already told Xandra he was on board with the plan, and now he'd acquired a mentor in the form of this bizarre old leather queen, living in a council flat penthouse furnished like a stately home. The time for Craig to call a halt, he realised, had passed. He'd just have to bite his tongue and try to be as supportive as possible when, as it surely would, the whole thing went pear-shaped.

That first night, when it was 'Robbie this' and 'Robbie that', Shane couldn't shut up about the guy. Since then, however, he'd grown more secretive about the connection. As far as Craig could tell, he mainly zyped White from home, which made sense while they plotted behind Mel's back. But he also made a point of going into another room to talk to Robbie if Craig happened also to be in the flat. It felt like a deliberate attempt to keep him at arm's length, and it left him wondering why.

It was clear from Shane's account that this White character revelled in his own cut-glass version of shadiness. Was he steering Shane down such a dodgy path that Craig mustn't know about it? That would be alarming. What if Shane ended up not just jobless and ridiculed, but in jail? Visions of handcuffs, prison bars and reporters camped outside their flat spooled through Craig's mind. Breathe, he told himself. Catastrophising, as the therapists called it, benefited no one.

On the other hand, maybe it was shame that made Shane exclude Craig from his machinations. He'd stabbed Mel in the back; there was no getting away from that, even if Xandra had sharpened the dagger and put it in his hand. Any decent person – and Shane *was* a decent person – would feel remorse, just as Craig was mortified at having drunkenly approved the whole shabby operation. Should he take the first step in admitting his own regret? Might that make it easier for Shane to open up?

A couple of weeks after Shane's return from Silicon Valley, they treated themselves to a rare Sunday in the West End: morning service at St Anne's, followed by an early lunch in Wardour Street, then a wander through Carnaby Street and Bond Street. Craig had half a mind to bring it all out into the open but, in the end, he couldn't bring himself to spoil the mood. They spent such little quality time together.

Enjoying the window-shopping, they stopped outside Smythson's and gazed at the immaculate display of leather-bound notebooks and diaries with matching bags and briefcases.

'You said I should keep a journal,' Shane said.

'I did. Come on, I'll treat you. To celebrate your new job.' Craig was aware, as he made the offer, that he was compensating for his private reservations.

'Are you sure? I was joking. All this stuff costs a bomb.'

'I said I'm buying.'

The damage turned out to be about four times what Craig had expected. It took an effort to disguise the shock. 'Just make sure you use it, now I've spent half this month's mortgage on it,' he said.

Shane promised he would, and he'd been as good as his word. Craig often saw him scribbling away in the calfskin volume at the end of the evening. He continued to worry that Shane had private qualms about the lengths to which his new job would oblige him to go. If only Craig knew for certain, he might be able to raise the subject with confidence and attempt to find a way out of the whole mess.

One night, while Shane was in the bathroom brushing his teeth, Craig finally plucked up the courage to look at the journal. The idea had been knocking around in his head for a few days. It could do no harm to have a quick glance.

Shane kept the diary in the Ikea chest of drawers – white Malm, like all their bedroom furniture – on his side of their bed.

As Craig lifted the journal out of the top drawer, he saw a pile of Valentine cards, all from himself, stacked below it. The top one was the first he'd ever sent to Shane: a heart filled with red glitter. He remembered choosing it in Paperchase. He flipped the card open. In his own hand the message read: 'The first of many, I hope. With love xxx'.

The innocence of the inscription made him smile, but it also served as a rebuke. After a moment's hesitation, he returned the journal to its place in the drawer, unopened. They'd built their relationship on trust. He wouldn't dishonour it by sneaking around reading private diaries, however selfless his motive.

By the time Shane returned from the bathroom, Craig was back under his own side of the duvet. He remained concerned about his husband's bizarre situation at Orange Peel. But he was relieved that he himself hadn't overstepped the line.

8

In the difficult interregnum between the board meeting and Mel's formal departure, Shane knew that the staff at Orange Peel were speculating furiously about the reason she was going, and whether her exit was really voluntary. Since Mel was bound by a non-disclosure agreement, there was no danger of her telling them the truth, even if she had any friends or allies among them in whom to confide. Shane gave nothing away either, so no one had any idea what was really going on. However, he worried how the hell he was going to tell them about the charity's change of direction. They would need to know about their new remit eventually, but he hadn't a clue how he was meant to break it to them.

Xandra advised him to settle in first, without rushing into any premature disclosures.

'Remember you're starting with a natural advantage,' she

said, over a drink in a Shoreditch wine bar, the evening before he was formally due to take over. 'Mel wanted to close the place down and put them all out of a job. You're the one who stepped in to save them. Once they know that, they'll have a high tolerance for any changes you make, because the alternative would have been much worse. You've been loyal to them and they'll return it.'

'Yes, I can see that. Provided they're aware of it. That Mel wanted to make them all redundant and I saved the day, I mean.'

'You'll have to tell them, won't you? I suggest you assemble them for a pep-talk tomorrow. Paint it as a new dawn. They'll love you for it, you'll see.'

He did as she suggested. They usually grumbled about such gatherings, but on this occasion they clustered around as soon as he called for their attention.

'I'm aware there's been a lot of confusion about what's been going on,' he began. 'I've also overheard some understandable worries about all our futures at Orange Peel, amid rumours that we might be about to shut up shop.' They were all staring intently at him, the most captive audience he'd ever had. 'And there was, I'm sorry to say, some truth in those rumours.' The collective gasp was audible. He allowed his words to sit unchallenged as he gazed dolefully back at them. This was his moment and he meant to make the most if it. 'I'm afraid that Mel, who built this organisation from nothing and did an amazing job of making it what it is today, really did want to close nearly everything down, with the loss of most of your' – he corrected himself – 'of *our* jobs.'

Directly in front of him stood Erika, a fast-talking German in her mid-twenties who headed the social media team. She had tears in her eyes. Shane had always liked Erika. They got on well and had sometimes socialised.

'I'm also sorry that I haven't been able to say anything to reassure you while those rumours were circulating. Believe me, I wanted to, and now, finally, I can. The good news is that the board strongly disagreed with Mel's vision for our future, or lack of it. So strongly, in fact, that there was a parting of the ways and I was asked to take over. And I'm happy to be able to tell you this morning' – at last he broke into a smile – 'that there won't be any job losses. The Orange Peel Foundation remains open for business on my watch.'

The fear gave way to actual cheers. Ellie rushed forward and hugged him. Xandra was right: for all of them, he was an instant hero.

For almost all of them. 'And the bad news?' called Ollie, one of the graphic designers, from the back of room. Gloom returned, and smiles turned to frowns.

'The best news of all is there is no bad news,' said Shane. 'It's all good news. I know, right? But it's true.'

It was not a complete lie. Ollie was no doubt thinking of pay cuts all round, or a mere deferral of Mel's closure plans. None of that was going to happen. In that sense, he wasn't lying.

'You may notice some changes of style and emphasis. If some things seem puzzling at first, don't worry. You have my word that everything I do is designed to strengthen and expand our role and to guarantee a future for us all. As I say, I'm lucky enough to have the full backing of the board, and I know I can rely on you all to give me your full support too.'

As he turned away, they all clapped. They'd never applauded Mel. Xandra had called it exactly right: they were much more likely to give him the benefit of the doubt now, because they knew how much they owed him.

It was an excellent start, but he knew he had to move forward with caution. He certainly mustn't spring all the changes on them at once. That would be a sure way to burn through all the credit he'd just banked. Incremental was the way to go: softly, softly, turning the ship around so slowly that they wouldn't even notice it was pointing in the opposite direction. It would be a major challenge, but it might also be the making of him. After all, if he could pull it off with his own staff, there was a chance he could do it with the world at large.

His first step on the route to Orange Peel 2.0 was rebranding. From its earliest days, the foundation's logo had been a simplified version of the orange-peel projection: the original deconstructed citrus. It was coloured orange, naturally, and had a primary-school feel: big, bold, sans-serif typography that wouldn't be out of place in an early-learning ABC. It conveyed the message that map projections were fun, friendly and accessible to everyone. This insignia had done the job magnificently, helping make Orange Peel one of the best known and most trusted charities in the country.

Clearly, Shane mustn't do anything to squander that. Joey Talavera had approached them because Orange Peel's reputation extended globally, and success depended entirely on the maintenance of that international standing. Shane's job was to persuade people to cast aside beliefs they'd always considered unshakeable; if they listened to him, it would be not as an individual, but as the head of a body they trusted. Brand recognition was crucial to that.

Nevertheless, the current logo was no longer fit for purpose, for the simple reason that the deconstructed orange only made sense if everyone agreed the earth was round. If the peeled skin had to go, that presented an opportunity to ditch the childish graphics and replace them with something much more sober and authoritative. It also made sense to do this early on, before any other change of direction became apparent. That way, the new branding would have a chance to bed in, soaking up all the trust, affection and goodwill in which the present one currently flourished.

He delved into the files to find out who'd designed the original logo. It turned out to be an established firm of brand consultants who were still going strong, so he sent them a brief for a replacement design, and they sent back an array of options which he shared with the board. Xandra and her colleagues chose something dignified: the name of the foundation, in a traditional stockbroker-style font, without any other artwork, in a crisp, resolute black.

That was the easy part. Now he had to present the rebranding to his staff.

His head of communications was a sharp-suited Geordie called Jem, virtually the only man in the office not to have a beard. The birth of his first child had left him hollow-eyed and less dapper of late, but he was all too alert to the implications of the makeover.

'Out with the old, eh?' he said, when Shane asked him into his office to preview the design. 'What's the concept here? No offence, but it looks quite strait-laced and safe. Is that the shape of things to come?'

'I wouldn't say that,' said Shane, truthfully. 'We're growing up, that's all. We've spent years building up authority, and now I want to put that authority to good use. To do that, we need to look the part.' That wasn't bad, considering it was completely off the cuff.

'No problem. I actually quite like it. Everyone knows who we are nowadays, so we don't need a picture of orange peel to explain the name, do we? And we don't even need it in orange letters. It's assertive, in that sense.'

'I'm glad you think so. I do too.'

That was much easier than he'd expected. So far, so good. He'd signalled a change without being specific about what it was, and his explanation had been accepted. Hopefully that boded well.

Nevertheless, the rebranding was only a superficial tweak. If he was honest, it was a form of displacement activity: a way of convincing himself he'd made a start on his gargantuan task, without doing anything meaningful. He'd put a new emblem on the quarterdeck but hadn't started to change course.

A chance remark of Xandra's gave him an idea.

She'd taken to calling every week to receive a progress update, and to offer guidance and moral support. On this particular occasion, he was telling her about the range of academic studies that were now up and running, thanks to Dr Rao, from Oregon to Cape Town and Singapore.

'We truly are a global operation,' she said. 'I'm impressed.'

'You mean *worldwide*,' he corrected.

'Worldwide, global… Same differe… Oh, I see what you mean. We're going to have to stop using that word, aren't we?'

He'd meant it as a joke, but it set him thinking. Policing language was all the rage, and he was growing used to finding once-acceptable phrases now vetoed. Often there was no obvious difference between the approved term and the banned one: how would you explain to a Martian that calling someone a person of colour was deeply respectful but calling them a coloured person was beyond the pale? Unlike many of his peers, Shane viewed these battles over words as a diversion: in a world riven with injustice and inequalities of wealth, dictating people's vocabulary made activists feel better about themselves, but little else. Nevertheless it was the preoccupation of the age, and he might as well take advantage of it.

What would it take to get 'global' on the banned list? If he could pull that off, the benefits might be huge: it would throw an aura of negativity over anything involving the globe. From there, it was a more manageable step to the next stage, where belief in a globular earth was an ugly, unacceptable heresy. And it could all be done without any reference to flat-earthery; it was crucial not to show that part of his hand for as long as possible. Much better, and more achievable, to make the g-word unsayable by linking it to other, already discredited causes.

Happily, he had a perfect one in mind.

There was a certain beauty to all this, he saw, as he thought his plan through. It was a long game that only he and a handful of others knew he was playing. He remembered the day when he'd admitted to Robbie that he was nervous about messing up and looking ridiculous; he'd been serious about that, and until now he'd approached the whole enterprise with trepidation. It hadn't occurred to him that it might actually be fun.

He scheduled a meeting with Erika who, in addition to looking after social media, was the foundation's acting head of research.

'How is everything?' she asked, seating herself in the visitor's chair in front of his desk. 'Are you enjoying being in charge? Everyone's very happy they gave it to you, especially after we found out what Mel had in mind.'

'Thank you. I appreciate that. It's really good to hear.'

'Of course we're all keen to know what we're going to be doing. Everyone wants to play their part.'

'Excellent. That's exactly what I wanted to talk to you about. I'd like you to lead a research project on globalisation.'

'Globalisation?'

'Yes. You know, the way the structure of the world economy has transformed itself in the past twenty years or so, transcending national boundaries and impacting the lives of billions of people.'

'For sure. I know what it is. I'm just a little surprised because it's so different to map-making. But yeah, whatever you need.' Her perfect idiomatic English sounded gently incongruous in her clipped German accent. 'Any particular aspect of it?'

'All the bad stuff. Chapter and verse. All the ways globalisation has made the world a worse place. Particularly when it comes to racism. Make sure you focus on that.'

'Racism?'

'Yes. And inequalities. Get your team to give themselves a crash course.' Erika managed three colleagues: two on job share, the other full time. 'Read up, watch some explainers on YouTube, build up as much expertise as you can. Then start compiling some dossiers. You know, arranged thematically.'

'So the themes would be, like, "racism" and "inequalities" and…?'

'Other stuff like that, yes. All the nasties. I can see you've got the gist. Get really immersed in it and start presenting some findings in, say, a month from now?'

'Cool, yeah. No problem. Is this, like, a priority over all other existing stuff? Like, all hands on the pumps?'

'It is, really, yes. Go for it. Have fun with it. Well, not fun, exactly. Racism and inequalities aren't fun subjects, clearly. I mean, be creative. Think out of the box. Tell me a load of stuff I don't know. Things that will surprise people, as well as the obvious.'

'Got it. Leave it to us.'

'Thanks, Erika.'

'Thank *you*.'

Again, it boded well. They were so relieved still to have jobs, they'd do anything he asked with willingness and enthusiasm.

Despite his regular reports to Xandra, Shane treated Robbie as his real guiding light. Although he wasn't privy to the precise arrangement, he assumed White was on a hefty retainer to Joey as a round-the-clock consultant. He certainly seemed on permanent standby to provide a pat on the back and usher Shane towards the next task.

'How long is Erika going to take to deliver what you need?' Robbie wanted to know when next they spoke.

'I gave her a month.'

'Good. In the meantime, I'd set up some bots, if I were you.'

This was where Robbie was so useful. Shane vaguely knew that fake accounts, automated on an industrial scale, were part of the smoke and mirrors of social media, but he was still getting used to being the kind of shadowy player who dealt in such black-ops currency.

'Walk me through that. I don't really know how it all

works.'

'Well, if you want to make a particular word or expression socially unacceptable, you need some allies to agree with you and help you spread the word. In due course, if everything goes to plan, you'll have plenty of real people who'll do it of their own accord, with just a bit of nudging from you. At the moment, however, you don't have that, so you need some fake ones. Now's the time to get them up and running, building up a few followers, so they're in place when you're ready to start pushing your message out.'

'Is it legal?'

'If buying fake likes on social media were a crime, our jails would be full of celebrities. No, it's not illegal. But you don't want to get caught. It tends to tarnish the brand.'

'Yes, I can see that. So how do I go about it? Creating the bots, I mean. As well as not getting caught. I haven't a clue where to start.'

'Fortunately I do, so you don't have to worry about that.'

'I hoped you might say that.'

'Delighted to be able to assist.'

'What would I do without you, Robbie?'

'That's an academic question, because I'm here, at your disposal.'

'Thank you. So can I leave it to you? Or is there anything you need from me?'

'Yes, you can. I simply need to know how many bots you want.'

'What do you advise? Is there, like, a normal amount to choose?'

'I'd go with a thousand, for the time being. We can always make more later.'

'Cool.'

'And what do you want their profile to be?'

'Profile? How do you mean?'

'When you set up a fake account, on Facebook, Twitter, Instagram or wherever, it needs to appear as if it corresponds to a real person. With a real-sounding name, some kind of biography, a location and so on. And it must follow other accounts. You can tell a good deal about any user from the accounts they choose to follow. For example, if someone follows a bunch of Conservative politicians and nobody from any other party, it's a fair bet they're a Tory. If someone else follows lots of footballers but no cricketers, you can tell which sport they like; and probably also what team they support. If a third account follows the entire cast of *The Only Way Is Essex*, it's a reasonable guess they're under twenty-five. And so on.'

'Yes, I get all that. But why does it matter with bots? If they're only there for likes and retweets, who cares which accounts they follow?'

'It matters a lot. Think ahead to when you're ready to launch your campaign. Imagine you've got some killer tweet that says…I don't know…*Globalisation is horrid and if you use the word "global" you're horrid too…*'

'You know that's not a killer tweet, right? That's the world's worst tweet.'

'I know. Yours will be much better. That's why you have people like Erika. Let's say she's written it for you, and it really is a killer tweet. If you put a particular hashtag on it, that will tell your thousand pre-programmed bots to retweet it. They're your instant supporters, as we've said. The question is, who do you want them to be? For example, sixty-three percent of them could insist that Princess Diana was murdered by the Royal Family, which would be obvious from the kind of accounts they follow, and forty-nine percent of them might believe President Obama was born in Kenya.'

'No, definitely not. That's the last thing we want.'

'Why?'

'Because they're all cranks, and it would be obvious that the only people who supported us were lunatics. That would put all the sane people off, and they're the ones we want on our side.'

'Exactly! Now do you see why this matters?'

It was so obvious, when Robbie put it like that, that Shane was embarrassed to have asked. 'All right, so they need to be opinion-formers. And people with progressive views. That way, disapproving of the g-word becomes, like, a cultural thing.'

'Precisely. You want liberal millennials to collectively decide that the word "global" should never be used in civilised discourse. Once they've done that, they'll set about policing the internet to make sure everyone obeys. They'll enjoy that.'

'Amazing. They'll be doing our work for us. And nobody will ever find our fingerprints.'

'I'm glad to hear you're getting the hang of this. I knew you would. And what about location? Metropolitan, I'd say, wouldn't you? Urban, at the very least.'

'Yes, definitely.'

'And UK only? Or global?'

'You mean *worldwide*.'

'Just my little joke,' said Robbie. He was irritatingly difficult to catch out.

Shane considered for a moment. 'It should be the English-speaking world, because our messages are in English. Maybe a sprinkling of US, Canada, Australia and New Zealand? But still millennial progressives in cities.'

'Consider it done. How about seventy percent UK, and the rest divided between those other countries?'

'Perfect.'

'Good. We have a plan. Let me go away and talk to my good friend Dr Frankenstein at the bot laboratory, and he'll make us one thousand latte-drinking, avocado-loving hipsters on three continents before you can say Christopher Columbus.'

'He doesn't really call himself Dr Frankenstein?'

'No, that's just my little *bêtise*. You don't need to know his name.'

'Don't worry, I don't want to. Out of interest, though: where is this lab? What country, I mean. We won't end up in hock to the Russian mafia, will we?'

'No fear of that. It's not in Russia. The best bot-farms for our purposes are in countries where they speak good English. India and Bangladesh, for example. In our case, I shall be placing a discreet call to Lapu-Lapu City, the click-farm capital of the Philippines. More than that, I will not say.'

'Awesome. Will you let me know when they're ready for action?'

'I will indeed, but you'll probably know anyway, if you keep an eye on your Twitter account.'

Sure enough, in the next few weeks Orange Peel steadily acquired hundreds of new followers on Twitter. The surge was so dramatic that Erika flagged up the news in an email.

Shane pretended he didn't already know. 'Brilliant. It's testament to all your hard work and the great content you're putting out,' he replied.

To her credit, she refused to accept the plaudits. 'I haven't been doing anything different to normal,' she said, when he stopped at her desk to congratulate her in person. 'Usually, if you have a rush of new followers, it's because of one tweet that's done particularly well. But this isn't like that. They're just coming in a steady stream, with no obvious prompting.'

It was important that she didn't get suspicious and start looking more closely at the profile of the new followers. Anyone with an eye for this kind of fakery might recognise them as bots.

'I wouldn't overthink it. It's really good news. Take it as a vote of approval for everything you're doing. I certainly do. Keep up the good work!'

'Thanks. By the way, our globalisation research is nearly ready. I'll have something for you by the end of the week.'

A couple of days later, she delivered as promised, sending him a folder headed 'Globalisation Dossier'. Inside were various Word documents with thematic titles, as he'd requested: not just Racism and Inequalities, but also Carbon Emissions, Tax & Regulation, Economic Fragility and Populism. Each one consisted of an overview, followed by a bullet-pointed list of factoids. These lists were full of punchy stuff: transnational corporations that paid virtually no tax by domiciling themselves in tax havens; the erosion of local cultures and languages as the same companies took over the world; the catastrophic domino effect throughout the world of the US banking crisis, which had taken the entire international economy down with it, and so on.

The final document was labelled Positive Impact. At the top of the first page, inside square brackets, Erika had written a note: *I know you said to focus exclusively on the negative, but we did find quite a lot of positive stuff too. It's well documented, eg the World Bank report on p2 below that found poverty in India and Indonesia was cut in half by globalisation. Even if you don't want to quote from this material, I hope it's useful for context.*

He closed the document and dragged it into his trash folder. Context was for pussies.

A week later, the social media team were ready to launch Orange Peel's Spotlight on Globalisation campaign. Ollie had made a series of striking graphics, and Erika had scheduled tweets and Facebook posts to go with each of them. A new tab on the foundation's website – now redesigned with less brash fonts and colours to match the sober rebranding – navigated to a Spotlight on Globalisation page, in which the research information was laid out in punchy format. Everyone had done a superb job.

His complacency was disturbed when Laura, his head of training, tapped at his door.

'Are you busy, Shane? Can I have a word?'

Of all the staff, Laura was the only one who intimidated him, mainly because she was more than twenty years his senior. A contemporary of Mel's, with a helmet of short, steel-grey hair and an equally steely glare, she'd been with Orange Peel almost from the outset. He couldn't blame her if she struggled to accept his leadership because of his youth alone – quite apart from any qualms about the new direction. Her approach today could only mean bad news.

'Sure, yes, of course. Come in.' He gestured for her to sit. 'How are the schools materials going?'

Laura and her colleagues were working on a new range of work-packs, tied to the campaign.

'Fine. No problem at all. Everything Erika gave us was really clear. Meticulously researched and sourced, so there's no issue there.'

'Good.' It was clear there was an issue somewhere.

'It's just that...' She hesitated.

'Go on.'

'Well, I'm not being funny, but none of us are sure why we're doing it.'

'Doing what?'

'Campaigning against globalisation.'

He felt himself reddening like a teenager. 'But if Erika's dossier was very clear... Isn't that reason enough?'

'It's not that I disagree with it, because I don't. All I mean is, I don't see why *we're* doing it. It's so different to anything we've done before.'

He tried to quell his rising panic, telling himself it was absurd to be intimidated. 'If you agree with it, then why not?' Did he sound too defensive? And a bit squeaky?

'I just don't see how it fits in with our remit. I honestly don't mean to be obstructive. It would simply be helpful to know where we're coming from, if we're doing presentations on the subject.'

'What's our motivation, you mean?' He attempted a laugh. 'That's what actors say, isn't it?'

'Do they?' She seemed determined not to cut him any slack.

He took a deep breath. 'Look, Laura.' He hated it when people used his own name to his face, because it was patronising. With the boot on the other foot, he found it emboldened him. 'You remember what I said on my first morning? There might be some changes of emphasis, to make sure we have a future? Well, this is an example of that. The board and I have concluded there's a role for us in this area. I know it's a departure from our previous work, but that's because our focus was always very narrow. In the past, we were only interested in maps. That's to say, the graphic representation of places. Now we're more interested in the people who live in those places. But the idea of place still holds it all together. Think of it as a move from physical geography to human geography. It's still geography. Makes sense?'

She was frowning heavily at the start of this ad hoc pitch. However, she gradually brightened as he neared the end. When he finished, she actually smiled and nodded. 'Thanks. That really helps.'

'Really? I mean, brilliant. Is there anything else I can help you with?'

'No, all good now, thanks.'

'Awesome. See you later then. And thanks for all your hard work.'

He let out a long sigh as she closed the door behind her. That had been his toughest challenge yet, but somehow he had risen to it. How long could he continue doing this before he stumbled?

As Erika's tweets started to go out, it was time to mobilise the army of bots.

'Can you ask Dr Frankenstein to start retweeting?' Shane asked Robbie on Zype.

'I will indeed. Is that all you want them to do?'

'What else is there?'

'They can comment. Spread the enthusiasm, sing your praises. Hurrah for Orange Peel. That sort of thing.'

'Awesome. Go for it. Do you need me to script any of it?'

'No, Frank can do all that. That's what we're paying him for.'

'He's Frank now, is he?'

'It's easier than saying Dr Frankenstein every time. I rather like it, don't you?'

'I don't know. I've no idea what he looks like, so I can't say if Frank's a good name for him or not.'

'And you're never going to, so you'll have to take my word for it.'

'Deal. Send Frank my regards and tell him to give it his all.'

Within days, Erika was expressing her delight at the initial response to her campaign.

'People seem to really like all this stuff,' she told Shane when he checked in for a progress update. 'I was worried they might be puzzled by it, because it's so different from the work we've done before, but it seems to have struck a chord.'

'So you're beginning to see there's method in my madness?' He said it loudly to make sure Laura, a couple of desks away, could also hear.

'I never said you were mad,' said Erika, reddening, which Shane took as a sign she'd been saying precisely that behind his back.

'Don't worry, it's just an expression.' Since her English was almost perfect, she knew that already; it was his way of throwing her a forgiving lifeline. 'Keep it up, anyway. Let me know if you have any problems.'

Not that there would be. This, after all, was the straightforward part of the operation. The next phase was what really mattered, and it was a job for Frank and his bot army, not Erika.

'So you're ready for Phase B?' asked Robbie, when Shane called to report on the encouraging results so far.

'I think so.' It made him queasy just to think about the next stage of their scheme, because his entire strategy depended on it. When they'd first talked about it, he was so pleased with the idea, but his confidence ebbed as the moment of truth approached. What if the bots were ridiculed? Or worse, ridiculed *and* rumbled as an army of fakes? 'This part won't be traced back to us, will it? It still feels way too early for Orange Peel to be advancing this kind of message.'

'Relax,' said Robbie. 'Frank will have a way of planting the seed and making it grow without any involvement from Orange Peel. Your current campaign is the inspiration, that's all.'

'Good to hear. Do you need anything at all from me?'

'Just your green light to proceed.'

He swallowed, suddenly feeling the burden of office. 'You've got that.'

'Good man. Watch this space.'

Shane needed no bidding to do that. He monitored Twitter in every spare moment. He watched the progress of Erika's anti-globalisation campaign, which continued to receive a healthy level of support. He also searched on Orange Peel's name, to see what kinds of conversation the campaign prompted. The results, again, were positive. They were winning lavish praise from their natural supporters for a stance that seemed to press all the right buttons, and nobody seemed bothered by the new direction.

All this, however, was still just the prelude to the main

event, which depended on Dr Frankenstein and his bots. That came a couple of days later, as Shane scrolled through his Twitter feed at home while an exhausted Craig dozed in front of a Netflix zombie drama.

He'd learned how to fine-tune his search to show everyone who'd retweeted any of Erika's messages with a comment of their own. Some of these were obviously authentic humans, with long histories of interaction on all kinds of subjects, as well as plenty of legitimate-looking followers. In the main, however, they were the bots, recognisable by handles with lots of random digits, picture-free avatars, and too-perfect English account names: the likes of John Williams, Jane Wright, Steven Matthews, all baptised at the font of a fake-name generator. It was obvious to Shane that Sally Jenkinson (@saljenk07342), who loved President Obama, hated bigotry and lived in Brighton, was actually one SIM card in a stack of fifty, held together by a grubby elastic band, in a backstreet basement in Lapu-Lapu. He reminded himself that he'd known next to nothing about bot farms a couple of weeks earlier, and it wouldn't have entered his head to question the integrity of any Twitter account, let alone one that tweeted complimentary comments about Orange Peel. For all the ugliness that social media generated, most of the internet remained in that happy state of innocence.

Craig was gently snoring and the zombies were at bay when he found the tweet he'd been hoping for.

It came from Mollie Thomas (@theept), health psychologist, Gemini, based in Bristol. Quoting an Orange Peel tweet, it read: *I hate globalisation so much, I've stopped using the word 'global'. I say 'worldwide' instead. Who's with me? #NoToGlobal.*

So far, this message had received 51 likes and nine retweets

— all, presumably, from fellow bots. As Shane watched, the totals clicked up: 52, 57, 61 likes; 11 retweets. Frank's foot-soldiers were on the march.

He clicked on the *#NoToGlobal* hashtag to see if anyone else had taken up Mollie's call. Sure enough, one or two had begun to do so. *I'm horrified by the evils of globalisation, To show my disgust, I'm no longer using the word 'global'. It's 'worldwide'. Say it with me: #NoToGlobal* said Sofia Burgess (@Itimpookind), an ESL teacher from Edinburgh. Evie Wells (@Loded1976) of East London took much the same view, and their comments were now getting likes and retweets of their own. As far as Shane could see, the process so far was entirely circular, with all the support coming from fellow bots, but that was only to be expected. He switched back and forth, checking the lengthening list of accounts liking or retweeting the three posts, to see if any were real. None seemed to be, but it was early.

The zombie action was reaching a climax. The howls and screams were finally loud enough to wake Craig.

'Have I been asleep? What did I miss?'

'I haven't really been watching. I think the zombies are losing. Rewind if you want to recap.'

'Do you want to watch something else?'

'No, it's fine. I'm kind of...' He trailed off.

'Addicted to your phone? No kidding.'

'We're having a big moment, that's all.'

'Why, what's happening? Has Orange Peel done the decent thing and come clean about its new beliefs?'

'God, no. It's way too early for that. Slowly does it, step by step. But some of those steps are more significant than others, and we're in the middle of a major one right now.'

'What does it involve?'

'It's complicated. It may be better if you don't know.' He'd barely told Craig anything about his long discussions with Robbie or the strategy they'd devised. That was mainly because Craig worked such long hours and they saw so little of each other, but he realised he was acquiring the habit of secrecy.

'You're practising the dark arts, are you?'

'Something like that.'

'And you could tell me, but you'd have to kill me?'

'Pretty much.'

Craig hit the rewind button on the remote, reversing through the zombie rampage to the calmer scenes where he'd first closed his eyes. 'Fair enough. Your shenanigans are probably more than my poor, tired brain can cope with.'

'Shit!'

'What?'

Shane was too stunned to reply.

'What?' repeated Craig.

'Something amazing has just happened. The background is too complicated to explain, but there's stuff happening on Twitter right now that's really important to us.'

'Yes, I gathered that.'

'I mean, we've got some, erm, allies involved who are tweeting some of our key messages. I want them to do well, but there's a danger they may not because they're a bit...'

'Mad?'

'Bold.'

'So what's just happened?'

'It's unbelievable. I never in my wildest dreams thought it would go this well so quickly. One of the messages has only been retweeted by Lateefa Latif!'

'Who?'

'Don't you know her? She's massive on here. She's an actress, I think, although I've never seen her in anything. The important thing is that she has, like, a gazillion Twitter followers. Let me check…yes, 1.2 million.'

'Is that a lot?'

Craig didn't even have a Twitter account, rather to Shane's relief.

'That's loads. She's on it a lot, and lately she's become famous for allying herself with all kinds of progressive causes. Minority this, diversity that…'

'Not your obvious flat-earther, then.'

'No, but she's just retweeted one of these actual tweets. That's, like, epic. I really can't believe it.'

The tweet in question, Mollie's, was getting even more attention now. It was already up to 780 likes, and the counter was clicking up ten at a time thanks to Lateefa's intervention.

'So it's really happening, the Talavera plan?' said Craig.

'We've got a long way to go yet, but this is a brilliant start. You know what? I think it really may work.'

For three months, the fleet explored. As the admiral knew from the writings of Marco Polo, there were more than seven thousand islands in the Sea of China. They seemed to be sailing from one to the next without ever finding the mainland.

He claimed every island they encountered, no matter how small, for the kingdoms of Aragon and Castile. At each landing, he gave the place a name – San Salvador, Santa Maria de la Concepción, Fernandina, Isabela, Juana, Española – to replace the primitive descriptor used by the natives. Thus he baptised these new territories. On every foreshore, he erected a stout wooden cross, beside which Escobedo recited his formal declaration of Spanish ownership.

Their original set of captives escaped at the first landfall. The admiral blamed himself for allowing them ashore to help interpret. They promptly hared off into the interior.

His men gave chase, but pursuit through the knotty jungle undergrowth was futile. For the sailors, it was impossible to cross such terrain at any speed.

Fortunately, the mishap did not tarnish their reception: at this and every other landfall, the Indians offered yams to eat, fresh water to take back to the ships, and gifts of cotton, cinnamon and pepper, as well as the aromatic dry leaves whose smoke they taught the sailors to inhale. These folk were quick to laughter, never displaying the slightest hostility. They cheerfully bartered all their weapons, which were little more than reeds with sharpened tips, for the beads and bells the admiral offered.

It seemed to give them pleasure to follow a command. If only Torres or the admiral himself could pick up their language, he would be able to give them orders. Their own slow progress in this regard frustrated him, as did his lack of booty to take back to their majesties, to repay their confidence and their investment. Talking birds and aromatic weed were interesting novelties, but the king and queen expected gold.

Of each new island chief, the admiral therefore asked the same questions. How far was Quinsay, the magnificent capital of the Great Khan? Where were the other wondrous cities of the Khan's realm? And where, in God's name, were the gold mines?

He knew the gold was there somewhere. There had been no sign of it on the first island but, as they continued to explore, he began to see small quantities everywhere. The Indians wore it in their noses and ears. Once they understood how much the admiral prized it, they presented it as a gift, without any apparent notion of its value.

That increased his determination to trace its source.

Whenever he asked, they would reply by pointing, which encouraged the admiral at first, until he noticed that one would point this way, another that. Either they did not know where the mines were, and simply wanted to please him by giving some answer rather than none, or they did not understand the question. Once again, the lack of common language was a major impediment. The only real solution was to take a party of Indians back to Spain where they could learn Castilian and come back to interpret on future voyages. But that would mean crossing the Ocean Sea at least twice more. Having come further west than any other European had travelled, the admiral could not bring himself to return home yet.

For three months they sailed about the archipelago, no closer to discovering the gold mines of Cipango. The weather did not help: fine rain, an apparent trifle at first, but so relentless it drenched them to the core. It drenched their spirits too.

In the last week of December, as they hugged the northern coast of Española – where the local king, Guacanagari, had shown them great hospitality – the rain finally stopped. It left behind a light breeze, ideal for sailing, and a feeling of seasonal wellbeing. The admiral increased the wine ration on the *Santa Maria* to celebrate Christmas Eve. By nightfall, the breeze had fallen away completely, leaving a dead calm. The admiral slept sounder than he had for weeks.

He was woken by a cry of alarm above his head.

'What the devil?' he muttered, rising from his bed.

At the tiller, instead of the usual helmsman, was the beardless boy who had first spotted weed in the sea. There was a look of terror on his face and he was trembling, even though the night was warm.

'What is it, boy?'

'I think we're aground, sir. I felt it just now. It was very soft, but we've stopped moving. I didn't see anything, sir. It must be a low sandbank.'

'Or a reef, the devil take you.'

There was enough moonlight to see that they were surrounded by flat, calm water, still some distance from the shore. But that did not mean the water was deep. They had encountered offshore reefs before.

'Forgive me, sir.' The boy began to blub.

'The fault is with the lazy drunkard who let you steer. You'll both be flogged for it, have no doubt of that. But first we have more urgent concerns.' He put his hand to his mouth and roared: 'Captain! Look lively, man! We're aground. Secure the longboat astern. Anchor it fast.'

The ship was already listing, and now the current drove her further onto the reef. Had it really come to this, sailing three thousand miles across the Ocean Sea, only to wreck his flagship in a flat calm?

'Cut away the mainmast,' he ordered, as the tilt grew more pronounced. It was a drastic step, but they had to lighten the ship to have any chance of floating her free.

The men set to work and the mast was cast overboard, but to no avail. When the sun rose, the *Santa Maria* lay on her beam ends across the sea, her planking open to the waves.

The *Pinta* and the *Niña* were out of sight while all this was happening. Instead, help came from the Indians of Española, who arrived with great promptness: scores of naked tribesmen in their dugout canoes paddling out to empty the ship of her provisions and the precious cargo the admiral had acquired – including all the gold. Their efficiency, and their unquestioning support, touched him deeply. Looking at the contents of his ship laid out on the beach, and watching the *Santa Maria* sink slowly beneath the sea, he wept uncontrollably.

The Indians attempted to console him, and he tried to make them understand that his tears were not entirely of dejection, but also of relief and thankfulness to receive such kindness. These were the gentlest people in the world, wholly without greed, who loved their neighbours as they loved themselves and never stopped smiling. He wished he could convey the depth of his gratitude.

'Do me the honour of dining aboard another of our ships,' he told Guacanagari, miming the eating of a feast and pointing at the *Niña*, which had belatedly come into view and was now moored offshore.

Not only did the king consent, he agreed to wear the shirt and breeches the admiral presented as a gift. This was a blessing: even in the interests of friendship, the Europeans did not have the stomach to break bread at their own table with a naked man.

At the end of the meal, where the lack of common language was no barrier to conviviality, Guacanagari smiled and bowed. Then, by means of similar mimes, he invited all the sailors to sup in his village a few hours later. It would be their second Christmas feast of the day.

When the Europeans came back ashore, their hosts duly presented a spread of rock lobsters, game and cassava bread. The admiral and his men did their utmost to do justice to this bounty, which was surprisingly good for the primitive setting. The happiest of the company was the idiot boy who had put them aground: he had dodged his flogging, so far at least, and gorged himself as only a youngster could.

In all their communications so far with the Indians of these islands, one word stood out in their conversation: 'Carib'. As far as the admiral understood, the Caribs were a neighbouring people, as fierce as the Indians themselves were gentle. Ferocious raiders, these monsters ate human flesh. It was no wonder they inspired such terror.

At this feast, once again, he heard them mentioned.

'Be assured, we will defend you,' he told Guacanagari. 'You are our friends. While you are not Christians, I see in you the natural Christian virtues, and your goodness shines powerfully in everything you do, for all your primitive ways and your ignorance of the civilised world. You have my solemn promise that we will always stand with you against the Caribs. Under our protection, you need fear no longer.'

His listeners nodded and smiled in appreciation, but the admiral was not convinced they completely understood. Keen for them to appreciate his sincerity, he ordered a couple of his men back to the pile of ship's salvage on the beach, to fetch a lombard and musket.

'These are our arms,' he told Guacanagari, once they had returned. 'With these to defend you, the Caribs will flee for their lives and never trouble you again.'

With a nod, he bade his men discharge the weapons into the air. Two thunderous explosions shattered the stillness of the night and, all around them, Indians clapped their hands to their ears and flung their naked bodies to the ground.

Fearful that he had gone too far, the admiral helped Guacanagari to his feet. 'There is no need to fear us. It is the Caribs who will fear you,' he said, but he could see awe in the chief's eyes and on the faces of all the villagers.

In that moment, he saw that taking gold back to their

majesties need only be one objective of this historic voyage. Here was the chance for an altogether different undertaking, nobler and more ambitious in its scope. He would establish a defensive fortress on this very spot, as an outpost of their majesties' Christian realm, which would protect these simple, gentle people in perpetuity.

Because the day was the twenty-fifth of December, he would call it La Navidad.

9

Of all Mel's regrets about her time at Orange Peel, the greatest – greater than inviting Xandra to chair the board or hiring Shane, greater even than agreeing to let that traitor accompany her to California – was signing a gagging agreement.

What she should have done, she realised not long afterwards, was fight them all the way. If she'd refused to sign on the dotted line, they would have sacked her anyway, but she could have taken them to court for unfair dismissal. She would almost certainly have won the case, thereby exposing their mercenary hook-up with Talavera for all to see.

Xandra must have realised that, which was why she'd sprung the whole thing so publicly and so humiliatingly, in front of Shane and the rest of the board. That also explained the huge sum of hush-money. Mel didn't think of herself as a mercenary person, but the cash had been hard to resist, particularly with them all ganging up. As they all stared at her in that boardroom, the prospect of going to court, with its stress, worry and unpleasantness, was daunting. Any compensation award from a tribunal would have been paltry compared with what Xandra was offering. They were effectively giving her three or four birds in the hand, instead of one in the bush. From that perspective, signing was a no-brainer.

Only later did she see the flaw in the logic. Yes, the deal gave her far more money than a court would have done, but cash only had value if you were prepared to spend it.

Not touching the money wasn't a conscious decision, not at first. She stashed it, divided into safe clumps in case of another financial crash, in what each bank continued, quaintly, to call its savings account, even though it paid annual interest of less than half a percent. Then she left it alone while she licked her wounds and wondered what to do next. The windfall made many things possible, but she shied away from the obvious options, such as a month or two in the Maldives or moving to a three-storey pile in Chiswick.

Only gradually did she realise she wasn't touching the Talavera lucre on principle. This was the prize for which she was meant to trade her soul, and she'd gone most of the way there, by signing the agreement and depositing the cheque. But the bargain was only complete if she used the money. If, instead, she let it sit undisturbed, she hadn't gone the full Dr Faustus. She might even, very slowly, begin to recover her self-respect.

She considered giving it all away: just getting shot of the whole damn lot, thereby earning instant redemption. She could think of umpteen deserving causes, but something held her back. Again, it was just a feeling at first, rather than a fully baked thought, but eventually she was able to spell it out: by keeping the money intact, she was leaving open the possibility of returning it, in case she ever decided to break her side of the agreement and tell her tale.

She had no immediate intention of speaking out. Still reeling from the shock of having the organisation she'd built from scratch stolen from under her nose, her only wish was to be left alone. But knowing what she did about Shane's intentions, she couldn't help keeping tabs on Orange Peel. She set up an anonymous Twitter account to snoop undetected on their social media output. She noted the change in logo, and understood why the orange peel had to go, but the globalisation campaign puzzled her. Then she noticed a cohort of excitable young people trying to ban the word global, and she began to see the point. The zeal with which their call was taken up alarmed her. She'd assured herself that Talavera's crackpot plans had no chance of success, but Shane seemed to have a talent for this. He must be getting help from somewhere, which he could doubtless afford to buy, no expense spared; nevertheless, she'd underrated him.

That prompted her to reassess her own role. If Orange Peel had an achievable plan to junk centuries of scientific knowledge and foist Talavera's lunacy on the world, good people had a duty to stop them. Correction: good person. She was the only one with the slightest inkling of what was afoot.

The prospect of intervening so soon filled her with dread. In considering breaking her silence, she'd imagined several years passing before she did so – long enough to regain her confidence and rebuild her life and reputation. Now, only months after the coup, she still had bruises to nurse. She was in no state to step back into the ring.

Agonising over the dilemma, she called Rachel. She'd already dropped hints to her old friend about the involuntary nature of her departure. Now she unloaded everything.

It took Rachel a while to absorb the story. 'I'm so sorry, Mel. I understand why you didn't, but I wish you'd told me sooner.'

'I know I should do something to stop them, but I don't think I have the strength or the courage,' said Mel. 'In fact, I know I don't.'

'If you want to fight them, you don't have to do it all yourself,' said Rachel. 'Why don't you start sharing the burden?'

'Isn't that what I'm doing, by telling you?'

'I'm nobody. Tip off someone more important. A journalist. Someone you've never met before, so no one can connect them to you. You don't need to tell them everything. In fact, you don't even need to tell them who you are. You could contact them anonymously to say they should keep an eye on Orange Peel, without going into any specifics. If you choose the right person, that'll fire their curiosity and you won't have to do anything else.'

'It's not a bad idea. An investigative reporter, you mean?'

'Yes. Maybe not even an established one. Someone just starting out might be better. This could be their big chance to make a name for themselves.'

'So I'd be doing them a favour?'

'Exactly.'

'Who, though?'

'No idea. I don't know any journalists. That's your area, not mine. It can't be anyone you know personally, though, for the reasons we've agreed. Think it over. Once you put your mind to it, I'm sure you'll be able to find the right person.'

Mel wished she shared her friend's confidence. She didn't know many young people, and she didn't read the kind of shoestring websites and blogs for which a would-be investigative hotshot might write, while awaiting their big break. Nevertheless, she could see the sense in what Rachel proposed. She would try to broaden her reading. Perhaps some suitable candidate would come into view.

They did so a few weeks later, more by accident than Mel's design.

Shaken by the possibility of Talavera's ideas taking hold, she'd taken to searching the internet for articles about flat-earthism, to see how much traction the notion already had. She also set up a Google alert for articles with 'flat earth' in the headline.

The piece that dropped into her inbox wasn't about flat-earthism at all. It just used the expression to grab attention. 'Why 9/11 conspiracy theorists are the new flat-earthers,' the title proclaimed.

But Mel read it anyway. It seemed well argued, and the journalist had the sort of credentials she and Rachel had discussed: one or two *Guardian* bylines, which signified ambition, but mainly much smaller websites and her own blog. That sort of writing must pay woefully, if at all. Comparing it with her own early career as a well-paid staffer on a national paper, enjoying lots of perks, Mel wondered how any of these young journalists survived nowadays. In that respect, at least she was doing this young woman a favour by providing her with a potentially lucrative, career-making story.

She drafted a message on the contact form of the journalist's website.

In the name field, she called herself 'An Insider', and she invented a fake hotmail address to go in the email field. In the space for messages, she wrote: 'If you want a good story, keep an eye on the developments at the Orange Peel Foundation. They're changing direction and they don't want anyone to notice, because they have a massive secret to hide. If you study their Twitter feed, you'll begin to see what's going on. It's too risky for me to identify myself or tell you more, but do some digging of your own. You won't regret it.'

With that wording, she'd barely broken the terms of her gagging order, because she hadn't disclosed anything of substance, but she hoped it was tantalising. Who wouldn't start paying attention to Orange Peel after receiving a message like that?

Hitting send, she felt calmer than she had for weeks.

10

Shane was proud of how far they'd come in five short months.

A small but growing segment of hyper-progressive opinion now considered it distasteful and offensive to use the word 'global'. This wasn't just the view of his bot army – swollen in number to two thousand – but also of a growing number of flesh-and-blood humans. These were mainly the self-flagellatory sort who followed Lateefa Latif and wanted to publicly shrug off the privileges into which they believed they'd been born. But they were actual people.

The vast bulk of the population remained unaware the g-word had fallen out of favour, and would have scoffed at the idea if they had known. But that wasn't the point. For Shane, the object of the exercise was to plant a seed. It would sink its roots out of sight, with only a tiny shoot to show for itself, but shoots turned into trees if they were left alone. Whenever he saw a teenage zealot berating someone on Twitter for using the banned term and thereby colluding in the evils of globalisation, he felt a thrill of dendrological pride.

In another triumph, Dr Sonali Rao of the Peter Amber Institute of Palo Alto, California was now a fashionable figure among the liberal intelligentsia. This followed the publication by VICE.com of a long read based on her paper about *The Truman Show*. Groaning under the weight of its academic jargon, the study itself was all but incomprehensible to lay readers, but the feature translated enough of the original into plain English to make it readable, while preserving sufficient direct quotes and Bakerian buzz-phrases to emphasise the importance and profundity of the writing. Impressionable readers came away believing it wasn't just possible, but was actually a moral imperative, to doubt the evidence of their senses.

To Shane's surprise and delight, he didn't need to deploy his bot army to popularise this article: it became a massive talking-point on social media of its own accord. Dr Rao's own Twitter following increased tenfold as Lateefa Latif pronounced her an important visionary.

It didn't hurt that Sonali was young, brown and photogenic. She was invited to write her own version of the VICE story for an opinion slot in *The Guardian*. So fulsome were the comments below the line – and not just from Shane's bots – that she became a regular contributor, writing about the Peter Amber Institute's ongoing research projects on the othering of the South, the patriarchal nature of establishment cartography, and so on. Readers signalled their own progressive credentials by sharing the article and parroting Dr Rao's Bakerian theory as cutting-edge thought.

Mindful that Joey and the board were expecting results,

Shane decided the time had come to take his campaign to the next level. The immediate task was to integrate some of these newly fashionable ideas into Orange Peel's training programme.

The programme was part of the Zest Badge scheme, which had been Mel's proudest achievement. To qualify for a badge, the applicant – a business, institution, charity or government department – promised to use the orange-peel projection whenever it published a map of the world. In return, it was allowed to display the Orange Peel logo. Everyone from corporate lawyers to the spooks at MI5 used the badge to present a benign public face. The scheme humanised them on the cheap, and around a quarter of the working population now worked for a Zest Badge employer. The only other requirement for scheme members was to host a training session for staff, which Orange Peel provided for a fee, with obligatory refresher courses every three years. Mel had realised they couldn't get away with charging schools, so she devised a more benign-looking way of signing up the teaching profession: they accessed all the training materials online as part of Orange Peel's contract with the Department of Education. It was a beautifully designed scheme at every level and, since it was it held in such unchallenged esteem, it was the perfect vehicle in which to drive forward Shane's own plans.

The obvious next step was to develop a module within the Zest Badge training scheme on, say, the artificial division of the earth into two hemispheres and its effectiveness in diminishing the South. An idea that was currently all the rage in the wackier corners of social media would thereby make the leap into the mainstream. Nobody would ever challenge it, because no Zest Badge holder wanted to lose their accreditation.

This was much more of a plunge than tweeting about worldwide inequalities or manoeuvring a secret army of bots; to publicly champion Sonali's ideas was to cast Orange Peel adrift from the shores of sanity. But that was what Shane had signed up for, in saying yes to Joey, so at some stage he had to cut the tether-rope. The trick was do it stealthily, so nobody noticed they were no longer on dry land.

To put the plan into action, he needed Laura's support, as head of training. Given his nervousness around her, she was the last colleague he'd have chosen to launch his most sensitive initiative to date. However, if he wanted to incorporate Sonali's jargon-ridden claptrap into the training package, there was no alternative. On the upside, Laura had been far more co-operative than he expected when she queried the anti-globalisation campaign. Maybe she was mellower than he thought.

He broached the subject by email, attaching a link to the *Guardian* article under the simple message: 'I'd like to incorporate these ideas into our training materials, if possible. Can you let me have your thoughts?'

He could see her desk from the internal window of his office. He watched her read the email as it arrived, click on the link and then get up from her seat and stride in his direction.

Fearing the worst, he lowered his head over his keyboard and feigned surprise at her knock. 'Laura! I've just this minute sent you an email.'

'I've just read it. I thought I'd come and tell you straight away, rather than write back to you.'

'OK. Is there, erm, a problem?'

'A problem? No, I love it! I actually read all that stuff when it was first published the other week and I thought it was really interesting. I've been an admirer of Jared Baker for ages and I'm so pleased his ideas are finally hitting the mainstream.' She was beaming.

'Wow, Laura. That's awesome.' He resisted the urge to give her a hug or a triumphant high-five. 'I had no idea you were a fan, but I'm overjoyed to hear it. I really am.' Deception was becoming so central to his working life, he relished every chance to be completely sincere.

'It'll make such a nice change. To be honest, I was getting tired of presenting exactly the same argument about Mercator, year after year. Obviously that's central to everything we stand for, so I'm not saying we shouldn't do it. But it will be great to have something new to present. And something so important and challenging, too. Really, Shane, you've made my day.'

'And you've made mine.' Again, with complete candour.

'Can I take it that this is our new direction?'

'You can indeed. Now that we've won the argument with map projections, the board are very keen to go down a more, erm, ideas-driven route. There's all this exciting work being done by disciples of Jared Baker, as you say. A lot of that is currently confined to academic circles, so we think there's a role for us to bring it to the public, or at least to opinion-formers, in a more accessible way. Much as Sonali Rao did in the *Guardian* article I sent you.'

'I like her approach. She seems an important new voice.'

'Doesn't she? Actually, I may be able to hook you up with her. I'm sure she'd be happy to give any guidance for your new presentation.'

Laura's eyes lit up. 'You know her?'

'I've never met her, but I know how to reach her.'

'She runs some research institute in California, doesn't she? Part of Stanford University?'

'I think so.' Laura didn't need to know that Sonali was still in Calcutta – or Kolkata, as Shane tried to remember to call it.

'Do we have links with them? That would be so exciting. No disrespect to Mel, but it did feel like we were in a bit of a rut. It would be wonderful to freshen everything up with some cutting-edge ideas.'

'We don't have a formal link, but I happen to know that Sonali has commissioned a piece of research about the azimuthal projection in the United Nations logo, which I think you'll find fascinating. I'll organise an email introduction and you can take it from there. How does that sound?'

'It sounds brilliant. Thank you, Shane.'

Once again, he'd won her over. This was going better than he had any right to expect. He watched her return smiling to her desk, then scrawled himself a Post-It reminder. *Get Cyrus to introduce Laura to Sonali. Make sure Sonali knows not to mention that Cyrus is her boss.*

With Laura's enthusiastic co-operation, the training programme was up and running as Shane approached his six-month anniversary at the helm.

This was great progress by any reasonable standard, but it was never fast enough for Joey. Their billionaire backer sent a barrage of Zype messages wanting to know when they were going to state explicitly that the earth was flat, rather than just tiptoeing on the fringes of the subject.

Whenever he received one of these complaints, Shane zyped back to explain why the process couldn't be rushed.

Couching it as gently as he could, he tried to make Joey understand that flat-earthery was an alarming proposition for 99.9 per cent of the world's population (at a conservative estimate). To have any chance of surmounting this daunting obstacle, they had to move by stealth, shifting the debate so gradually that nobody noticed they were being manipulated.

He knew Joey understood this in principle, which was why he'd approached Orange Peel in the first place, but he clearly had a hard time accepting it. His complaints returned again and again to the same argument: if everyone were given the facts as he himself understood them, surely they'd recognise the truth of them?

Try as he might, Shane could not bridge this gap in perception, and the Joey problem began to worry him. As Xandra and Cyrus were never slow to point out, their benefactor could easily take his money elsewhere if he thought they were dragging their feet. Sooner or later, Shane would have to grasp the nettle – or make Joey think he had grasped it.

'As ever, I think you'll find the bots are your friends,' said Robbie, on one of their own regular Zype calls. 'Whenever there's something you're nervous of saying out loud, get them to say it for you. That's the beauty of them.'

'Yes, of course. And then hope some loon like Lateefa Latif takes it up.'

'Lateefa Latif?' Robbie didn't follow social media as closely as Shane.

'She's a huge deal on Twitter and she likes Sonali's stuff. The madder the better.'

'I approve of her already. All power to her elbow.'

'So we need to up the ante, but let the bots lead the way?'

'Exactly.'

'In that case, we need to decide what we want them to say. Shall I draft something and let you pass it to Dr Frankenstein?'

'Yes indeed. I think, on this occasion, you do need to give him a precise script. Then we'll let him do his magic with it.'

'He really is a godsend.'

'I'll be sure to pass on your appreciation. He takes great pride in his work and loves to give satisfaction.'

Shane was never sure when Robbie was being serious. In his own imagination, 'Frank' was a lowlife who ran a sweatshop and cared only about getting paid, but that might be way off the mark. He could just as well be a teenage geek in a bedroom, and 'he' might be a she. Not that it mattered. The important thing was getting the job done.

He set to work writing some talking-points for the bots. He got the idea for the first one while he was channel-hopping one evening. He caught part of an ITV4 show called *Holidays Down Under*. 'While it's winter for you in the UK,' prattled the presenter, 'it's glorious summer here in the southern hemisphere.' A light bulb came on in Shane's head, and he reached for a pen and paper. He wrote a couple of lines, read them back, did some crossing out, wrote some more, then looked at it again. *Personally I always try to avoid northern hemisphere-specific seasonal language. Instead of 'this summer', I specify the months I mean, or Q3. Because it might be that season for me, but it's not for everybody.*

Was it too ridiculous? He couldn't quite tell. The next morning he forwarded it to Robbie, to send to Frank. Later in the day, he put part of the text in a Twitter search to see if the tweet had appeared, and sure enough, there it was. A few of the bots were gamely kicking it about. Frustratingly, though, it hadn't achieved traction.

Resolving to try harder, he got his next inspiration from snooping around flat-earther sites. In the normal, sane world, there was no need for a word for believing the earth was round; it was like having a special term for people who thought water was wet or the sun was hot. However, the hard-core cranks *did* have such a word, in order to revile their opponents. They called them 'globularists'. That was a mouthful, but saying 'I oppose globularism' sounded a good deal saner than 'I believe the earth is flat'. It also looked and sounded like 'globalisation', which Shane's target demographic already agreed was a terrible evil. This was a much better idea. 'Globularism' was the perfect keyword for the bots to use.

He crafted a new series of tweets, sent them off via Robbie, then felt confident enough to ping a memo to Joey: 'I've just initiated the next phase of the plan, which will make the conversation much more explicit. I think you'll be pleased. Watch this space.'

The following day, an account in the name of Hollie Iqbal (@Thema0897) retweeted one of Ollie's Orange Peel graphics about the othering of the South with the message: *It's high time we recognised globularism itself as a racist construct.*

This did much better than the tweet about the seasons, and it got far more attention than an account with only 147 followers would normally expect. Initially, the support came from accounts with equally low numbers of followers, all liking and retweeting away in bottish solidarity. Once again, Frank had programmed them to boost the original post at delayed intervals, rather than all at once, which would help extend the longevity of the message. Then, gradually, both the tweet and its sender started getting support from genuine accounts. By the time Lateefa Latif stepped in, Hollie Iqbal had more than 3,000 followers. This was a major development: the bot had crossed the species barrier and now had a genuine human audience.

Erika knocked on Shane's door. 'Just to let you know that one of Ollie's graphics is getting amazing traction,' she said.

'That's good to hear. You're doing a great job.'

'Again, this has nothing to do with me. Someone used Ollie's artwork and tagged us into it, which is the only reason I know about it.'

'Awesome. Provided they're not saying anything negative about us. It means we're central to the conversation even when we're not taking part in it.'

'Yes absolutely. It's just that...'

'Go on.' He had an idea what was coming. If the team were going to react badly to Orange Peel 2.0, this was how it would happen.

'Well, it's going off in quite a weird direction, that's all. I just wanted to make you aware of it, in case you had a problem being associated with something like that.'

'Something like what? What does it say?'

'It effectively says you're a racist if you don't agree the earth is flat.'

'Really?' He hoped his look of surprise appeared sufficiently spontaneous. Behind the façade, he was panicking. Had he encouraged Frank to go too far, too soon?

'Well, that's not literally what it says. Can I show you?'

'Please do.' He logged onto Twitter and allowed her to guide him towards Hollie Iqbal's tweet. Fortunately, this was the kind of platform that could keep a secret: there was nothing to show he'd looked at it many times already.

'There it is,' she pointed.

'I see.' He made a show of reading it carefully, which gave him time to think of a response to Erika. This wasn't the time to take her into any kind of confidence. Instead, she needed reassurance that she wasn't part of something lunatic. He put his head on one side. 'It's not really saying that, though, is it? It doesn't say anything about the earth being flat.'

'Well, no. Not in so many words. But that's what she means by "globularism", isn't it? It's the theory that the earth is round. If she's saying that theory is a racist construct, she must think the earth is flat.'

He frowned. 'Must she? I don't read it like that. What I see is someone beginning to question certain assumptions that we're supposed to take as gospel, which some of the most progressive thinkers – the philosopher Jared Baker, for example – are starting to challenge.' He warmed to his theme. 'To me this represents the first, erm, salvo in a fascinating new debate. We may not agree with every conclusion or implication, but it's brilliant to be associated with this new strain of thought. It's the future, and we should be excited to be part of it. Don't you think?'

She looked unconvinced as he started this speech, but the force of his enthusiasm seemed to overcome the worst of her doubts. 'If you're sure it's all right,' she shrugged.

'I really am. It's all good, trust me.'

When she had left, his sigh of relief was strong enough to rustle the papers on his desk.

A few days later, Erika knocked again.

'Have you heard of a freelance journalist called Ginny Pugh?' she asked.

'No, I don't think so. Who is she?'

'She's not that established, I don't think. She's had a couple of bylines in *The Guardian*, but so has everyone. Otherwise it's mainly stuff on her own blog.'

'So... What about her?'

'She tweets a lot. Mainly dismissive stuff about identity politics. She's got a real bee in her bonnet about that. And I did see her making some snarky comment about Orange Peel.'

'What did she say?'

'That we've been losing the plot lately, by associating ourselves with Sonali Rao and Jared Baker. She says this latest thing about globularism shows we're getting into bed with flat-earthers.'

'That's clearly ridiculous, as we discussed the other day. Besides, even if you accept her take on that globularism tweet, which I don't, it had nothing to do with us.' Robbie had briefed him on this. When attacked, the first thing to do was deny aggressively.

'I know. She seems to be condemning us for something we never said.'

'Of course she is.' Then play victim, to make this Pugh character look like the offender. 'Apart from anything else, it's completely defamatory. Embracing progressive Bakerian thought doesn't mean we have any truck with flat-earthery. Any suggestion that it does is outrageous.'

'Shall I respond? Or should we send her a legal letter?'

'No, don't do anything for the moment. Not unless she's getting lots of attention for it. Is she?'

'Not so far. She doesn't have many followers.'

'In that case, it's best not to reply. Keep an eye on her,

though.' An idea had occurred to him. 'Maybe also do some digging? Read back in her blogs and poke around in her tweeting history to see if there's anything embarrassing. Just in case we need it.'

'All right. Is there anything in particular you want me to look for?'

'Yes, actually. See if she's ever written or tweeted anything about Christopher Columbus.'

'Right.'

'And keep me informed.'

'Got it.'

'Thanks, Erika.'

When she'd closed the door behind her, he hopped onto Ginny Pugh's Twitter feed. There was only one tweet about Orange Peel, which read just as Erika had described, but it was enough.

It was highly unlikely that Pugh knew anything about the Talavera connection, but she'd scented that something was up, and she was on to them. If she pursued the matter any further, something would have to be done about her.

Which also presented a useful opportunity.

11

Jem, Orange Peel's Geordie head of comms, appeared at Shane's door.

'Are you up for doing interviews yet?' His expression suggested he was asking more in hope than expectation.

Shane had fended these approaches off ever since Mel's departure. Had she quit in more normal circumstances, a valedictory newspaper profile would have been an ideal tribute. As matters were, however, press was the last thing they needed, and the board had decided on a media blackout, to avoid any public scrutiny of the sudden change at the top. Shane had relayed a sanitised version of this to Jem – 'we want to keep everything very low key' – and reporting of the changeover had been limited to a paragraph in the charity trade press and a story in the eco website *Earth News*.

Since then Jem, frustrated and underemployed, had

revisited the subject every couple of months or so. Every time, Shane knocked him back as gently as he could. Today was no exception.

'It's still a bit early, mate. My brief is to reposition the organisation subtly, without any fanfare, and I don't have anything to discuss in public at this stage, Sorry, I know I always say that. But I promise I'll let you know when the position changes.'

This time, however, Jem was not deterred so easily. 'It's just that we do have a specific media request. It's the first since you took over, so I thought you'd want to know.'

'What kind of media request?'

'An interview.'

'To interview me?'

'Yes.'

'That's flattering, I guess. Who's it from?'

'Someone called Ginny Pugh? She's had a couple of bylines in *The Guardian*, but she's mainly a blogger, I think.'

'Really?' Pugh clearly meant business. 'It's still a no. If she represented an actual publication or had a proper commission, it might be worth considering. But I'm not going to change the policy for a no-marks blogger.'

'No problem. I'll put her off.'

'Good man. Thanks.'

Jem disappeared, leaving Shane to appraise this new situation. He'd have preferred to bait this shadowy adversary at his own pace but, since she seemed determined to pick a fight, she could have one.

He tapped out an email to Erika. 'Hi. Did you manage to dig anything up on that Ginny Pugh?'

A reply came back almost immediately. 'I've got a few links

that may be useful. I'm putting them in a dossier for you. It's nearly ready. With you in about ten minutes, OK?'

Ten minutes later he was poring over Erika's document. She'd done a comprehensive survey, going back over Pugh's four-year Twitter history, all her blog posts and any public bylines. Much of it, Erika stressed, was unremarkable, but a few selected highlights – presented as a series of links, each labelled with a date and a line of explanation – had made the exercise well worth while. For anyone who knew how to use it, there was ammunition here.

Shane kicked back in his chair and considered his next step. It was time to break the policy he'd just restated to Jem and begin talking to journalists after all. Just not to Ginny Pugh.

He stepped to the door of his office. 'Actually, Jem, can you get in touch with Ricky Simpleton and invite him to lunch?'

Jem stood up and ambled over, grinning. 'Don't call him that! One of these you'll say it to his face. Or I will. Either way, he won't be pleased.'

Ricky Singleton was the editor and proprietor of *Earth News*. Prone to see the world in strict black and white, with no grey, he used his website as a personal vanity project and for blatant score-settling with anyone who crossed him. In an age of controversy, this did at least secure his articles a wide reach. Fortunately, he'd decided early on that Orange Peel was on the side of the angels and had made it his business to cheerlead whatever the foundation did. This won him Mel's gratitude, if not her respect. It was she who coined the unflattering nickname, which suited him so well that it stuck. Shane had all but forgotten that Simpleton was not Ricky's real surname.

'Sorry, you're right. But can you give him a call?'

'Any preference on dates?'

'Sooner rather than later. Try next week, or the one after.'

'And where d'you want to take him? Gino's?'

Gino's was their local trattoria, known for its vast bowls of pasta and lethal Valpolicella.

'No, let's spoil him. See if you can get a table at La Limace. That'll make him feel loved.'

'Wow. He really is in your good books.'

'He will be if he plays ball,' said Shane, under his breath.

Ricky Singleton sighed with pleasure as a waiter ladled a portion of lobster bisque into a bowl on the starched tablecloth in front of him, and placed a dish of mussels and white fish beside it, for him to assemble his own bouillabaisse.

'I don't know what I've done to deserve this, but it's really hitting the spot,' he said, leaning forward to smell the aroma of the dish. Tall, with wiry hair and the complexion of porridge, he had dressed for the occasion in suit and tie. 'The one time Mel took me for lunch, it was to a cheap and cheerful Italian place near your office.'

'Gino's?'

'Probably. Not that I was complaining, of course. But this place is in a different league.'

Mel didn't have the luxury of charging her expenses to a Californian billionaire, Shane thought, but Ricky had no need to know that. 'I'm glad you approve,' he said, cutting into his own steak. 'You're the first member of the media I've invited to lunch since I started this job, so I thought it would be nice to push the boat out.'

'Brilliant,' said Ricky, struggling to scoop a mussel out of its shell with a spoon.

A more sophisticated guest might have acknowledged the honour, but Shane hadn't sought out Simpleton for his brains or charm.

'And how's it all going?' Ricky continued. 'I don't suppose you want to tell me the real story of why Mel left in such a hurry?'

'There's nothing to tell. Mel set up a charity from scratch. It went on to achieve everything she'd ever wanted it to do, at which point she decided her work was done. I was humbled to be asked to step into her shoes, and I only hope I do half as good a job as she did. I'm sorry if you'd prefer something more scandalous, but the truth can often be disappointingly dull. However,' he rushed on, as Ricky showed signs of wanting to argue, 'I do have something I want to tell you about which I think you'll find interesting.'

'Oh yes? What's that?'

'Well…' Shane had rehearsed this speech meticulously and it needed delivering with care. 'I don't know how much you've followed this but, in the past few months, we've built on our success in cartography by taking more of a public stance on, erm, human geography. Highlighting the unheralded consequences of globalisation for the disempowered and the left behind, for example.'

'Yes, I've seen some of that. I did wonder what—'

'And that led us into a new and fascinating area,' Shane continued, anxious not to be blown off course. 'There's a whole field of study in universities across the world which is beginning to challenge some of our most basic assumptions about the earth and the way we represent it to ourselves. Some of this is quite complex, but the key idea is fairly simple. Namely, we live in a world where privilege and inequality have been entrenched for centuries, and it's possible that much of what we consider to be objective reality may be a social construct. Perhaps it's designed to reinforce the structures on which that privilege and inequality depend.'

'Such as?'

Was Ricky's wrinkled forehead a sign he thought Shane was talking rubbish? Or was he just frowning with the effort to keep up? Either way, the only option was to press on.

'Such as the artificial division of the world into two hemispheres. We end up treating the South as lesser than the North, don't we? What if that was the point all along?'

His guest shook his head. 'It's not artificial. The equator is a real thing. It's the midway point on the surface of the sphere between the two poles, which mark the axis of rotation.'

This was not a good time for Ricky Simpleton to start being smart. 'That's what we've been traditionally taught. But this new thinking – its advocates call it the True Earth movement – is beginning to question those assumptions. The whole concept messes with your head at first, I know, because it's so challenging. But that doesn't mean it's wrong. Think of it like quantum physics: just because something presents itself to our senses in a particular way, that doesn't mean it's really like that.'

Ricky put his head on one side, considering the question. The genuinely intelligent response at this point would be to tell Shane to stop talking cobblers. He hadn't done that, which was encouraging.

Shane pressed on. 'We've deliberately put ourselves at the forefront of all this. That hasn't been without risk, because we're challenging all kinds of vested interests, but it's paying big dividends in terms of support from the public, particularly from progressive millennials. That's why I thought you'd be interested. They're your main target demographic, aren't they?'

'Definitely.'

'I'd obviously be more than happy to put you in touch with some of the most important academics in this field, such as Dr Sonali Rao of the Peter Amber Institute in California. You may have seen her articles in *The Guardian*? She's in the vanguard of all this, and it would reflect brilliantly on *Earth News* if you did an interview or profile. This debate is going to get more and more central over the next few years. If you get in at the start, by offering your support to the pioneers, you'll really own the story.'

Ricky nodded. These, presumably, were concepts he could understand.

'There's also going to be some pushback. Between ourselves, there's quite a battle coming and it may get messy. But the controversy will give you something to get your teeth into. You journalists like nothing better than covering a dust-up, don't you?'

'I wouldn't put it quite like that. But tell me more.'

Shane dropped his voice and leaned across the table confidentially. 'Have you heard of a journalist called Ginny Pugh?'

'Can't say as I have.'

'She writes for *The Guardian* a fair bit, and she has positioned herself on the conservative, populist side of all this. As you can imagine, it's easy to ridicule some of these new ideas if you appeal to the lowest common denominator, which is what populists always do. It's even easier when you're backed by rich and powerful right-wingers in the US.'

'Is she?'

'Oh yes. I can send you chapter and verse, but the simplest way to see for yourself is to google Ginny Pugh and Christopher Columbus. Turns out she's a big fan, which tells you all you need to know about her.'

There was a smidgen of truth in this. Erika had dug up an article Pugh wrote for an obscure online publication expressing disquiet at the fashion, mainly in the United States, for tearing down statues of historical figures who'd fallen from favour. Most frequently toppled was Christopher Columbus, about whom Pugh insisted she had no illusions. She acknowledged that his arrival in the Caribbean led to the extinction of the indigenous Taino people – Shane had made a point of remembering their name – and that the subsequent settlement of North America was a catastrophe for the continent's original inhabitants. She merely wanted to point out that the extermination of Native Americans in the seventeenth, eighteenth and nineteenth centuries couldn't be laid at the door of a fifteenth-century explorer who never set foot on the mainland. Furthermore, rampaging mobs weren't best-placed to deal with nuanced questions of historical responsibility.

Unsurprisingly, this article generated a storm on Twitter. Angry keyboard warriors who read no further than the headline – 'Why we should think twice before knocking Columbus off his plinth' – condemned it out of hand. Meanwhile, on the other side of the political divide, religious conservatives loved it. Pugh won praise from the Association for American Freedom, the equally right-leaning Heritage Union and the ultra-traditionalist Sons and Daughters of Columbus.

'I don't know if you've seen the new acronym for people like Pugh,' said Shane. 'They're becoming known as TERGs, short for True Earth-Rejecting Globularists. I predict that coinage will enter the language as the battle-lines form.'

It would if Shane had anything to do with it. Before leaving the office, he'd sent an encrypted memo via Robbie to Lapu-Lapu City, asking the bots to start using phrases such as 'all TERGs are racists' and 'die TERG scum'. They shouldn't spell the acronym out. Nor, for the moment, should they direct the expression at any particular individual. That way, people would become curious about the phrase, and its correct use would be a badge of belonging for those who understood what it meant.

'I can't say I've noticed,' said Ricky.

'I bet you will from now on. Like red Peugeots.'

'I'm still not clear where this Ginny Pugh character fits in. Has she been attacking your work?'

'Good question. Not as yet, but I'm almost certain she will. She's been sniffing around, and I know the signs. That's why I wanted to tip you off at this stage, so you'll know the background when it actually happens. I really hope you'll take our side and we'll be able to rely on your support if the situation gets nasty. More wine, by the way?'

Ricky turned out to be a fan not just of the Pouilly-Fuissé, but also of Sauternes with dessert. By the time they finished their coffee, petits fours and digestifs, Shane was confident that the bill of two hundred-plus pounds would be (Joey's) money well spent. *Earth News* would do the necessary when the right time came.

After her initial brush-off from Jem, Ginny Pugh came back quickly, saying she'd secured a commission from the *New Statesman* to write about Orange Peel's apparent new incarnation. One morning, Jem put his head around Shane's office to door to update him.

'Maybe you ought to take her to lunch too,' he said. 'It doesn't need to be La Limace. I'm sure she'd be happy with Gino's. Or I can take her, if you prefer.'

'No, I don't want to do that.' Jem's would be a sensible strategy if the aim was to befriend Pugh and stop her doing a hatchet job. But that wasn't what Shane had in mind. 'She's not getting an interview and she's certainly not getting a free lunch. Ask her to submit her questions in writing and find out when her deadline is.'

'But—

'Sorry, mate, but my mind's made up on this. If it goes pear-shaped, it's on me not you. But trust me: it won't.'

He hoped not, anyway.

Pugh's written questions, when they arrived, were pugnacious. However, she had phrased them inexpertly if she wanted to elicit answers of anything more than one word.

First, was it true that Mel Winterbourne was sacked? Second, if so, could Shane confirm that she'd been removed over a fundamental difference about strategy? Third, what was that strategy? Fourth, what was the rationale for embracing Bakerian social and philosophical thought, in the way that Orange Peel seemed to have done, when this was so far from its original purpose? And fifth, did Shane acknowledge – this was clearly meant to be the zinger – that questioning the division of the world into hemispheres, and other Bakerian positions which the foundation had embraced, strayed into the domain of flat-earthism?

Jem was clearly outraged. 'The woman's off her nut. She must be, even to think about calling us flat-earthers. And it's libellous if she prints that.'

'I told you she was trouble,' said Shane. 'No amount of lunch would have fended this off. Not even at La Limace. Fortunately, the responses are straightforward. Tell her, in this order...'

Jem stood ready with notepad and pen.

'One: no. Two: see above. Three: to build on the great achievements of my predecessor, for whom I have boundless respect. Four: see three. Five: no, and any suggestion that the Orange Peel Foundation subscribes to flat-earth beliefs is not only laughable, it's also defamatory.'

'Wow. That's telling her.' Jem finished scribbling. 'The only thing is, it sounds like we're going to war with her. Do we really want to do that? Mightn't it be better to have a chat on the phone and clear up any misunderstandings? I can do it, if you don't want to speak to her. It may not be too late to win her over. Otherwise, we're guaranteeing we make an enemy of her.'

Again, this was the right advice if the idea was to stop hostilities escalating. Shane wished he could take Jem into his confidence, but the latter's reaction to Pugh's final question showed it was far too early for that.

'Look, mate, I hear your objections and I understand the point you're making, really I do. But, like I said before, I need you to trust me on this one. I'd love to explain it all to you, but I'm bound by confidentiality at this stage. It may not look like it, but I honestly know what I'm doing.' Or so he prayed. 'Just bear with me, and all will eventually be revealed.'

Jem withdrew once more, looking less than convinced. There would be mutterings, Shane knew, but that couldn't be helped. If it worked, his plan would bind the staff to the project on which they had unknowingly embarked, because it would make them feel besieged. Once that happened, tribal loyalty would kick in and make it much easier to coax them, step by tiny step, towards Joey's ultimate destination.

Ginny Pugh's article, when it appeared, didn't hold back. Under the deceptively mild headline 'Has Orange Peel lost its way?', it rehashed the history of the foundation under Mel's leadership, emphasising its benign aims and warm place in the nation's affections, then painted the story of her departure in lurid terms. Pugh cited Shane's own monosyllabic responses as corroboration that he had something to hide.

In the second half of the article, she analysed Orange Peel's activity since the change of leadership, tracking the anti-globalisation campaign and noting how it had been used by other activists to fuel the claim that 'global' was a racist word. Without being able to find a definite tie to Orange Peel, she also took aim at the jargon-ridden arguments of Sonali Rao and Jared Baker. 'It astonishes me that I should have to type this sentence,' she wrote in her final paragraph, 'but, if you strip away the trendy vocabulary, these *soi-disant* visionary thinkers are driving us towards the logical conclusion that the earth is not round, but flat. It saddens and alarms me in equal measure that a charity as well-regarded as Orange Peel seems, despite its blanket denial, to have pitched its tent in the centre of this lunatic encampment.'

Shane had to admit he was impressed. Pugh had put two and two together and made not six, five, or even four and a half, but a perfect four. Fortunately, she'd missed a lot of the story: there was nothing about Joey and she seemed to have no inkling that the Peter Amber Institute was an Orange Peel front. That was a relief, not least because it showed she had no real sources. However, he had to give Ginny her due: she'd worked a hell of a lot out on her own.

Not that he would utter a word of that praise out loud, save perhaps to Robbie. In his head, Shane was already drafting a furious letter to the *New Statesman* to express astonishment that they'd given space to a pack of baseless and damaging insinuations that were a figment of a bad journalist's over-active imagination.

Before that, however, he had a call to make.

The phone was answered on the second ring.

'Ricky? It's Shane Foxley at Orange Peel. How are you doing? Have you seen the *Statesman*? Quite an attack, isn't it? Listen, mate. If you want to tell the world about Ginny Pugh's connections with the religious right, and her passionate devotion to the cause of Christopher Columbus, today would be a perfect day to do it. What d'you say?

'You will? Good man!'

PART TWO

HolbyFan @holbyfanhatestergs
I hate Tergs. They're no better than Nazis and they turn my
stomach. If I see one today I'm going to punch them
RT 57L 787

Jeremy Pennington @jeremy_pennington_74
What's a Terg?
RT 0 L 2

HolbyFan @holbyfanhatestergs
Vermin in human form. The lowest of the low
RT 29 L 238

Dennster @true_earth_matters
Not sure they're even human
RT 13 L 250

Jeremy Pennington @jeremy_pennington_74
It was a serious question. What is a Terg? I keep seeing the
word but I don't know what it means
RT 0 L 2

Globy Dick @GlobyDick
Maybe I can help. Terg is a term of abuse which is short for
'True Earth Rejecting Globularist'. It's a way of censoring
people who don't believe in medieval superstition and who
believe the earth is round, even if that (allegedly) offends
people from the southern hemisphere
RT 14 L 68

Sally Jenkinson @saljenk07342
STFU Terg
RT 4 L 95

Trent Meyer @meyer_the_fire
I'm from the southern hemisphere and it doesn't upset me
RT 1 L 15

Sadie @sadie93ozumvjfs
You're white though, aren't you?
RT 0 L 62

Trent Meyer @meyer_the_fire
Yes. What difference does that make?
RT 0 L 8

Sadie @sadie93ozumvjfs
[rolling eyes emoji] None at all mate [laugher emoji]
RT 0 L 64

Dennster @true_earth_matters
The whole point of globularism was to demean the
indigenous people of the countries in the so-called
southern hemisphere. If you're white, you arrived there
through imperialism so you're part of the problem
RT 17 L 194

Globy Dick @GlobyDick
What the hell are you on about? Can you even hear
yourself? The whole point of 'globularism', as you call it,
was to describe the shape of the earth
RT 2 L 16

Dennster @true_earth_matters
OK Terg
RT 0 L 83

Globy Dick @GlobyDick
OK flat-earther
RT 0 L 5

Dennster @true_earth_matters
Read a book
RT 0 L 43

Globy Dick @GlobyDick
After you, mate. Maybe you should start with Copernicus
RT 0 L4

Sally Jenkinson @saljenk07342
STFU Terg
RT 0 L 21

Sadie @sadie93ozumvjfs
Hahahahaha! Copernicus was another white guy
RT 0 L 32

Globy Dick @GlobyDick
Out of interest, are you black or white yourself?
RT 0 L8

Sadie blocked **Globy Dick**

replying to **Dennster**
Trent Meyer @meyer_the_fire
What makes you think 'globularism' is an imperialist
project? That's ahistorical bull
RT 1 L 23

Dennster @true_earth_matters
Are you serious? Have you ever heard of Christopher
Columbus?
RT 2 L 54

Trent Meyer @meyer_the_fire
What does Columbus have to do with anything?
RT 0 L 6

Dennster @true_earth_matters
Do you Tergs know nothing? He only invented the idea that
the earth was round
RT 8 L 101

Trent Meyer @meyer_the_fire
No he didn't. Don't be ridiculous. Nobody has seriously
believed the earth is flat for the last 2,500 years. Not until
you lot started drinking the Kool-Aid
RT 3 L 41

Dennster @true_earth_matters
Please. It's a documented fact that Columbus had to try
and persuade the Council of Salamanca that the earth
was round, but they didn't buy it. And none of his sailors
wanted to go on the voyage because they thought he was a
globularist nutter
RT 9 L 124

Trent Meyer @meyer_the_fire
It's not documented fact. It's pure fiction. It was made up
by the writer Washington Irving in the 1820s to create an
origin story for the United States. The Council of Salamanca
was never even a thing
RT 1 L 27

Dennster @true_earth_matters
Washington Irving? Right. Another white guy
RT 3 L 46

Mekell King @pointymekell
I'm black. It doesn't upset me if anyone says the earth is round. I'm comfortable with basic facts
RT 5 L 64

Dennster @true_earth_matters
Have you ever heard of internalised racism?
RT 0 L 14

Mekell King @pointymekell
Seriously? You're going there? You, a white dude, are actually calling me, a black woman, racist??
RT 7 L 89

Dennster @true_earth_matters
How do you know I'm white?
RT 0 L 65

Mekell King @pointymekell
You are, though, aren't you?
RT 1 L 75

Dennster blocked **Mekell King**

replying to **Dennster**
Trent Meyer @meyer_the_fire
If you knew anything about history, you'd know the world's leading thinkers have all believed the earth is round since Pythagoras in the 6th century BC. Plato said the earth was a globe. So did Euclid. So did Archimedes and Aristotle 1/...
RT 8 L 90

Trent Meyer @meyer_the_fire
The Greek mathematician Eratosthenes used geometry to calculate the earth's circumference in about 250BC and got

it nearly right. The Romans believed the earth was round. So did St Augustine, the Venerable Bede and Thomas Aquinas   2/...
RT 7 L 84

Trent Meyer @meyer_the_fire
You can disagree with all those learned historical figures if you want, but don't tell me everyone was a flat-earther before Columbus. That's a downright lie   3/3
RT 5 L 79

Dennster @true_earth_matters
Sorry, Terg, but you don't know what you're talking about
RT 8 L 118

Trent Meyer @meyer_the_fire
Actually I have a doctorate in the history of science. What's your qualification?
RT 6 L 89

Dennster blocked **Trent Meyer**

Sally Jenkinson @saljenk07342
STFU Terg
RT 0 L 57

1

Ginny had arrived early. Self-conscious about her limp, she preferred to get settled behind the speakers' table than to make a later entrance, with more eyes on her.

She watched the invited audience straggle in, dripping water from their raincoats and furled umbrellas. Generally over forty, some a good deal older, they almost all arrived singly, leaving shy gaps in the rows of hard plastic chairs, and casting discreet glances at their neighbours as they settled down to wait for the meeting to start.

Each of these people was an unexpected activist, an angry citizen who'd refused to bow to the compulsory new orthodoxy and had found solace among strangers on the internet. Given the risks, many of them hid behind satirical Twitter handles: Globy Dick, Sir Edwin Landsphere, Copper Knickers (to goad the anti-Copernicans) and Tergy

McTergface. Ginny knew who was coming, because she'd done the final mail-out providing details of the venue (left as late as possible to thwart saboteurs). But she couldn't match names to faces. In the dangerous world of anti-flat-earth activism, hardly anyone used their real image in their profile picture.

Some she did recognise. There were the casualties of the lunacy who had become minor celebrities: Diana Dorado, the Surrey geography teacher sacked for using a globe in her classroom, and Captain Wilf Phillips, the airline pilot, dismissed in a similar cause célèbre. Also present were the fearless Professor Cora Odell, Lorraine Churcher, the columnist who'd made her name writing about her experience of being transsexual, but was now a staffer covering all sorts of subjects for the *Daily Chronicle*, and Garrett Walsh of *The Bystander*, who'd lately established a following as a lugubrious guest host on *Have I Got News For You?* This last pair had each used their status as licensed contrarians to chart a steady descent into medievalism that the rest of the media had studiously ignored.

In the five years since Ginny first started looking into Orange Peel, there'd been some spectacular changes. Every child in Britain under the age of twelve was convinced the earth was flat, because that was what they were taught. Teenage schoolchildren were less sure. However, if they did believe the earth was round, they knew it was profoundly insensitive and offensive to say so. Many university students, particularly in the humanities, considered it their moral duty to make sure no one did say so, and they hunted transgressors like beagles on the scent of heretical foxes. Adults fell into three groups: cheerleaders for the True Earth sensitivity movement, some even more zealous than the students; anyone employed in the public or charity sector, whose jobs depended on paying lip-service to the baffling and ever-changing new ideas; and the large majority, who were dimly aware of a controversy and preferred to give it a wide berth, or as yet had no inkling of it. In addition, there were the dissidents, the Tergs, who could see what was happening and were desperate to reverse it. But they were so few as to be statistically negligible.

On a personal level, these five years had been the worst of Ginny's life, which was saying something, considering how badly she'd been bullied at school.

She'd been so excited when the *New Statesman* agreed to take an article from her. Even though she was still groping in the dark back then, the story would surely fascinate readers, challenging their complacent notion that progress travelled only in one direction. All being well, it would also be a defining moment for her own career.

That last part, at least, turned out to be true.

Her piece had only been online for an hour or two, and the print edition of the magazine wasn't even out yet, when the backlash began. *Earth News*, a website she'd barely heard of until that point, unleashed a personal assault of breathtaking ferocity: she was a racist, a passionate admirer of Christopher Columbus and all his most terrible works, and she'd spent years cosying up to the religious right in the United States. These claims rested on the softest of foundations: one obscure article whose misleading headline (not written by her) had won her the approval of an audience she'd never normally dream of cultivating. But those details didn't matter in the frenzy of the pile-on. Her friends did their best to calm her down, saying it was just the internet, and the mob would scent some new, fresher blood in twenty-four hours' time. This seemed a decent call, but they turned out to be wrong. The keyboard zealots refused to let it drop, and *Earth News* continued to feed the frenzy by dredging up further tenuous connections to show Ginny in a bad light. In one especially bad week, the site published nine articles about her. She thought of suing, but a solicitor pal said the idea was a non-starter unless she was rich or supported by generous backers.

Amid the horror of it all – which made her physically ill, vomiting at first, then bed-ridden with a three-day migraine – she couldn't stop thinking about how fast *Earth News* had turned its research around. The website was clearly primed and ready to go. The advance briefing could only have come from Orange Peel.

The storm eventually abated, and at least the *Statesman* kept her article online, defying calls for its removal. Licking her wounds, she was surer than ever that something sinister was afoot at the charity. When an invitation arrived to take part in a debate at the Cambridge Union, she thought reason had at last prevailed. She imagined she'd be able to discuss some of the odder aspects of the affair – such as the sudden, inexplicable conviction in radical circles that it was racist to think the earth was round – in a calm, cerebral environment.

She couldn't have been more wrong. When she arrived, the Union building was already besieged by noisy demonstrators, most with their faces hidden behind balaclavas. She had to have a police escort just to get inside, with the chants of 'die Terg scum' ringing in her ears. As a result of juvenile arthritis, her left leg was significantly shorter than her right, and she'd rarely felt so conscious of that disability. Aside from how vulnerable it made her feel, her back screamed with knock-on pain from her uneven hips as she was hustled through. Shaking and on the verge of tears, she needed to make a massive effort just to walk out onto the platform. Rattled, she spoke badly and her attempt to defeat the motion – *This house believes the division of the world into hemispheres is designed to further white privilege* – was a humiliating failure.

In the aftermath, she suffered a full nervous collapse. Persona non grata in the media, she couldn't get commissioning editors to reply to her emails, let alone give her work. Falling back on meagre savings, she shut herself away in her flat, barely getting out of bed. Without a series of postal orders from an anonymous benefactor, forwarded from the *New Statesman*, she couldn't have paid the rent. She had no idea who this life-saver was, but she sobbed with gratitude every time a new instalment arrived. Their generosity contrasted with everything else flung in her direction, particularly on social media. After a while she stopped checking Twitter, for fear of the abuse she'd find in her notifications, but she also hated the idea of allowing the insults and slanders to go unchallenged. As the mere sight of her phone began to make her nauseous, she eventually buried the device in the bottom of her wardrobe.

She spent the best part of a year in this broken state, until gradually the cloud lifted. She found a few editors prepared to publish her work, as long as she steered well away from anything involving the geography of the earth. She didn't argue.

Meanwhile, others began to pick up the torch in response to the steady assault on Copernican reality being waged in universities, the media, left-of-centre political parties and the public sector, with Orange Peel apparently pulling all the strings. It was now agreed across the public realm that the g-word was unacceptable. Anyone on *Question Time* saying 'global warming' instead of 'climate change' could expect a barrage of hisses and boos. Even Conservative politicians, looking for cost-free ways to modernise their image, began to go along with it. Meanwhile the word 'globularist' had become a term of abuse, denoting an unpardonable position that was hurtful to the people of the South. If the refuseniks ever countered that a globularist merely believed the earth was round, and anyone denouncing them must therefore be a flat-earther, the curtain was hastily lowered on the discussion amid complaints that this was filthy Terg logic. All the while, angry young people, many with green or purple hair, bombarded the internet with dogmatic claims that the earth was definitely flat, that Einstein and Stephen Hawking (as well as George Washington) famously thought so too, and any reactionary boomer who said otherwise ought to read a science book and STFU.

It made the world of Kafka seem measured and fair.

Fortunately, the small but growing band of heretics refused to be cowed. The sackings of Dorado and Phillips, plus an unpleasant controversy involving Sir Beowulf Fitch, rallied more supporters to the cause. More publicity followed when Dorado and Phillips both sued for unfair dismissal. The result, in the case of the former, was horrific, with a tribunal judge ruling that some of her subsequent tweets about her sacking showed evidence of beliefs 'unworthy of respect in democratic society'. Nevertheless, it boosted the resolve of those with eyes to see the absurdity.

The real wonder was that they were still so small in number, but Ginny blamed the media. The language of most news reports on the subject, filed by young journalists who had imbibed True Earth dogma, was designed to obfuscate: Dorado, they recited, lost her job after refusing to modify her lessons to respect the opinions of vulnerable minorities and insisted on using discredited teaching materials. It took blunt-speakers like Churcher and Walsh to use terms that readers might actually understand and explain that she'd refused to bin her globe.

With these developments, Ginny's own confidence had slowly returned. The newly minted activists, defiantly dubbing themselves the Terghood, looked on her as their spiritual leader and she'd gradually grown back into the role. She was still a hate figure for the zealots, but she was no longer their only target, which meant she no longer felt so vulnerable or isolated. Tonight's meeting was the brainchild of a group of these newcomers. Ginny had helped with some of the organisation and agreed to be the main speaker. The private security team checking names on the door had triggered a momentary flashback to Cambridge but, now that she was inside and watching the audience gather, she was glad to be part of it.

One face, next to the wall in the back row, caught her attention. Half a face, really, because its lower part was wrapped in a scarf and only the eyes and bridge of the nose showed beneath a green velvet peaked cap, pulled down low. This clear attempt to go incognito had the opposite effect, drawing Ginny's attention. It was a woman, clearly; tallish, maybe in her fifties. Their eyes met for a moment, then the disguised figure looked down, so only the top of her cap was visible. That sudden flinch spoke of more than just shyness: it felt like a move to evade recognition. Were the eyes familiar?

Beside Ginny, Benny Houghton, the veteran freedom-of-speech campaigner, who'd agreed to act as chair, called the room to order.

'Thank you all for coming to this, the inaugural meeting of the group we're calling Action to Prevent Flat Earth Lunacy,' he began. He still had a Northern accent after thirty years in London. 'That's Apfel for short which, as any linguists among you will know, is German for apple. It seems like a fittingly Newtonian response to a flat-earth organisation named after an orange.'

Several members of the audience laughed and someone started clapping, which triggered a full round of applause. Everyone seemed giddy with subversive excitement.

'We all know why we're here,' Benny continued. 'In a moment, I'm going to introduce Ginny Pugh, a woman of exceptional bravery. She was the first to draw attention to Orange Peel's frightening campaign, and she's paid a high personal price for doing so. I'm sure she'll give us a much better overview of the extraordinary situation in which we find ourselves than I can. However, if I were asked to summarise where we are, I'd put it like this. A bizarre ideology that tells us it's progressive to rip up everything we know about the world around us has somehow taken hold of our schools, universities, media, politics and institutions, both public and private. Anyone challenging that belief is liable to be sacked, as some people here tonight know to their cost. At the same time, most people in the country don't know this is going on, and certainly haven't considered the logical consequences of the ideology, because the takeover has been accomplished by stealth. And if we try to tell them, we're denounced either as crazy scaremongers or as Tergs – often both at the same time. That's the dilemma – the fact that most people don't even realise this is happening, but they don't like being told – which I hope we can address tonight. Let me stress that the point of this meeting is not to tell each other stories of how crazy everything is becoming, because frankly we all know that already. Our aim, rather, is to come up with a plan of what we're going to do about it. With that in mind, it's my great pleasure to introduce…'

Ginny rose to her feet amid a torrent of clapping, trying to ignore the malign electric spasm that ran up her back. She was about to start speaking when a couple of people in the second row stood up too, still applauding. Before she knew it, the entire room was on its feet. The last time she'd tried to address a meeting, in Cambridge, the audience bayed at her. But these people thought she was a hero. It was overwhelming, and she blinked back tears as she smiled her thanks and motioned them to sit back down.

'Thank you for that, from the bottom of my heart.' Her voice cracked with emotion. 'I can honestly tell you, that's the nicest reception I've ever had. Although if you know anything about my recent history, you'll know the bar isn't especially high.' That made them laugh, which helped ease the emotional intensity. She knew she could carry on now without breaking down in tears.

Benny had asked her to tell them about the anonymous tip she'd received, and everything that happened next. Accordingly, she told them how she'd started looking at Orange Peel's output, and had been particularly struck by the lurch into Bakerian gibberish. Then came the initial brush-off when she asked for an interview, followed by a second refusal, even after she'd followed their instructions and obtained a proper commission for her article.

'They told me to submit a list of questions and I thought, well, maybe Shane Foxley, their new CEO, is still very shy and he doesn't want to talk to the media, so I did what I was told and I sent them my questions.' She'd never seen an audience so rapt. No one was fiddling with their phone or fidgeting. All eyes were fixed on her. 'It was when I got the answers back that I was certain the tip-off was sound and Orange Peel was up to something peculiar. They were downright rude, and I remember thinking, it was like they were actually trying to make an enemy of me. Looking back, I think that's exactly what they were trying to do. Why else was *Earth News* ready and waiting to do a demolition job on me as soon as my article was in print?'

They continued to listen intently, tutting and gasping in the right places, as she recounted the horrors of the social media dogpile, the shock of being picketed in Cambridge, and the physical, mental and professional toll it had all taken. Then she took a more upbeat turn, deliberately lifting the mood as she celebrated the contribution of people in the room, as well as some of those not present, who had shone a light on the lurch into medievalism mandated by Orange Peel and its supporters in the name of progress.

'I don't pretend to have the solutions,' she said, coming to the end of her presentation, 'but the fact that we've all assembled here tonight is a major step forward. For that, I thank every single one of you, and I look forward to hearing where the discussion takes us.'

When the applause had died down, Benny threw the meeting open, and a fortyish man in a grey polo-neck raised his hand in the second row.

'Go ahead,' said Benny. 'Will you start by introducing yourself?'

'Sure. Good evening, everyone.' The guy had a full-on London accent, rather than the milder, estuary version. 'My name's Dave, but you probably know me better as Globy Dick.'

The audience broke into a collective smile of recognition and someone called, 'Hi, Globy!'

Dave laughed. 'All right, you can call me Globy if you like. It's better than calling me Dick. Although that has been known, trust me.' He was good with an audience and was clearly enjoying himself. 'I'd like to say two things, if I may. The first is positive, and that's to echo what Ginny has just said: it's brilliant that this meeting is happening, especially when you think how difficult the other side have made it for us to speak at all, with their insults, their threats and what-have-you.' Heads nodded all around the room. 'But the other thing I want to say – and I apologise in advance for bringing the mood down – is more negative. While you were talking, Ginny, I did a quick head-count. There are forty-eight of us here. That's not a bad turnout considering how hard it's chucking it down out there, and I know that large oak trees grow from tiny acorns. But I'm feeling small and powerless at the moment. We've all seen what we're up against and my question is this: what the hell can we do to stop it?'

From her vantage point at the front, Ginny watched the smiles of a few moments earlier turn to shrugs and sighs. Globy wasn't wrong when he said he was going to depress everyone.

Another hand rose.

'Go ahead, Cora,' said Benny.

'Thanks. Hello, everyone. I'm Cora Odell, professor of geography at Birkbeck. Dave makes a good point. We're a limited number of people attempting to take a stance against an opponent with massive support.'

It was polite of her to introduce herself, because there was no need. Everyone in the room had seen Cora wipe the floor with various opponents on *Newsnight* or *Channel 4 News*, on the rare occasions when those programmes had dipped a toe into the controversy.

'I'm sure everyone in the room is familiar with the difficulties encountered by academics whenever we've tried to stand up for science and rationality,' she began. 'Take it from me, a black woman attempting to argue that it's not racist to believe the earth is round: I know all about the madness that's taking over.'

She gave a throaty cackle, and the room laughed with her, although everyone knew there was nothing funny about the way she'd been treated. Her publisher had cancelled her most recent book after a revolt by its younger members of staff.

'Of course, there have always been cranks in universities churning out incomprehensible nonsense on some subject or other. You can't stop them: it's part of what universities are for. The problem comes when the nonsense, which is often poorly understood by the people who create it in the first place, crosses from academia into real life. In ordinary circumstances, nobody would give a monkey's that some junior researcher at Berkeley or Goldsmiths is wasting time and money trying to prove that the most basic scientific truths are social constructs designed to justify an imperialist world order. But these aren't normal circumstances, because this nonsense has become fashionable, and it's hard to stand in the way of fashionable ideas.'

No wonder Cora had made a name for herself via her books and media appearances: she was a superb communicator.

'But we have to remind ourselves that these ideas are only fashionable within a very small part of society and most people don't support them. Why aren't they speaking out in larger numbers? Either because they don't know what's happening, or because they're afraid of losing their jobs. That means we have two tasks. First, to spell out loud and clear, at every opportunity, that these so-called True Earth sensitivities are a Trojan horse for flat-earthism. And second, to challenge the stranglehold that Orange Peel has on so many employers via its Zest Badge scheme.'

Amid the applause for Cora, another easily recognisable figure raised his hand.

'Yes, Wilf,' said Benny. 'Go ahead.'

'Thanks. For those who don't know me, I'm Wilfred Phillips and I lost my job with everyone's favourite budget airline, iFly, after I invited passengers on the right-hand side of the aircraft to look out of the window if they wanted to see the curvature of the earth.' With his neat haircut, his thick beard shadow and his square jaw, he was the airline pilot from central casting, even if tonight he was dressed down in a scruffy jumper and an outsize parka. 'I admit I was being deliberately provocative, giving two fingers to the official airline policy of not saying anything to upset the True Earth crowd. So I wasn't surprised when a passenger reported me, but I expected a slapped wrist. I wasn't prepared to be sacked for gross misconduct, with no right of appeal. And no other airline will employ me.'

This much of the story was well known already, having

been covered widely in the national media – although most journalists had obscured the facts by saying Phillips had 'mocked True Earth philosophies', rather than describing his actions in a neutral way.

'Sorry, Benny. I know you said you don't want to rehash stories that everyone knows already, so I'll get to the point. What infuriates me about my story, aside from the loss of a career I loved, is the dishonesty. Every pilot, every air-traffic controller, every executive on the ground, knows what shape the earth is. Otherwise, their planes wouldn't get you to most of the places you want to go. The real lunacy is not being able to say so. As you'll probably know if you've flown in the past couple of years, the airlines have all taken the route maps out of their in-flight magazines and they've got rid of the location tracker from the display on the back of your seat, just to avoid telling a basic truth about the shape of the earth. And if we ask ourselves why they're doing this, I actually disagree with Cora. My bosses at iFly certainly did care about their Orange Peel accreditation, so that may have been their main motivation at the beginning. Now, though, I think they're more scared of the kind of passenger who complained about me. We've created a generation of science-denying idiots who all think they know more about science than anyone else. People like my former bosses are literally terrified of them.'

As he finished, more hands went up.

'What I want to know,' said a fiftyish man with a shaven head and a wild salt-and-pepper beard, 'is—'

'Can you introduce yourself?'

'Sorry, Benny. I'm Mike. What I want to know – and, as I was going to say, I haven't seen anyone come anywhere near explaining this – is *why*. Why the hell is this happening?

Where's it coming from? People always say you should follow the money to understand who's behind things that don't otherwise make sense. I get that. With something like climate-change denial, for example, it's obvious the oil companies had an interest in trying to convince people that man-made climate change wasn't real. But that doesn't work here. Who has a financial stake in forcing us to believe the earth is flat? Does anyone know? What am I missing?'

'Is it the Russians, perhaps, or the Chinese?' said a well-spoken woman in thick glasses and a misshapen hat, who introduced herself as Tricia, adding, to laughter, that people might know her better as Copper Knickers. 'Chaos and division in the West are good for both of them. Maybe that's what's happening here.'

A few people tittered, not taking the suggestion seriously.

'So you reckon Shane Foxley's getting paid in roubles?' called someone.

'Through the chair, please,' said Benny, raising his voice to restore order. 'I've got a number of people wanting to speak, starting with—'

'Sorry to butt in, chair, but I think I can settle this argument,' said a voice from the back of the room.

It was the mysterious woman in the green cap. She'd risen to her feet to make her intervention, allowing the scarf to fall away from her face. Ginny realised with a gasp why she'd looked so familiar earlier.

'You'll have to wait your turn,' said Benny, barely hiding his irritation. 'There are several other—'

Ginny leaned across and touched his arm. 'Let her speak,' she whispered. 'Don't you recognise her?'

Benny frowned, clearly harassed. 'No. Who is it?' he

muttered back.

'Just let her say what she wants to say. Then you'll see.'

He sighed and turned back to the disruptive woman. 'Go on then.' Under his breath, audible only to Ginny, he added: 'If you must.'

'Thank you, chair,' said the woman. 'As I say, I'm sorry to barge in, but I think this will be of great interest to everyone here, and you all need to know it before you go any further.'

'Would you start by introducing yourself?' interrupted Benny, still peevish.

'Forgive me. Of course. My name is Mel Winterbourne. I was the founder of the Orange Peel Foundation and I was its chief executive until five years ago, just before it took the strange turn you've all been talking about. You all want to know why it happened, and Mike's dead right to say you should follow the money. That's where I can shed some light. If you'll hear me out, I can tell you precisely where that trail will lead.'

2

Mel was horrified BY the savaging of Ginny Pugh. Having thought she was doing the young journalist a favour by tipping her off about Orange Peel, she was consumed with guilt when she saw how Ginny was pilloried.

'What can I do to help her?' she said to Rachel back then, after they'd both read the account of Pugh's barracking at the Cambridge Union. 'I got her into this mess. I can't just abandon her.'

'It's not your fault,' said her friend. 'You're not the one abusing her. If you blame yourself, you're letting Shane Foxley off the book, and that ghastly *Earth News*, not to mention all the trolls and woman-haters trying to destroy her life.'

'That's true in the abstract, but it doesn't help Ginny. The fact remains, she wouldn't be suffering this character assassination if I hadn't chosen her to share my own burden.'

'It speaks well of you that you care. Maybe you could get in touch properly and offer her some moral support? I'm sure she'd appreciate that.'

Mel did want to reach out to Ginny in some way, but she found herself more nervous than ever of putting her own name in the fray. In the end she took the coward's way out and started sending small financial contributions, in the form of postal orders – a refreshingly old-tech way of sending money anonymously, which she was surprised to find still existed. This meant breaking her resolve not to dip into Talavera's hush-money, but it was a worthy cause. She took the opportunity to move the rest of the cash out of the low-paying savings accounts and into a decent investment fund. That way, she'd still be able to pay the whole original sum back if necessary.

Later, as the controversy built up steam, other journalists such as Lorraine Churcher and Garrett Walsh tried to make contact. Mel was relieved to see Ginny no longer bearing the sole brunt of the True Earthers' vilification, and felt less guilty about her own silence.

It was the public monstering of her old friend Beowulf Fitch that finally spurred her to more public action. The polar explorer was doing media interviews to promote his latest book, about a typically gruelling trek across the Arctic, when he was asked what he thought of True Earth sensitivities. His interviewer no doubt calculated that Fitch would be the last man ever to defer to a bleeding-heart fad imposed on the world by student radicals. Sir Beowulf duly obliged, with a tirade about a generation of idiots who could barely find their way out of their own bedrooms without Google Maps, and who had the nerve to tell him the earth was the shape of a frisbee.

'I won't be told by a bunch of mollycoddled halfwits that the poles are a figment of my imagination,' he thundered. 'Unlike them, I've actually been to both of them. So far, it's cost me three fingers and two toes. Were they a figment of my imagination too?'

It was rousing stuff, which made Fitch a hero for the Terghood and sounded like plain-spoken common sense to most of his natural readers. But it was anathema to True Earth zealots and their appeasers. #FascistFitch trended for two days on Twitter, the rest of Sir Beowulf's media tour had to be cancelled amid the threat of walkouts from key production staff, and Amazon withdrew the book from sale. The explorer was eventually forced to issue a statement apologising for his unforgivably inflammatory remarks, avowing his willingness to educate himself about the need for True Earth empathy and promising to make a donation to Orange Peel, as well as to do better in future.

It pained Mel to see him so humiliated. The statement had clearly been drafted for him and issued in his name, and he might never even have seen the wording, so she didn't believe for a moment that he had really recanted. Getting your PR consultant to issue your apology on your behalf was the twenty-first-century equivalent of Galileo muttering defiantly *eppur si muove* – 'yet still it moves' – after his own humiliating climbdown on the relationship between the earth and the sun. The fact that Fitch didn't mean it was scant consolation, however. What mattered was his public stance, and the fearless Sir Beowulf Fitch had been bullied into kneeling before the altar of Bakerian lunacy.

For Mel, enough was enough. She could remain mute no

more.

She set up a Twitter account which she called Nægling, in honour of the original Beowulf's trustiest, most ancient sword; it was a reference that few, if any, would understand, but it made her smile. In this guise, she became an active member of the online Terghood, as familiar a voice as Sir Edwin Landsphere, Globy Dick and the rest.

As her confidence grew, she resolved to make proper contact with the movement. Not with Ginny, this time – she had done enough damage in that quarter already. Instead, she drafted a discreet message in her head to Lorraine Churcher, signalling that she might be prepared to break her silence at last. She was on the point of sending it when she, or more accurately Nægling, received an invitation to a secret but potentially historic meeting at Carnarvon Hall, the traditional rallying place for radicals and dissenters in Bloomsbury. The Tergs were getting organised.

It was five years since she'd spoken in public and she'd fretted all through the meeting about how to intervene and what to say. She was embarrassed by her ill-judged attempt at disguise, which seemed absurdly melodramatic, attracting rather than deflecting attention. Instead of hiding away at the back, she should have sat up front with her old friend Cora, who would have calmed her nerves, but it was too late for that.

When she finally found the courage to speak up, she made a hash of it, butting in out of turn and putting the chair's nose out of joint. But she saw Ginny interceding on her behalf, which gave her the confidence to press on. Introducing herself by name had exactly the effect she'd hoped. People in the rows in front of her swivelled to look at her, including

Cora, who flashed a reassuring smile. She began by explaining about the gagging clause, saying that speaking out now meant she'd probably have to pay the money back. She saw the admiration in their eyes. They'd have been astounded if they knew quite how much she was prepared to return, but that would also allow them to quantify her original betrayal. Then she moved on to the story itself. She watched their mouths fall open, more or less in unison, when she got to the crux of the matter: yes, Orange Peel had an agenda and a paymaster, and yes, it was every bit as bad as they'd feared.

When she eventually sat down, silence fell. Even the chair seemed dumbstruck. Then, suddenly, everyone seemed to come to life and hands shot up all over the room.

Dave, aka Globy, seemed to catch the mood. 'I can't get over it. These Silicon Valley characters made all their money out of technology, which is basically a form of science. Why would they want to deny some of the most basic scientific observations? And Joey Talavera, of all people. I'm not a big fan of billionaires as a rule, but I genuinely thought he was one of the good guys. How the hell did he become a flat-earther? I mean, what's going on his head?'

'Frankly, I'm not sure I care, Dave,' said Cora. 'The point is, the world needs to know it's being manipulated at the whim of one powerful, obscenely wealthy man. We've said all along that Orange Peel has been captured by some crazy force. Now we can show it's even simpler than that: it's been captured by one sole nutcase, who happens to have more money than half the rest of the planet put together and wants to impose his crazy ideas on the rest of us.'

'It's not really up to us, though,' said Ginny, from the top table. 'It's your decision, Mel. Are you willing to make your testimony public?'

Mel shrugged. 'Of course. Why else am I here? I've already gone public by saying what I've said tonight in front of several journalists.'

'Thank you, Mel,' said Benny Houghton, his irritation apparently forgotten. 'I'm sure I speak for everyone here when I say how much we appreciate your bravery. It can't have been easy to come here today. Can I suggest we cut the meeting short so you can speak to the journalists among us in more detail? Perhaps other people can continue the discussion informally. Sorry, Tricia, did you want to say something?'

Tricia, aka Copper Knickers, was waving her hand urgently. 'Thanks, Benny. Can I just inject a note of caution? Is it such a brilliant idea to go public with the Joey Talavera connection? I mean, people love the guy. He's gorgeous, he cares about the environment, he's got one of the brighter Vardashians for a wife and he's the most admired tycoon on the planet. Isn't there a danger the True Earth cause will become more popular once the public know he's behind it?'

One or two people nodded, swayed by the argument. For a fleeting moment, Mel felt relief at not having to tell the world her story after all, but then Ginny chipped in, saying people had a right to know where the insanity was coming from, and the room fell in behind that view. Benny proposed a vote, and Tricia was the only one against; even then, she only half-raised her hand, as if she'd lost faith in her own case.

A small group of them adjourned to the nearby Black Lion. Mel huddled with Lorraine, whom she instantly liked, and the guy from *The Bystander*, who was harder work. They'd agreed they would each talk to their editors, and whoever could get the story published first would have the scoop. Once Mel had answered all their questions, they both rushed off before last orders, anxious to start work. Ginny, who'd been sitting at a separate table with Dave and Tricia, called Mel over.

'You must be exhausted after all the attention, Mel,' said Tricia. 'Let me get you another drink.'

'I'll get them,' said Dave. 'It's my round.'

'I'd love one, whoever's buying,' said Mel. 'Sauvignon blanc, please. Large, if possible.'

'Same,' said Ginny. 'Although a small one will do for me.'

'Coming right up.'

Tricia headed off in the direction of the ladies', and Mel dropped into a chair opposite Ginny. It was their first moment alone together, which Mel had been dreading, not knowing how she'd begin to explain herself. But it was a night for getting rid of secrets, so she'd better just—

'Was it you?' said Ginny, before she had a chance. 'Sorry to be so blunt but…well, I've always wondered if it might have been, and now I think it must have.'

'Who tipped you off, you mean? Yes, it was. I'm so sorry. At the time, I truly thought I was doing you a favour. I had no idea how badly it would turn out.'

Ginny's eyes moistened, then she composed herself. 'Why me, though? That's what I never understood.'

'Believe it or not, it was pretty random. I wanted someone I didn't know already, and I also thought they should be young and ambitious. I looked around and I found your name. I think you wrote something that mentioned flat-earthers in the headline.'

Ginny smiled. '*9/11 conspiracy theorists are no better than flat-earthers?*'

'That sounds about right. It caught my eye. I hope one day

you'll forgive me for thrusting this burden on your shoulders.'

Ginny reached across the table and squeezed her hand. 'I've forgiven you already. You changed my life, and it was terrible for a while, but after the meeting tonight, I'm glad to be part of it.'

Mel managed a smile back. 'I'm not sure I completely believe you, but thank you for trying to make me feel better.'

'You should believe me. That's not all I meant, though, when I asked if it was you.'

Mel felt herself blushing. 'You'll have to be more specific.'

'The postal orders.'

'Oh yes. So they arrived? I never knew if they were being forwarded or not. I crossed them, so that only you could use them, but you pay for them in advance, and there's no way of knowing if they ever get cashed or not.'

Ginny laughed. 'Trust me, they were cashed. Honestly, thank you from the bottom of my heart. I don't know how I'd have managed without them.'

'I'm glad. It felt like it was the least I could do. And strictly speaking, it's not me you should thank. The money came from Joey Talavera.'

'It was yours to give, so it came from you. I'm so grateful, truly I am.'

'Me too,' said Dave, arriving back from the bar with three wine glasses and a pint pot wedged awkwardly in a two-handed grip.

'Sorry?' said Mel, startled.

'Ginny said she was grateful to you, didn't she? So am I. It's an amazing thing you did, coming to this meeting tonight.'

'Ah, yes, I see.'

'It must have been a hard thing to do,' said Ginny, embracing the change of subject, as Tricia also rejoined them.

'So everyone keeps saying, but it's nothing compared to what you've been through, as you well know.'

'You lost your charity, your brainchild. That can't have been easy,' said Tricia.

'It wasn't. But I didn't get turned into a hate figure, like poor Ginny did, thanks to Shane.'

'So you think I'm right that it was Shane?' said Ginny. 'It wasn't just Ricky Singleton at *Earth News*?'

'Ricky Simpleton, we always used to call him. No, of course it was Shane. I can imagine it was useful for him to have a bogey-figure. You came along at just the right time.'

'What was Shane like, when you worked with him?' said Dave.

'Reasonably bright. Ambitious. I didn't have him down as quite so scheming. Or competent, for that matter. Not that he was incompetent. It's just that this has been such a slick operation. I assume he's had help. The board chair, Xandra Cloudesley, was always extremely well connected. I'm guessing she found someone to teach Shane some of the nastier tricks he's pulled off.'

'Like who?' said Dave.

'I've no idea. What sort of person do you go to if you want to convince the world of some massive lie? Some shadowy manipulator, I imagine. It won't be a name any of us have ever heard before. It will be someone super-discreet, who knows how to remain in the background.'

'Like a kind of ultra spin-doctor,' said Ginny.

'Exactly.'

'To me,' said Tricia, 'the big mystery is still why. I know you've explained that Joey Talavera is paying for it. But what's in it for him? It won't make any more people use Zype. Why go to all this trouble?'

Mel shrugged. 'Does there have to have been a reason? He's one of the richest men in the world, if not the richest, and he's also crazy. There's nothing new about that. Think Howard Hughes, Ivan the Terrible, Kim Jong-un... Being filthy rich detaches you from reality. Our Mr Talavera has all the possessions he could ever need, so now he wants something more elusive than that: he wants the whole world to believe the same warped nonsense as he does. To be honest, I don't give a toss why he believes it in the first place. Why should any of us care? The important thing is to stop him imposing it on the rest of us.'

'Let's all drink to that,' said Dave, raising his glass.

3

Shane was in the office when he received a Zype message from Robbie White.

'Could you come and see me? Sooner rather than later. Something's come up. Best discussed face to face. This afternoon, if possible.'

This was unnerving. In the five years that Shane had known him, Robbie had always exuded calm, to an almost pathological degree. He soothed and reassured. But now, something had clearly rattled him.

'Sure,' Shane thumbed back. 'I can move a meeting and be with you at two. Should I be worried?'

'I'll tell you when I see you,' came the reply, which did nothing for Shane's own nerves. He'd hoped for a simple 'no'.

He took a taxi from Shoreditch to the Chaucer Estate. It had been more than a year since he'd visited. The lift groaned and whined more than ever, as if it were begging for oil, and Shane had visions of getting stuck between the floors. The compartment no longer stank of weed; instead it bore the unmistakeable aroma of Jeyes Fluid. At least he wasn't high when he reached the top.

Robbie, on the doorstep, looked grave. 'Thank you for coming so promptly,' was all he said, ushering his guest indoors.

Shane installed himself in an oval-backed chair in the drawing room, and noted that he wasn't even offered refreshment. 'Do we have a problem?'

'Life may well have become more difficult all of a sudden,' said his host, perched on a matching chair. 'One of my sources in the Terg movement tells me they've got as far as setting up an organisation. They're calling it Apfel, short for Action to Prevent Flat Earth Lunacy. The name itself is clearly problematic. They had their inaugural meeting last night, in Carnarvon Hall in Bloomsbury.'

Shane frowned. 'They were bound to do something like that eventually. Did your source tell you how many people came?'

'Forty-eight.'

'Is that all? If you'd said two or three hundred, I'd be more worried.' For this, he'd dropped everything? He'd expected a crisis.

'Ask not "how many", but "who".'

When Shane was in a good mood, he found Robbie's gnomic manner idiosyncratic and charming. At times of stress, he wished the guy would talk like an ordinary mortal. 'OK. Who was there?'

'Your old friend Ginny Pugh, unsurprisingly. Benny

Houghton in the chair. Cora Odell. Lorraine Churcher and Garrett Walsh. Again, no surprises. And Diana Dorado and Captain Wilfred Phillips.'

'The usual suspects, as you say. Is that any great cause for alarm?'

'And Mel.' Robbie said it drily, but this was his bombshell.

Its effect was suitably explosive. 'Mel? No! What about her gagging order?'

'What indeed.'

'Maybe she was just there to listen. Do we know if she spoke?'

'We do, and she did. According to my informant, she sang like the proverbial canary.'

'You mean about…everything?'

'If you're asking whether she mentioned our friend in California, I'm afraid the answer is yes, very much so.'

'Has she lost her mind? She'll have to pay back every penny we gave her, plus interest. I can get the solicitors onto it right away. They'll take her to the cleaners.'

'I'd hold off on that that for present.'

'Why?'

'Let's not reveal our advantage. They don't know that we know. I'd rather keep it that way for as long as possible, until we find out precisely what they're planning to do. And let's face it, the money is the least of our problems. Bolting horses and stable doors, and all that.'

Shane could see he had a point. 'What are they planning to do? Do we know?'

'Their immediate aim is to get Mel's account into the press. The *Chronicle* or *The Bystander*, or both. If they succeed, it will be extremely damaging all round, as I don't need to tell you.'

Shane was already picturing the headlines. 'We have to stop them.'

'I think I can probably handle that. There are some useful levers we can pull – or rather that Joey can pull, once I show him where they are.'

'That's reassuring, at least.'

'It is, but life is bound to get trickier. We won't have the free run we've enjoyed until now.'

'I still can't believe she's done it. It's treachery. We gave her enough of Joey's money to live in comfort for the rest of her life. Now she thinks she can throw that generosity back in our faces. Xandra will go berserk when she hears.'

'To be fair, we – or, more accurately, you – did stab her in the back first. Frankly, I didn't think she had it in her, but I have to admire her sense of principle. She's prepared to give all the money back. She admitted as much at the meeting. She can't have touched it, which means she's been anticipating this moment and biding her time.'

'I don't see anything to admire.'

'Having respect for one's enemy is the best way of beating them. Just look at Churchill and Rommel. We should certainly increase hostilities. They're openly calling us flat-earthers. That's damaging. We need to fight back and tell the world it's a disgraceful slur.'

'Joey won't like that.'

'Never mind about Joey. He's the paymaster not the strategist. Remember the key routine when under attack: first, deny aggressively, then play victim, to make your opponent look like the offender, whether their point is valid or not. In this case, that means discrediting Apfel before they even get off the ground.'

Shane nodded. 'Can your source tell us any more about them?'

'I've told you everything they told me. To be honest, you've got all you need to know. Remember, we're not trying to engage with them, to take their pronouncements at face value and enter into a civilised debate, or any such nonsense. Our aim is to cut them off at the knees before they start to walk.'

'Throw any kind of mud we can find,' Shane agreed.

'Any mud at all. The more the better. Brand them a hate group. Everyone loves to hate a hate group nowadays, don't they? That will make other Tergs think twice before pinning their own colours to the Apfel mast.'

'We can certainly do that.' Under the leadership of Erika, who had evolved to become a True Earth believer, Shane's social media team had adapted superbly to the Orange Peel 2.0 era. This kind of operation would be second nature to them now. 'It will definitely up the stakes, won't it? It may even strengthen us. With hindsight, Ginny Pugh was too soft a target, especially with that limp, which ruined the optics. A nasty bunch of establishment figures frothing at the mouth because we've dared to talk about racism is a whole different ball-game. Who wouldn't love to hate them?'

For the first time since Shane's arrival, Robbie managed a smile. 'Your enthusiasm restores my confidence,' he said. 'Apologies for my slight wobble. Please ignore that moment of weakness. Now, shall we have a glass of sherry before we gird our loins and sally forth into battle?'

Orange Peel √ @OrangePeelFoundation
We're disturbed to hear about a new group calling itself
Apfel, short for Action to Prevent Flat Earth Lunacy, which
held an inaugural meeting this week and plans to campaign
against the True Earth movement 1/5

Orange Peel √ @OrangePeelFoundation
The group's name should immediately alert people to its
hate-filled nature. By characterising True Earth sensitivities
as 'flat-earth' beliefs, they're belittling and demeaning the
many legitimate concerns that minorities have raised about
globularism 2/5

Orange Peel √ @OrangePeelFoundation
For centuries of colonialism and imperialism, those
concerns have been brushed aside. At last, thanks to our
work and that of many other people all over the world,
they're being heard, but Apfel now wants to silence those
voices. Why? The answer is clear: white privilege has been
challenged 3/5

Orange Peel √ @OrangePeelFoundation
There's a name for people who defend their privilege in this
way. We will be attacked for it, but we're not afraid to call
them what they are. They're racists. Furthermore, the word
'lunacy' is openly ableist and sanist 4/5

Orange Peel ✓ @OrangePeelFoundation
We therefore urge our followers to shun Apfel and call it what it is: a hate group. We believe in freedom of speech but not in the peddling of hate. This group has no right to make minorities feel unsafe and undo the progress we've made. We'll oppose it with our last breath 5/5
RT 679 L 3.5k

HolbyFan @holbyfanhatestergs
Thanks so much @OrangePeelFoundation. You're an inspiration. Don't worry, we'll fight and destroy these racist Terg scum
RT 67 L 987

Freddie Daneford @FredoDTweets
They disgust me. I hate them so much
RT 328 L 1.2k

Sally Jenkinson @saljenk07342
Tergs don't deserve to live. We have to drown this hate group at birth
RT 74 L 975

Globy Dick @GlobyDick
I was at the meeting. There were several black people there. Are they racist too, @OrangePeelFoundation?
RT 2 L 23

Sally Jenkinson @saljenk07342
STFU Terg
RT 14 L 348

Globy Dick @GlobyDick
What a mature response
RT 0 L 21

Sally Jenkinson and **Orange Peel** √ blocked **Globy Dick**

Dr Cora Odell √ @that_geography_prof
I was at the meeting too, @FredoDTweets. Am I racist?
RT 1 L 51

Sadie @sadie93ozumvjfs
Coconut
RT 5 L 865

Dr Cora Odell √ @that_geography_prof
I'm sorry?
RT 0 L 46

Sadie @sadie93ozumvjfs
You literally co-founded a hate group with racist agitator
Ginny Pugh. STFU racist Terg scum
RT 93 L 758

Dr Cora Odell √ @that_geography_prof
There's certainly a racist here, Sadie, but it isn't me. I'd say
it's the person who thinks all black people are flat-earthers
RT 6 L 47

Sadie @sadie93ozumvjfs
Reported
RT 0 L 125

Sadie reported **Dr Cora Odell** √ for targeted harassment

Freddie Daneford @FredoDTweets
Same
RT 0 L 114

Freddie Daneford reported **Dr Cora Odell** √ for
targeted harassment

HolbyFan @holbyfanhatestergs
I know where you live @that_geography_prof. You'd better keep the fire extinguisher handy
RT 24 L 208

Dr Cora Odell √ @that_geography_prof
Just to let you know I've notified the police about the clear threat of violence in your last tweet @holbyfanhatestergs
RT 3 L 42

> **HolbyFan** reported **Dr Cora Odell √** for targeted harassment

4

Ginny prided herself on avoiding clichés, but it was hard not to think of the highs and lows immediately after the Apfel meeting as a rollercoaster. First came the euphoria of meeting fellow dissidents in the flesh and hearing Mel's extraordinary disclosure. Then came the brutality of the Orange Peel counter-attack. They'd all known that Shane Foxley would hit back, but the suddenness and ferocity took them by surprise.

On the day of Orange Peel's Twitter broadside, Ginny held an anguished Zype conference with Mel and Benny Houghton.

'How did they know about the meeting?' she wanted to know. 'Do you think they had a spy in the room?'

'A few people from the meeting tweeted about it afterwards,' said Benny. 'Orange Peel could just have taken their information from that.'

'I don't think anyone tweeted the name Apfel or spelled out what it stood for,' said Ginny. She'd been searching, and the Orange Peel tweet was the first mention.

'I wouldn't be surprised if we do have a mole,' said Mel. 'It's what I'd do, if I were Shane.'

Amid the turmoil and the uncertainty, a Google calendar alert, popping up shortly after the call ended, jerked Ginny back to normal life. She'd completely forgotten she had a hospital appointment the following morning.

When she was thirteen, she'd noticed a painful swelling in her joints. Her body was undergoing other changes at the time, so at first she thought this was all part of the same rotten deal. When she eventually spoke up about the soreness in her knees and elbows, her mother assured her it had nothing to do with the other, more expected upheaval and took her to the doctor. He, an Iranian with a soft voice and a sad smile, broke the news about the juvenile arthritis. He sent her to a specialist, who prescribed steroid injections at first, then a different course of medication, and eventually the swelling and the pain went away. However, the specialist warned this might not be the end of the story, and he was right: the disease had messed with the growth of Ginny's bones. Had it done so in a symmetrical way, in an equal opportunities attack on both sides of her body, the consequences might have been more bearable, but that wasn't the case. Instead, Ginny's left tibia, as she learned to called her shin bone, was significantly shorter than the right.

The medics gave her shoe lifts, which only partially straightened her. She learned to compensate by hoiking up her right hip, despite warnings that she would suffer in later life as a consequence. At that age, later life felt like a remote problem compared with the need to stop the morons at school calling her Peg-Leg Pugh (which was not only nasty but stupid: she had a wonky leg not a wooden one). So she persisted in trying to lift one hip high enough to outsmart her mismatched legs, but it was a lose/lose situation, because it didn't banish the limp and, as predicted, there was much more pain waiting further down the line.

When she reached that point, she found ways of tuning out the spasms and relentless aches. Sitting down was helpful; drinking wine, even more so. But she had a personal trainer friend who knew about joints, discs, tendons and muscles – how they could make your life a misery and how you could fix them. She did the background reading that Ginny would have done, had she not been so busy drinking the pain away. This friend discovered that surgery was possible, but you had to nag for it, even to be considered. After all that effort on her behalf, Ginny felt obliged to take an interest and, once she sobered up, she realised her friend was completely right. Asking for a referral, she joined the queue for an initial consultation. That had been nearly a year ago. Missing the appointment today would have been a disaster.

The tube was snarled up so her journey was fraught. Fortunately, she'd given herself more time than she needed, so she had ten minutes in hand when she arrived at St Mary's. She followed the signs to the Outpatients reception on the first floor.

'The name's Pugh, to see Dr… Hang on…' She looked down at her hospital letter. 'Actually it doesn't say the name. It just says I'll be seen by a consultant from the department.'

'That's fine, dear,' said the receptionist, a tiny, wizened woman who moved in slow motion and spoke in a kindly, island lilt. 'It should be Dr Kamara today, but he's been delayed, so it may be another member of her team.' Frowning at her screen though the bottom of her milk-bottle bifocals, she clicked her tongue as she jabbed at her keyboard. 'This is running very slow today.'

She gave every impression that she was the slow one, who wouldn't cope if the software loaded any faster. But perhaps it was true, and she'd simply slowed to the pace of the hospital IT system.

'There it is. Finally. Take a seat, dear. Someone will call you.'

In the waiting area, a dozen or so people were watching an old episode of *A Place in the Sun* with grim resignation. Sitting in an empty row, Ginny pulled out her phone, eager to check if there was anything in the *Chronicle* yet. Frustratingly, internet reception was terrible. Google took forever to load and even longer to search. No wonder everyone else was looking at the TV.

'Welcome back. Before the break, we met Ben and Tilly from the West Midlands, who are looking to buy a holiday home on Lanzarote after they fell in love with the island during a family holiday four years ago. They're particularly drawn to the resort town of Playa Blanca in the south of the island and have their hearts set on somewhere with a sea view...'

Her search finally loaded. There were no bylines for Lorraine Churcher in the *Chronicle* that day. What about Garrett Walsh? *The Bystander* often compensated for its time-lag as a weekly magazine by posting online content faster than the daily papers. After a couple of false starts where it refused to do anything at all, Google slowly began to search.

'They're calling in the skills of property expert Jason to find the home of their dreams for their budget of £250,000.

They've already seen one villa on a brand-new development, a little further out of town than Tilly had hoped. Now Jason has a second property to show them. The question is, will this one hit the spot?'

At last the results screen appeared, with all the most recent articles by Garrett Walsh in *The Bystander*. There was one piece about the True Earth movement, but it was three months old; nothing more recent showed up. Ginny told herself to be more patient. She'd waited five years for this scandal to get the attention it deserved. Another day wouldn't hurt.

But she couldn't help herself.

She and Lorraine had swapped numbers on parting the other night, so she thumbed out a text. 'Hiya Lorraine. Ginny here. Hope you're good this morning. Any joy placing the story? Hope so. Let me know. Gx'

She hit send and stared at her screen, waiting for a response. The phone remained defiantly silent, and her eyes wandered to the TV. Ben and Tilly were examining a two-bedroom duplex apartment in a popular (according to Jason) residential area. The accommodation consisted of an open-plan living area, a kitchen area with terrace access and sea views, plus two bedrooms (generously sized, in Jason's view) and two bathrooms, plus the use of a large communal pool. But Tilly was turning her nose up, not keen on the tiles in the kitchen and hoping for a larger terrace. Spoiled mare.

Her phone pinged with a text from Lorraine. 'Not quite as smooth as I'd hoped. There may be an obstacle. Don't worry, though. I haven't given up.'

This was not good. 'What obsta—' she started texting, but she was interrupted by a voice calling: 'Virginia Pugh?'

She waved acknowledgement, switched her phone to silent

and got to her feet, wincing. She'd wondered if she ought to exaggerate her limp to make her point, but there was really no need.

The doctor himself had called her name: around her own age, no more than mid-thirties, so perhaps not a full consultant. He led her along a windowless corridor and into a side room, where he held out his hand.

'I'm Dr Gerrard, a member of the orthopaedic team. Have a seat.'

Pasty, with receding curly hair, he frowned slightly as he sat at his desk and looked over the notes in front of him. Ginny hoped that was just his concentration face, not a sign of anything worse.

He looked up. 'So, Virginia…'

'It's usually Ginny, actually.'

His eyes widened in a split-second of alarm. She'd learned, since acquiring notoriety, to recognise this reaction. Very few people had heard of her, but if they had, they might well hate her. She never knew when she was going to encounter one of them. On this occasion, she evidently had.

The doctor was clearly trying to be professional as he launched into a recap of her condition and the possible surgical solutions, but the effort was visibly a strain, not least because he seemed determined to avoid eye contact. It was irritating, but she needed this consultation, so she told herself not to take umbrage. Not to express it, at any rate. She glanced at the lanyard around his neck to make sure she remembered his name – Dr Craig Gerrard – in case she ever decided to register a complaint about his rudeness, then tried to focus on what he was saying.

'There are two basic solutions: lengthening the shorter leg

or shortening the longer one. Since shortening is a much smaller procedure than lengthening, we tend to advise that option wherever possible. We remove a segment of the bone on the longer side – in your case, the right tibia – and fit it in place with a metal rod inserted into the intramedullary canal, the cavity inside the bone. The tibia can safely be shortened by a maximum of three centimetres. Looking at your notes, that should be enough to adjust your leg-length discrepancy, but we'll need to get you X-rayed to take a precise measurement.'

He scrawled something on a pad of printed forms and tore off the completed sheet.

'If you hand this in at reception, they'll book you in. Do you have any questions or worries about the procedure?'

She'd written a list, which she fished out of her pocket. What was the recovery time from the surgery? Would there be pain afterwards? What was the chance of success? What, in the worst case, could go wrong?

He talked her through the answers and she noticed how good at this he was: giving clear replies in non-technical language without talking down to her. She'd have felt lucky to be in his care, if only he'd deign to look her in the eye.

He finally did so as he saw her to the door, offering her his hand. She was astonished to see his own eyes full of tears.

'I'm very sorry for everything that's happened to you,' he said.

Perhaps she'd read him wrong in assuming he was hostile. But maybe that wasn't what he meant either. 'Well, it hasn't been easy having a limp, and the pain has been getting worse,' she said cautiously, 'but I'm glad I'm in your hands now.'

He shook his head with a hint of irritation. 'Not that. What I want to say is… No, I shouldn't have started. It's unprofessional. It's just that...well...I can help. I'm in a particular position which means that...'

He seemed tongue-tied with nerves, and she'd have helped him out, but it was such an abrupt change from the doctor-patient relationship of a few moments earlier, and she found it hard to adjust.

'Look, I have your address on your notes,' he said. 'Do I have your permission to send you something? Then everything will become clearer.'

His eyes widened in entreaty. He wanted her to let him help her, in whatever mysterious way he proposed.

'Sure. Yes. If you think... I mean, I don't quite understand, but...'

'You will understand. Trust me.' Then he was back to consultant mode. 'Goodbye now. And don't forget to hand in your X-ray form at reception.'

5

For Craig, finding himself face to face with Ginny Pugh was the answer to a prayer. Literally. Only a few days earlier, he'd slipped into the hospital chapel trying to find an answer to the dilemma that increasingly plagued him.

For five years, loyalty had told him to stay out of his husband's affairs and allow events beyond his control to take their course. Every other impulse – decency, empathy, moral responsibility – countered that the malign sway of Orange Peel was within his control; what's more, the current global (yes, he still used that word) fiasco was partly his fault in the first place. If he'd put his foot down at the outset and said no, this was a ridiculous thing to get involved with and Shane mustn't touch it, however tempting it might be financially, everything might have turned out so differently. Instead, he'd actively encouraged it.

In money terms, it certainly had been a no-brainer. A couple of years after Shane ousted Mel, they traded their flat in Plumstead for a four-storey Georgian house in Greenwich – on the west side of the park, not the tatty downriver end – where their neighbours were bankers from Canary Wharf. With a view of the Royal Observatory at the top of the hill, they were the envy of all their contemporaries. But at what other cost?

Shane continued to freeze Craig out of day-to-day developments at work, confiding instead in the ubiquitous Robinson White. Craig held to his vow to offer support should it be needed, but otherwise not to interfere. He grew used to the role of bystander, rarely offered confidences and not asking for them either, for fear of what he might be told.

That it should be Ginny Pugh, of all people, who walked into his consulting room felt particularly symbolic. The nastiness directed at her five years ago was so public that Craig of course knew her name. That Shane was prepared to spray such vitriol at her, wrecking her life and reputation on a whim, had come as a shock. It made him realise quite how dirty his husband was prepared to play, showing a ruthless side in Shane that he'd never known existed.

Unfortunately, once seen, it was hard to unsee.

He understood the principle well enough: Shane's project required an enemy, a target against whom hostility could be whipped up. But this adversary wasn't a character in a video game to be blasted out of existence, or a chess piece to be knocked off the board. Ginny was flesh and blood, and entirely blameless, as far as Craig could see; even if she wasn't, she didn't deserve the treatment she received. But Shane didn't view her like that. He seemed to revel in the bullying.

Craig tried to mention it at the time.

'You're talking about this Ginny Pugh as if she's done something terrible,' he said one weekend, when Shane had been glued to Twitter for hours, all but hugging himself with glee as he watched the pile-on. 'Her only crime is to notice that Orange Peel has junked its founding mission in favour of something odd. If you weren't part of it, you'd be on her side.'

Shane didn't look up. 'But I am part of it. She's a hack trying to make a name for herself by bringing me down. It's her or me.'

'Yes, but…'

'But what?'

His jaw was clenched, which Craig recognised as his defensive tell. If Craig pressed the point, they would row. He hated rowing, because Shane was much better at it and always won.

'Nothing,' he sighed.

He had to conserve his energy for work. That was his excuse for letting it go, and it was true, as far as it went. Determined to survive his training, he got through his first year as house officer, then slowly climbed the hospital ladder, from senior house officer to registrar and now senior registrar. His guilt about not spending enough time at home steadily subsided. Each immersed in their own job, he and Shane became the classic workaholic couple who studiously ignored the growing chasm between them.

For Craig, the newspapers were a better source of information about the goings-on at Orange Peel than anything he heard from Shane. A journalist on the *Chronicle*, Lorraine Churcher, followed the whole business closely and wasn't afraid to speak out. Craig read her work online and wondered what would happen if she knew the full story. Would that make the madness stop?

One question had long intrigued him. He didn't ask it, because not talking to Shane about Orange Peel had become their unspoken arrangement, and he didn't want to spark hostilities. Not everyone shared his discretion, however.

'So, Shane, I've been dying to know,' said Craig's mother, down from Berkshire one spring weekend. 'I've been reading about all this True Earth stuff. Do you really believe in it?'

Shane shot a suspicious look at Craig, as if to ask if he'd put her up to this.

Craig shrugged his innocence. His mother was more than capable of making mischief on her own, without his encouragement.

Shane was forced to apply himself to the question. 'I certainly believe there's a strong case for reconsidering the way we look at the world. Whether we like it or not, everything we think we know has been shaped by the social and political power structures within which we all exist. They could easily skew our perceptions without our noticing.'

Craig's mother frowned. 'You'll have to make allowances, Shane. Bear in mind I'm from a different generation. Could you translate that into English?'

Craig suppressed a smirk. Approaching her seventieth birthday, his mother was nobody's fool, but she wasn't above pretending.

'Sorry, Maureen,' said Shane. 'Let me give you an example. There's a tribe in New Guinea that doesn't have words for colours. All they have is "light" and "dark". If they can't talk about colour, do they even see it? They can't see the difference between yellow and red, which for them are both "light", any more than we can see the difference between the fifty types of snow the Eskimos have.'

'Isn't that a myth?' she said. 'And aren't you meant to say Inuit now?'

Craig glowed with private filial pride.

'Maybe not quite fifty, but they have more words for it than we do,' said Shane. He maintained a polite façade, but Craig could see he was needled. 'Or there's the Hopi tribe of Native Americans, whose language doesn't break up time into units such as minutes, hours and days. It's a never-ending stream. That means the Hopi don't have any concept of wasting time. Do you see the point? We think of the difference between red and yellow or the passage of time as objective facts. But maybe we only think like that because that's how our language frames the world.'

'I think I follow,' said Maureen. 'So...if our perceptions have been wrong all along, do you really think the earth is flat?'

Craig concentrated on mopping a wine splash from the table with his napkin.

'It's more about asking the question,' said Shane. 'I'd rather expose some of our certainties to rigorous doubt than arrogantly assume we've always got everything right.'

That evasion sounded like a stock answer. He must often be asked this kind of question, just not in Craig's presence.

'But you don't like Tergs, do you?' Maureen continued. 'And they believe the earth is round. They're denounced all the time for saying so in public. If it isn't round, it must be flat, mustn't it?'

'I'm simply rejecting their certainty. That's what I find so disturbing about them.'

'So you don't know if the earth is flat or not?'

'No.'

'I see.'

'Who's for coffee?' said Craig. 'And then we should discuss what you want to do tomorrow, Mum.' Proud as he may have been, enough was enough. He didn't want an all-out battle in his own kitchen.

When she'd gone to bed, however, he felt emboldened by her forthrightness to revisit the subject.

'I was interested to hear the official line,' he said. 'You're still not coming out in the open with it, are you?'

'Coming out with what?' Shane's tone was frosty.

'That the earth is flat. That's the whole point of all this, after all. You're going to have to say it sooner or later, otherwise Joey'll pull the plug.'

Shane mouthed an angry *shut up*, pointing at the ceiling.

'She can't hear. She's going deaf,' said Craig, but he lowered his voice for the sake of argument. There was no point in opening too many fronts at once. 'It's true, though, isn't it? You can't keep denying it forever, otherwise you won't have fulfilled the brief and *Joey*' – it was his turn to mouth theatrically – 'will cut off your funding.'

'You say it like you've got a problem with my brief, as you call it.'

Craig shrugged and clicked the TV on, taking his usual refuge in passive aggression.

'You didn't have a problem when we spent the best part of a million pounds buying this house,' Shane persisted. 'And I don't need to remind you where most of that came from, do I?'

He didn't. That was the problem.

The conversation haunted Craig. It was the first time he'd been explicitly forced to acknowledge how much he'd benefited from Shane's deal with the devil. There he sat, in his beautiful home, thinking he occupied the moral high ground because he privately disapproved of his husband's behaviour. But who was he trying to kid? He was like the wife of a mafia don, affecting ignorance, but knowing deep down exactly how her life of luxury was funded.

The incident that pushed him a step closer to rebellion also involved his mother.

She was selling her house to move to a smaller place, and Craig had carved out some time to go and sort through the contents of his old bedroom. He was meant to divide the stuff into three categories, to take home to Greenwich, donate to a charity shop or throw in the bin. He looked at the array before him: his Goosebumps books, plus his Adrian Moles and his Harry Potters; a broken Wii console and a collection of Pokemon cards; a Buzz Lightyear who just needed a new battery; and his globe, a present from his grandparents on his father's side, the ones he rarely saw, for his tenth birthday. He remembered spinning it, enraptured, learning the names of countries and their capitals, and vowing to visit them when he was old enough. Aside from the nostalgia value, it was a finely crafted object in its own right, standing on a handsome bronze base. He wished he could take it home, but that would be too provocative. Reluctantly, he put it in the Oxfam pile.

A few hours later, back in Greenwich after a stressful drive across London, he found the latest article by Lorraine Churcher about the hounding of Terg dissidents. Her subject was the teacher sacked for refusing to junk a similar object on the orders of Shane's thought-police. Craig was angry on

Diana Dorado's behalf, but also for himself; it felt like the True Earth Taliban had raided his own childhood.

He knew he must take some kind of stance. It mattered for his own self-respect, if nothing else. For several months more he weighed his options. After a while, however, he realised that this latest indecision was yet another form of prevarication. It demanded a resolution, and not just for moral reasons. The turmoil in his head began to impair his judgement on the operating table. One close call alarmed him enough to prompt a visit to the chapel. The kind of Anglican who reserved his Christianity for Sunday mornings, Craig rarely troubled God with personal requests, and when he did, they were modest in nature, so this was a new departure. Sitting before the simple wooden cross on the altar, below an arch of grubby Victorian stained glass, he begged for direct guidance.

'Help me, Lord. Tell me what I should do. Please, I implore you, give me a sign.'

Ginny Pugh's arrival in his consultation room a few days later felt like an obvious divine response. He tried to focus on her surgical needs, even as his mind raced ahead. In blurting out, at the end of their ten-minute slot, that he meant to help her, he was finally taking the plunge.

She clearly had no idea who he was. Why should she? Afterwards, he realised this meant he could still back out, ignoring his own outburst, and do nothing. At worst, she'd think her consultant was weird.

But he'd made her a promise. Breaking it would be to take another step down the moral ladder. No, his mind was made up. In speaking out, however clumsily, he'd passed his personal point of no return.

Because he knew now what he had to do. *I can help.* He'd

known it as he spoke the words. It was a drastic course, and a betrayal of his marriage vows. But he'd remained silent long enough and he owed it to Diana Dorado and all the other innocent victims of this insanity to take the action open to him alone.

For what he had in mind, he needed the house to himself. He had a week off in a fortnight's time, mainly to catch up with sleep and binge on Netflix. Now that he'd made his move, however, it felt more urgent than that. So he jumped at the chance of a ward-cover swap at the weekend, which would give him the Monday free and the run of the house while Shane was at work.

He wasn't in the habit of going through his husband's personal possessions, so he felt a shiver of self-loathing as he opened the drawers of the little Danish rosewood nightstand – an upgrade from their his-and-his Malms, to mark their ascent in the world – on Shane's side of the bed. He wasn't even sure he was still looking in the right place, as he lifted out piles of credit card statements, warranties and receipts.

He found it in the bottom drawer. Although it now had a new home, no attempt had been made to hide it, which caused Craig a further pang of guilt. But this was no time for sentiment, he told himself, as he lifted out the tan leather journal.

Opening it now, and seeing the pages filled with his husband's slanting script, he wished he could scroll back to that Sunday in Soho, and tell Shane not to touch Joey Talavera's plans or his money. Had he done that, they wouldn't now live in this beautiful house and life would be much less comfortable. But neither would he be feeling sick to the stomach at the prospect of betraying the man he'd pledged to

235

love and honour until death did them part.

He forced himself to focus on the entries. He'd never found Shane's scrawl easy to decipher – an irony, considering *he* was the doctor – and this was no exception. It soon became clear, however, that most of the entries were from the very early days. There was an account of Shane's dealings with Xandra and Cyrus at the time of the California trip, including a record of the board meeting when Mel was sacked. Shane had clearly followed Craig's advice, back then, to keep proper notes with a view to protecting himself in case it all went wrong. After a while, however, he'd written in the journal only sporadically, and eventually the entries fizzled out altogether. Most of the pages remained blank.

While that was disappointing, Craig reminded himself that the early entries were the most important, because they spelled out the terms of the pact with Talavera. Any later material would be a bonus, but the structure of the initial deal was what mattered.

As he closed the book, he noticed something tucked away inside the back cover. It was a sheaf of three or four printed pages. He unfolded it and his mouth fell open when he saw what it was.

Perhaps this was another sign.

6

Still puzzled by her consultant's outburst, Ginny checked her phone as she waited for the lift back to the ground floor of the hospital. She'd forgotten about her unsent text to Lorraine, asking about the obstacle her fellow journalist said she'd hit. Whatever it was, it was clearly still causing stress. She now had a voicemail from Lorraine too.

'Ginny, sorry to bother you, but everything's frantic at this end. Can you call me as soon as you get this?'

That didn't sound good. Surely their plans to tell Mel's story to the world couldn't have foundered already?

Once she was back in the main entrance hall, Ginny found a seat with no immediate neighbours, and hit ringback. Lorraine picked up at the first ring.

'Sorry I missed you,' Ginny said. 'I was in the middle of replying to your text but then I had to turn my phone off.

What's going on?'

'I'm sorry to have pestered you, but my news editor is driving me crazy. He says he can't make an accusation against Joey Talavera without evidence to back it up. Mel's sworn word isn't good enough, apparently, which seems ridiculous to me. He wants corroboration. I've been trying to get hold of Mel, to see if she ever saw anything in writing, but she's not picking up. I've got to go into a meeting now. Could you do me a massive favour and carry on trying her for me? I've sent her a text, but I really want her to understand the importance of this. When we spoke to her the other night, she mentioned some document setting out the future of Orange Peel, which they showed her when they fired her. She said it mentioned Talavera by name. I need to know if she was able to keep a copy. Without it, I don't think they'll let me publish.'

'You're joking?'

'Sadly not. They're very jittery. Could you chase her for me?'

'Sure. No problem. Why the massive urgency, though?'

'You know what newspapers are like. Once they decide they're interested in something, they want it yesterday. If you're still talking about it tomorrow, it must be old news. Sorry to burden you with this, but I can probably get you an additional reporting byline, once we do publish.'

The professional credit, and whatever payment accompanied it, would certainly come in handy. 'No worries. Will you text me Mel's number?'

'Coming up. Thanks for this.'

'Oh, just one thing, Lorraine. I know you're in a hurry, but before you hang up…'

'What's that?' Lorraine sounded seriously harassed.

Gina dropped her voice, cupping the mouthpiece with her

left hand. 'Does the name Craig Gerrard mean anything to you? Dr Craig Gerrard?'

'No, I don't think so. Should it?'

'It doesn't matter. I've just had a strange conversation with him. I'm still trying to make sense of it. But if you've never heard of him, not to worry.'

'Sorry, no. Look, I've got to fly now. Thanks again for helping out.'

Mel's number arrived by text a few seconds later. Ginny dialled it, more to lodge it in her phone than in expectation of a reply, but a breathless voice picked up.

'Morning, Mel. It's Ginny Pugh here. I hope this isn't a bad moment?'

'No, it's fine. I've just got out of the shower, that's all. Did you call about ten minutes ago?'

'I think that was Lorraine. She left you a message, but she asked me to call you as well. She's in a flap, I'm afraid, because her news editor is being difficult about the story.'

'In what way, difficult?'

'He says he can't publish without independent confirmation.'

'You're joking!'

'That's what I said.'

'I'm prepared to breach the terms of my severance agreement, at great financial cost, to reveal how and why I was sacked. And they're fussing about corroboration? Why would I lie about something like that? They can always put it to Orange Peel and Talavera before they publish, allowing them a right of reply.'

'I know, I know. I'm just the messenger here. I completely agree with you, and I'm sure Lorraine has told them all that too, but she can't budge them. Can you think of anything at all that might substantiate your version? The confidentiality agreement you signed, for instance. Did it refer to any of this?'

'No, that was just a legal document, as far as I remember. It banned me from revealing anything I learned during my time at Orange Peel, on pain of surrendering the whole pay-off. It was all in lawyer-speak and didn't go into any specifics.'

'Lorraine mentioned another document. A report setting out what they were planning to do? You didn't manage to keep a copy, did you? If so, that would be a slam dunk.'

'I was in a daze at the time, so I don't remember, but I doubt I've got it. I can double-check in my files, if you like, but I'm ninety-nine percent certain I don't have it. There's no way Xandra would have let me keep it. '

'D'you mind doing that?'

'What, now? While we're on the phone?'

'If possible. Sorry, but I know that's what Lorraine would say. She said to tell you it was really urgent.'

Mel sighed. 'All right, if I must. But it's ridiculous of them to demand it.' She was breathing more heavily again, and Ginny pictured her going upstairs to wherever she kept her paperwork. She heard a drawer being opened. 'All that stuff is in here somewhere. I can't quite… Hang on, I'll put the phone down for a moment so I can use both hands. Don't go away.'

'I won't.'

A scruffy young man on crutches sank into a seat opposite Ginny. She twisted away, conscious that all talk was potentially dangerous.

'No, as I thought,' said Mel, back on the phone. 'All I've got is the gagging agreement, plus some follow-up paperwork that arrived later. It's all very dry and businesslike. I didn't think they'd have let me keep that other document. It was far too incriminating.'

'I can see that. The trouble is, we don't have anything to take to Lorraine's news editor.'

'I don't know what else I can do. Maybe we'll have more success with the other guy, Garrett Walsh.'

'Yes. Fingers crossed.'

'I guess that's part of the reason Lorraine's flapping, isn't it? She and Garrett presented themselves last night as only concerned for the greater good, without any personal agenda, but a journalist is a journalist. Don't take offence – I used to be one too. Lorraine doesn't want to lose the story to a rival publication. That's natural.'

'I suppose so.' Ginny felt disloyal for acknowledging the point, but she couldn't deny there was truth in it.

'Can I leave you to relay that to Lorraine?' Mel continued. 'If I think of anything that might help, I'll let her know. But I honestly don't think I will. All I can offer is my own testimony, and she's heard that already. I simply don't have anything else. In the meantime, let's keep our fingers crossed for *The Bystander.*'

'Yes, OK. There is just one other thing. I asked Lorraine just now, and she couldn't help, but perhaps you can.' Ginny dropped her voice again, conscious that she was still on hospital premises. 'Does the name Craig Gerrard mean anything to you? Dr Craig Gerrard?'

There was a pause as Mel pondered the question. 'I don't think so. Why do you ask? What's the context?'

'I've just had a hospital appointment—'

'Oh dear. Nothing too awful?'

'No, it's to correct something I've lived with for a long time, so I hope it will make my life easier.'

'That's a relief.'

'Thank you. Anyway, my consultant acted funny with me when he found out I was Ginny, rather than Virginia, as it says on my notes.'

'He recognised you as Queen of the Tergs?'

'I'm not sure I deserve that title, but yes, that's what I assumed. I certainly thought he had a problem with me. Then, right at the end of the consultation, he got emotional and burst out with some really unexpected stuff: he was sorry for everything that had happened to me and – get this – he could help. He said he was in a particular position that meant he could.'

'A particular position?'

'That was his exact phrase.'

There was another pause, then: 'What did he look like?'

'Mid-thirties, curly hair, receding slightly. Quite a nice face. And I got a bit of a gay vibe.'

'Now I come to think of it, his name *was* Craig. He was training to be a doctor and the description fits.'

'Who? Whose name? Do you know who he is?'

'Yes. If it's the same one, I've even met him a couple of times. He's Shane Foxley's husband.'

'Oh wow. What do you think he's planning to do?'

'Your guess is as good as mine. What else did he say?'

'Only that he had my address from my notes, so he's clearly planning on sending me something.'

'You should tell Lorraine. It may be the corroboration she's looking for. Provided we can actually trust him.'

'You think he could be trying to set me up?'

'We've both learned to our cost that this is a brutal game, so we can't rule it out, can we? Tread with caution, I'd say.'

'At the moment I can't do anything but wait.'

'That's true. Let me know if you hear anything further.'

The post didn't bring anything the following day, nor the one after that. When nothing arrived on the third day, Ginny began to think Dr Gerrard had changed his mind.

In the meantime, she heard that Garrett Walsh had run into the same problem as Lorraine. His editor at *The Bystander* was equally nervous of publishing on Mel's say-so alone. It was all a depressing anti-climax, after the excitement of the Apfel meeting.

Not that the national media was the only way of getting the Talavera connection into the public domain. The Twitter rumour-mill had already started to grind, with prominent Terg accounts talking about a household-name billionaire secretly funding the True Earth movement. None of those original accounts had actually used Talavera's name, either out of caution on their part, or because they didn't know it. The element of mystery made the story tantalising, even for people without strong opinions one way or the other. Suggestions bounced around the internet. Bill Gates? George Soros? Rupert Murdoch? Because he was so famous, Joey Talavera's name inevitably came up too, but only as one of a number of runners and riders.

However, tongues were clearly wagging in private. Four days after her hospital appointment, Ginny woke to find a message from a Twitter friend in Australia. Unusual in that he used his real name and picture, Trent Meyer was a clean-shaven, outdoorsy-looking professor of the history of science at a college in Tasmania. He was a good explainer and Ginny had picked up a good deal from his posts about the history of geographical inquiry. For example, she'd learned that every serious thinker since Pythagoras in the sixth century BC believed the earth was round. This flew in the face of the frantic rewriting of history by Shane Foxley and his True Earthers, who had convinced their acolytes that most people believed the earth was flat until the late fifteenth century, when the heinous Christopher Columbus spoiled everything. Trent dealt with these falsifications with endless wit and patience, which put him on Ginny's list of favourite Tergs.

She clicked his message open.

'G'day Ginny. I hope all is well up there in your evil racist hemispherical construct.' She smiled. Terg in-jokes were the best. 'I wanted to ask you about these Joey Talavera rumours. Are they true? I assume you'll know if they are. Don't worry if it's hush-hush, I'm not looking for insider dish. It's just that, if the story is true, there's an obvious historical angle that may be worth pursuing. If you're interested, I can gladly fill you in via a Zype chat.'

She sighed. You could always count on a historian to find an interesting historical angle. Interesting to them, anyway; whether anyone else cared was another matter. Amid the stress of trying to calm news editors' jitters and meet their demands for multiple sources, this wasn't a priority.

'Great to hear from you, Trent,' she thumbed back. 'Between ourselves, the rumours are indeed true. We're trying to get the press to run the full story, but even the friendly ones are nervous. You can imagine how frustrating it is. To be honest, I'm not sure I've got time to have a Zype. Do send over any thoughts/notes about your historical angle, though.'

She hoped that didn't sound too dismissive, but she couldn't afford to get dragged down a rabbit hole of irrelevance, with so many more important calls on her time.

As she hit send, she heard the sound of mail being squeezed through her letterbox. In her slippers, she padded into her flat's tiny hallway. Having convinced herself that Gerrard had changed his mind, she didn't expect to see anything other than pizza flyers and clothing collection bags. There was indeed a small pile of junk mail, plus a windowed manila envelope of the kind that only ever came from the tax office. But there was something else too. Poking out from beneath an estate agent's leaflet was the corner of a jiffy envelope, the smallest kind, about the shape and size of a mobile phone. She stooped to pick it up. Her name and address were block-capped in marker pen. Too neat for a doctor? There was nothing on the back.

She ripped the envelope open. At first, to her disappointment, it seemed to be empty. Then she tipped the package on end and gave it a shake. A small rectangular object fell out. It was a memory stick.

Hurrying back to her desk, her fingers shook as she fumbled to insert the stick in the correct slot of her laptop. Once it was in place, she woke up her screen, waiting for the new item to appear. She panicked for a moment as nothing happened, but then the flash-drive icon popped up, labelled 'For Ginny Pugh'. She clicked it open. Inside was a folder bearing the same label. Clicking on that, she saw that it contained a collection of photographs.

She opened the first picture, enlarging it to fill her screen. It was the opening page of a hand-written journal. The slanting script was not the easiest to read, but she could make out the first sentence easily enough:

Craig has persuaded me to use this journal to record the weird set of circumstances in which I seem to have got myself involved, so here goes.

'Oh wow,' said Ginny out loud.

She cast her eye over the other images. Most of them were of similar hand-written pages, but a group of four at the end seemed to be the pages of a printed document. She clicked on the first one, and read the heading.

'Oh wow, wow, wow!' she said, reaching for her phone.

Lorraine picked up immediately, wearing her brisk voice. 'I'm just going into a meeting, Ginny, so I'll probably have to call you back, unless it's very quick.'

'You'll want to hear this, trust me. You remember I asked if you knew a Dr Craig Gerrard?'

'Yes. And I didn't.'

'No, but Mel did. He's Shane Foxley's other half. And he's just sent me something in the post. I haven't looked at it all yet, because I wanted to tell you immediately.'

'And what is it?'

'Honestly, Lorraine, I think it's dynamite. It seems to be a complete photographic record of Shane's private journal. There's a fair amount to read, and the handwriting isn't always easy to decipher, but I'm looking at the first page now, and it seems to start when Shane first meets Joey Talavera at his house in Silicon Valley.'

'No! That's gold dust. Does it go into full detail?'

'I think so. It's written as if it's his private insurance policy, in case everything went badly wrong.'

'Brilliant.'

'But that's not the best part.'

'Really? How can it get better than that?'

'There's also a photograph of an internal document, written by Shane. It's headed *Orange Peel Foundation – a new direction: programme for expansion.* It's his blueprint for the way forward, setting out in black and white the entire rationale for their flat-earth collaboration with Talavera, including all the financial rewards. Honestly, it's gob-smacking.'

'Well done, Ginny. That sounds amazing. I can't wait to see it. Just as I was giving up hope, we may finally have caught the bastards red-handed!'

Ginny spent the rest of the day reading and transcribing the journal. That way, she could share it with those who needed to see it rather than passing on the pictures themselves.

Everything Mel had described was here, and much more. Although the diary seemed to have been started after Shane's return to London from California, it described his encounter with Joey Talavera in detail, paraphrasing the billionaire's diatribe about his flat-earth beliefs – George Washington? seriously? – and making clear that Shane thought the guy was mad. Later entries revealed the inner workings of Orange Peel's campaign, including the commissioning of bots for the initial dirty work, as well as the revelation that the Peter Amber Foundation was an Orange Peel front. Even at her most cynical, Ginny hadn't suspected that.

Seeing her own name liberally mentioned wasn't pleasant. Clearly, she'd fallen into a trap: Shane wanted an enemy and she'd knocked on his door offering to play the role to the full. She felt sick when she read his account of his lunch with Ricky Singleton at *Earth News*, as he briefed the journalist against her. This was no more than she'd already guessed, but it brought her no satisfaction to see her assumption confirmed.

Mel had said she thought Shane must have had someone to help him with these more devious elements of his plotting, and this too was borne out by Shane's accounts of his meetings and conversations with Robinson White. Ginny broke off from copy-typing to google White's name. She wasn't sure what she expected to find: a company website, a registered directorship at Companies House, a LinkedIn profile… In fact, there was nothing. The guy was completely off-grid, which was no mean achievement nowadays. She took it as a further sign that they were up against a serious player.

Once finished, she went through her text to mark up highlights, which she then assembled in a bullet-pointed summary. The effort should certainly justify a joint byline. Perhaps she would even get sole credit.

She called Lorraine again.

'What's the best way of pursuing this?' she said. 'Should I send the transcript and my summary to you? Or would it be easier if I pitched it directly at the news editor?'

'No, don't do that,' said Lorraine. 'I'm afraid your name still makes people nervous around here. It's better if you let me make the case. From what you've told me, the journal backs up everything Mel said, so it should deal with the objections here. What my news editor will ask, of course, is how we know it's real. Are you completely certain your source is genuine. I mean, is he really who he claims to be?'

'He didn't claim to be anyone. As far as I was concerned, he was just an orthopaedic consultant called Craig Gerrard who was seeing me professionally. When I mentioned him to Mel, she didn't know the name at first, but then she remembered that Shane Foxley's husband was called Craig and was training to be a doctor, and my rough physical description was a match. So we assumed that's who he must be. Then I got a memory stick in the post, containing photos of what appears to be

Shane's private diary, as well as a confidential Orange Peel document – strongly suggesting Mel's assumption was correct.'

'And the memory stick itself? Did it come with a note from Craig?'

'No, it was in a plain jiffy envelope. No note, no explanation, no nothing. But who else could it have come from?'

'I know, I know. I'm just trying to second-guess what our lawyers are going to say, namely that we're making lots of assumptions. All of them may be reasonable, but we're not certain about any of them. So, for a start, we need to confirm that your Craig Gerrard really is Shane Foxley's partner. Then you need to ask him if he sent the photographs. Finally, we need a sample of Foxley's own writing, so we can check that the diary really is in his hand.'

'OK.' Ginny was scribbling notes, trying to suppress her irritation at these demands, and to focus instead on how she was going to meet them.

'I'm afraid there's something else as well. Can we trust Gerrard? I mean, how do we know we're not being set up?'

'Wait till you read the journal. Why would anyone go to the trouble of fabricating all this? It would be a huge amount of work, just to make Orange Peel look like evil, manipulative bastards who've literally sold themselves to the highest bidder. If that's not the case, why would they want the world to think it is? It makes no sense.'

'True, but what if… Sorry, I'm only playing devil's advocate here… Years of bitter experience, I'm afraid. What if Craig and Shane have had a massive bust-up and Craig has faked the whole diary to get his own back?'

'And he just happens to have made up exactly the same story that Mel told us? Besides, I know Craig didn't write it himself. When I met him for my appointment, he wrote out a form for me to hand in at reception, and his hand was completely different. Besides, if we do manage to get hold of a sample of Shane's writing, we'll be able to show the journal is authentic, won't we?'

'I'm sure you're right. Craig must be for real. Don't you wonder what's going on, though? I mean, if he copied the entire journal to send to you, knowing that you'd try and get it in the papers, it's going to be completely obvious to Shane where it came from. Does that mean the relationship is on the rocks and Craig's planning to walk out? Or maybe they've spilt up already, and this is revenge after a messy divorce.'

'Yes, maybe they have. Mel said they were together five years ago, but anything could have happened since then.'

'In that case, you really do have to make contact with him, Ginny. Not just to confirm that he sent the photos. Find out why he smuggled them out to you, and what he's expecting us to do with them. If he's gone this far already, you may even be able to persuade him to speak on the record.'

'I doubt he will, but I can ask. I'm not sure how to get in touch with him, though. All I know is his job title.'

'Call the hospital, tell them you're a patient – which is true, isn't it? – and get them to page him.'

'Yes, that could work. Just one other thing…'

'What's what?'

'If I'm doing all this legwork, am I writing the story too? Or am I sharing a byline?'

Lorraine laughed. 'Don't worry, I'll make sure they give you the sole byline. Honestly, if we can make this story watertight, they'll probably decide they loved you all along and put you on staff.'

7

It was Saturday morning, and Craig paid a rare visit to the gym. They'd agreed that Shane would wait in for their Ocado delivery and he, in return, would make lunch. When he got back, he set about stir-frying some chicken, with pre-sliced vegetables from the delivery and black-bean sauce out of a sachet. Shane, in an unusually expansive mood, opened a bottle of wine.

'I've got some news I think you'll like,' he said, pouring two glasses as Craig plated the food.

Craig was instinctively wary. 'Oh yes?'

'We're going to California.'

'Really?' He set the plates on the table and they both sat down to eat.

'Really. Didn't I always promise I'd wangle a trip for both of us, so I could show you Joey's place?'

Craig spluttered as a beansprout went down the wrong way. 'We're going to Joey's place?'

'I knew that would blow you away. Do you want some water?'

Craig accepted the water and took a gulp to clear the blockage. 'When is it, though? I can't just book leave whenever I want.'

'I know that, which is why I've arranged for us to go the week after next. You told me you've already taken it off. You didn't have anything else planned, did you?'

'I was planning to spend most of it sleeping.'

'You can sleep on the flight. Which will be business class, of course. Joey's paying.'

Craig's eyes widened. While he loathed the idea of taking Talavera's hospitality, he'd never flown anything other than economy. Nevertheless, he was suspicious. 'What's the occasion?' he said.

'Occasion?'

'I mean, why now? Why's he paying for us to go now?'

'No particular reason. There have been various things going on lately. Potential hiccups. I won't bore you with the ins and outs. They simply mean I've been talking to Joey more than usual. But his paranoia is getting worse. He hates any form of internet comms, even Zype. He suggested it might be easier to do it face to face. And it was his idea for you to come.'

'Oh. Not yours, then?'

'Of course I want you to come. The place is amazing, and I've wanted to show it you ever since I first went there. I just mean it's a sincere invitation that came directly from him. He wants to meet you.'

This rang alarm bells, and Craig sipped wine to mask a

nervous swallow. 'Does he?' Had Talavera somehow already got wind of his treachery? The idea wasn't impossible. The guy was a billionaire who'd made all his money in digital communications. He must be able to monitor everyone on the planet.

'Don't look so worried. Hey, I know it can be daunting to meet someone so rich and glamorous. But underneath all that celebrity froth—'

'He's just like you and me?'

'Well, maybe not. But if I can handle him, so can you.'

'Right.' Craig forced a smile. 'It sounds awesome.'

'It will be, I promise. Apparently Krystal's going to be there this time, too.'

Craig barely slept that night.

He'd already been kicking himself for the sloppy way he'd conducted his skulduggery when he put the memory stick in the post four days earlier.

In his mind, it had all been clear. He needed to give Ginny Pugh some incontrovertible proof of everything that had happened, so she could expose it. If she used the diary as background – wasn't that what journalists called it? – Shane need never know how close to home the mole was. That would prevent an ugly domestic showdown.

The problem was, Craig hadn't specified the background-only part to Ginny. Caught up in the thrill of spycraft, he'd put the pictures in the mail without any kind of note or commentary. That cloak-and-dagger approach might have made him feel like a character from John Le Carré, but it was also stupid. He wasn't really doing it anonymously, because he'd told Ginny he was ready to help. If she hadn't worked out his relationship to Shane already, she would do as soon as she looked at the diary entries. So it was ridiculous not to have included some instructions.

If he'd been thinking straight, he'd have told her he had cast-iron evidence of scandalous behaviour at Orange Peel, and that he'd only hand it over on two conditions: she must swear not to use his name nor make any reference to the nature of the evidence – the fact that it was a journal – in anything she wrote. At the very least, he could have put a note in the package setting out those conditions and urging her to respect them.

And now here was Shane's bombshell announcement that they were going to Talavera's home, making his previous worries look like minor niggles. Was he walking into some kind of trap? Even if his betrayal wasn't yet known, anything could happen between now and their departure. In the best case, with neither Shane nor Talavera suspecting anything, Craig would have to spend a week, or however many days they were meant to stay, making nice with their host and pretending he was delighted to be there.

He listened to Shane snoring softly beside him. He envied him: capturing the world in a monstrous deception, yet able to sleep as soon as his head hit the pillow.

Eventually Craig dropped off too, but he woke at his normal time, feeling groggy and unrefreshed, and remained as edgy as ever. He got up and showered. By the time he'd made coffee, he had made a decision. He couldn't see any way of getting out of the California trip, but he could at least clarify matters with Ginny. As soon as he could get her contact details out of the patient records system, he would call her, spell out his concerns about the use of the journal material and throw himself on her mercy.

Sundays usually flew by, but this one went at a crawl as he counted the hours before he could get to work the next day and find Ginny's number. In his fretful state, he had a sudden realisation. He didn't just want to secure her discretion, important as that was. After years of carrying his reservations and remorse in silence, he now yearned to be able to talk honestly with someone who understood. His pledge of help, blurted out so clumsily in that windowless little room, was a plea for Ginny to be his confidante.

Monday finally came. He had an early-morning ward round, after which he planned to look up Ginny's number. Midway through the round, his pager vibrated. He stared in astonishment at the message on his screen: *pls call Ginny Pugh*, followed by her number. Was this another sign?

'Is everything all right, Dr Gerrard?' said the nurse with whom he'd been discussing a patient's knee surgery.

'Yep, sorry. Where were we?' He tried to concentrate, while also attempting to work out when and where he could snatch ten minutes to call Ginny back.

It was another half hour before he got the chance, from a landing outside the ward. That was what passed for privacy in a busy teaching hospital.

Ginny picked up almost immediately.

'It's Craig Gerrard here,' he said. 'I got your message.'

'Dr Gerrard! It's good to hear from you. I was nervous you wouldn't call.'

'Craig, please. Dr Gerrard is your orthopaedic consultant. I'm assuming you weren't calling me in that capacity.'

'No, you're right. I wasn't. Is that OK?'

'Normally it wouldn't be. In the circumstances, it's fine. In fact I'm very pleased to hear from you. I was planning on calling you today too.'

'Again, not as a patient?'

'Correct.'

'Right. Great minds, huh?'

'Look, I haven't got long. Why don't you go first and tell me why you were trying to get in touch?'

'Sure. It was… Sorry, it's a bit awkward… I received something in the post which I think can only have come from you.'

'Go on.'

'Well… Firstly, I want to say thank you. It's an amazing resource. And I understand you may not want to say "you're welcome", because that would be an admission that you sent it. But the thing is, before I or anyone else can use it, I do need to know it definitely came from you, to prove that what it showed was genuine. I'm sorry to be so blunt.'

'No, that's fine. Please don't apologise. Bluntness is what's called for.' He looked at his watch. He needed to get back to work.

'Hello?'

'Yes, I'm still here. Look, it would be better to talk about this in person. Can we meet?'

'Of course. When were you thinking?'

'Tonight?' Was that too needy? If so, he was past caring.

'Fantastic. I'll have to move something, but…'

'Or we could do later in the week if you prefer.'

'No, no. Tonight's great.'

'Good. Do you know Paddington Basin? There's a wine bar called The Wharf.'

'Not really, but I'm sure I can find it. What time?'

'Is six all right for you?'

'Perfect. I'll see you there.'

Predictably, he was delayed leaving work. He texted to say he was running late, paranoid that she'd have upped and left by the time he arrived. To his relief, she was still there.

'Sorry,' he said, spotting her at a discreet table at the rear of the bare-brick bar room, whose designers had aimed for warehouse chic, even though the building was brand new. 'Let me get you another glass of wine to make up for it. What was it?'

Five minutes later, he returned with two glasses of Merlot from the bar and sank into a soft leather armchair opposite her. He'd chosen the place because it was rarely busy. They could talk without having to shout above normal pub din. 'Cheers.'

She raised her glass. 'Thanks for the drink. And also for... well, you know.'

'You're welcome,' he said pointedly.

She laughed, understanding his meaning. Then she was serious again. 'Do you mind if I ask why you did it? It must have been a massive step for you.'

'Yes it was. That's why I wanted to talk to you. To be honest, I was reckless in doing what I did and I've been worrying ever since. What I should have said, if I'd been thinking straight, was that those journal entries were only meant as background, to let you know what's been going on. The enormity of it, I mean. I ought to have said that I didn't want you to reproduce them or do anything else to reveal to my husband that you've got them, because...' He sighed.

'Because, if I'm brutally honest with myself, I'm prepared to betray him, but I'm not yet ready for him to know I've betrayed him. Does that make sense?'

She took a sip of her wine and nodded. 'Of course. It makes perfect sense.'

'I know I should have told you that from the outset. But I didn't. Like an idiot, I sent you the pictures without establishing what you could do with them, so technically I can't stop you, if you want to splash direct quotes from Shane's diary all over the papers. All I can do is appeal to you not to do that, as a favour to me, because I'm not ready to turn my life upside down. Not just yet. And I know you must think I've got a nerve saying that, considering that my husband tried to destroy your life, but...'

She held her hand up to stop him. 'Listen, Craig. You're not Shane. I know that. You've proved it already and you don't have to carry the guilt for everything he's done. That's his responsibility, not yours.'

He sniffed back a tear, trying to cover it with a cough. That made matters worse, and what emerged sounded dangerously like a sob.

'Hey, relax,' she said. 'It really is going to be OK. We can use your material as background, because we already have very strong first-hand testimony from...well, from someone else who was once closely involved in all this.' Her phone was ringing but she ignored it. 'I've been working closely with Lorraine Churcher at the *Chronicle*. You know, the columnist?'

'The one who's always on TV? She's trans, isn't she?'

'That's her. The thing is, we were having trouble getting the story into the paper on the basis of that testimony alone, because the news editor wanted corroboration. And then you came along and provided what we needed. Honestly, it couldn't have come at a better time. I'm happy to give you my solemn promise that we won't reveal our source, because that's part of our code as journalists. In this case, the source is both you and Shane's diary. We won't reveal either of them.'

She glanced at the screen of her phone, which had stopped ringing. 'Hey, how weird! That was Lorraine calling, just as I was talking about her. Sorry, do you mind if I give her a quick call back? It could be important.'

'Of course not. Go ahead.' He watched as she pressed ringback and put the phone to her ear.

'Hey Lorraine. Sorry I didn't pick up just now. You'll never guess who I'm... What?!' Her eyes widened. 'Say that again... What's one of those when it's at home?... You're kidding me! Since when?... Bastard! And there's really nothing we can...?'

She shook her head in dismay as she listened. Lorraine, at the other end, was plainly furious. Craig could hear her voice from across the table.

'What is it?' he asked nervously, when Ginny eventually ended the call.

She closed her eyes as if trying to steady her emotions, then took a gulp of wine and said: 'Do you know what an anonymised privacy injunction is?'

'No.'

'Nor did I. It's apparently the new version of what used to be called a super-injunction.'

'I don't know what that is either.'

'I'm not completely clear myself, but it's basically a gagging device used by the rich and famous to put a blanket ban on the media covering a story that will show them in a bad light.'

'Can they do that? Even if the story's true?'

'Apparently.'

'And let me guess. Joey?'

'Correct. Our friend Mr Talavera has taken out a privacy injunction to prevent the *Chronicle* writing anything about this story, or even reporting that they've been banned from writing it. There's one on *The Bystander* too. That means everything we've been talking about is irrelevant. The only papers that are willing to run the story can't print a word of it.'

8

When she reached home, Ginny called Lorraine again.

'I'm still stunned by what you told me about Talavera's injunction,' she said. After two glasses of wine, she was steaming angry. 'It was all going so well. I was in a bar with Craig Gerrard, who poured his heart out to me. He confirmed that he sent the pictures, the diary is Shane's and they're still together – although only just, by the sound of it. We had everything we need to stand up Mel's version of the story. And now this. It's unbelievable.'

'Tell me about it. What an absolute bastard! The first I knew of it was this afternoon, when the editor called me in.'

'And there's no way round it?'

'I don't think so. These injunctions are scary things with massive penalties – jail for the editor, that sort of thing – so no one breaks them. There was a spate of them in the early

Noughties, and the details of some of the stories eventually slipped out. The most famous was designed to protect a shipping company that had been dumping toxic waste in West Africa, but then celebrities started using them to stop the tabloids writing about their sex lives. The legal procedure has evolved since then, so the orders now have to be issued publication by publication, rather than to the entire media at once, but that doesn't seem to bother Talavera.'

'It's outrageous. What about the freedom of the press?'

'Having enough money to get an injunction seems to trump that. The media can't even make a fuss about it, because they can't report the existence of the injunction. It's a totalitarian horror which makes me spit with fury, but there's nothing we can do about it.'

'What did your editor say?'

'He's as angry as we are, which is the only positive thing about all this. He was on the fence before, but he's now a convert: he's peaked and gone full Terg.'

'For all the good it will do.'

'Don't. I know.'

One question had been nagging at Ginny all the way home. 'What I'm really wondering is, how did he know?'

'Who? My editor?'

'No, Talavera. Nobody approached him for a comment, did they? So how did he know the story was coming?'

'His name has been mentioned on Twitter.'

'Rupert Murdoch has been mentioned on Twitter. And Bill Gates. Neither of them took out an injunction.'

'Neither of them was guilty as charged.'

'I guess not. But taking out an injunction is as good as saying it's a fair cop. You wouldn't do that on the basis of an idle Twitter rumour.'

'So what are you thinking?'

'That we really did have a spy in the Apfel meeting.'

'It's always been a possibility.'

'After reading Shane's diary, I don't think anything's too far-fetched any more. Especially with that character Robinson White involved. Did you read those parts of the journal?'

'I did and I know what you mean about him. Behind the eccentricity, he sounds a sinister piece of work. So we think the Terghood has been infiltrated by someone who got themselves invited to Carnarvon Hall? Do you suspect anyone in particular?'

'I did wonder about Globy Dick. What was his real name? Dave? I didn't think anything of it at the time, but now I know all about White, living in his weird Bond villain penthouse at the top of a Bermondsey council block, I started wondering.'

'You mean because Dave's a bit cor-blimey, he must live on the same estate?'

Ginny felt herself blushing. 'Perhaps not, when you put it like that.'

'You may be right in principle though,' said Lorraine. 'We know White is ruthless and extremely capable, so your theory is perfectly plausible. It may be wise to take precautions in future and not make big decisions in a group setting like that.'

Ginny sighed. 'It's academic, though, isn't it? Whatever decision we take, we can't actually do anything, because Talavera and his lawyers have tied our hands.'

'I know.' Lorraine sounded as gloomy as Ginny felt.

Aware that they were wallowing, Ginny remembered the other reason she was calling. 'There is something else I meant to tell you. I don't know if there's any way we can turn it to our advantage, but Craig's been invited to California.'

'To Talavera's place, you mean?'

He'd poured all this out later, over his second glass of wine, while Ginny switched to mineral water. He explained his worries about going. Ginny tried to persuade him how unlikely it was that he was walking into a trap. If Talavera and Shane knew their conspiracy had been rumbled, they simply wanted to spend time talking face to face, surely? Craig seemed to accept that, but he remained fixated on why Talavera had included him in the invitation.

'If they want urgent talks, I'll be in the way, won't I?' he said. He was convinced there must be some other reason.

Ginny did her best to calm him. It was more likely the invitation had been Shane's idea, she said, because he didn't want to make the long trip on his own. He'd simply told a white lie to make Craig feel more welcome. 'Far be it from me to defend your husband to you, after everything he's done to me. But he may genuinely have thought it would be nice to take you to stay with one of the richest people on the planet.'

That seemed to set Craig's mind at rest. It was only after they parted that Ginny wondered if the trip might present them with an opportunity.

'What did you have in mind?' said Lorraine.

'I'm not sure. It's just that, up to now, our plan has been to expose the conspiracy between Orange Peel and Talavera in order to show the world what the True Earth movement is really about. The injunction means we can't do that, so we have to think of other approaches. To be honest, I haven't got any bright ideas. All I know is that someone who wants to help us has been invited to stay at Talavera's billionaire lair.

That's got to be worth something, hasn't it?'

'How, though? You're not suggesting that Craig slip something into Talavera's tea, or whatever Silicon Valley billionaires drink, to make sure he never troubles the world with his crazy theories again?'

'No, of course not.' This hadn't occurred to her, and she tried to push the idea out of her head before it took hold. 'I was thinking more along the lines of...I don't know...trying to find out what makes the guy tick?'

'I'm not sure how far that will get us. He's a certifiable lunatic who happens to have made enough money to foist his crackpot obsession on the rest of the world, having helped develop the kind of technology that can make hundreds of millions of people as crazy as he is. That's what makes him tick. How does it help? Sorry, I don't mean to be negative, but what am I missing?'

'I don't know. It's just that having access to this amazingly powerful figure in his home environment, when his guard is down, feels like a big deal. Besides, what else do we have?'

'Nothing,' Lorraine conceded. 'Unless we can find a way of challenging the injunction. That would be my preference, but it may not be possible. In the meantime, it's obviously worth keeping in touch with Craig while he's there. You've got each other's numbers, haven't you?'

Ginny confirmed that they had. She and Lorraine agreed to call it a night, but to keep in touch, particularly if anything changed with regard to the legal situation.

She knew she ought to go to bed, but she was still wired. She wondered if Lorraine had told Mel what had happened. There was no harm in making sure, so she keyed out a text explaining the situation, in case Mel didn't know already, and suggesting they talk in the morning.

She remained furious and resentful. Aside from everything else, the squashing of their story by the lawyers meant she wouldn't get her promised byline or the cheque that came with it – let alone the job offer Lorraine had predicted. Although maybe she'd been joking about that. It was all right for Lorraine, with her staff job and her expense account. For Ginny, it meant all that work transcribing the journal would go unrewarded.

Her phone pinged with a reply from Mel, who had indeed been unaware of the latest development. 'I'm gutted to hear this,' she wrote. 'It's a real kick in the stomach. I've had a few of those already, so you'd think I'd be used to setbacks, but they don't get any easier to bear, do they? Let's talk tomorrow.'

Closing the text, Ginny saw a notification of a direct message on Twitter. It was from Trent Meyer. She clicked on the envelope icon to open it.

'G'day Ginny,' he wrote. 'I completely understand that you don't have time to Zype, what with everything else that's happening in London right now. You know people here are referring to the UK as Terg Island? Sounds wild!'

That at least cheered her up.

'You asked me to jot down some notes about the historical angle I mentioned re Joey Talavera,' he continued, 'so here goes. Before Joey, the most famous Talavera in history was one Hernando de Talavera, the Bishop of Avila and later the Archbishop of Granada, in the reign of Ferdinand and Isabella. As far as academic historians are concerned, he was a serious and decent character. He learned Arabic so he could forge a good relationship with the Muslims of Granada, and he opposed the Spanish Inquisition. In the popular imagination, however, the poor guy is remembered as the leader of the so-called Council of Salamanca, set up by the queen to examine Columbus' proposal for an expedition westward to the Indies. I say 'poor guy' because he opposed the trip and has gone down in history as the ultimate flat-earth drongo.

'The point is, I'm wondering how much of this Joey knows. Has the story got into his head and turned him into a flat-earther, as a perverse way of defending the family name? It sounds off-the-wall, I know, and I could be totally wide of the mark. But if I'm not, it could be important – because there's more to the tale than Joey may realise. I'll leave it there for now. Hit me up if you want to hear more.'

'Interesting,' she wrote back. 'To be honest, our main problem at the moment is trying to stop Talavera throwing his weight around with the legal injunctions he's taking out on the UK media. I don't mean to be dismissive but, in the mood I'm in, I don't give a monkey's how or why he got this crap in his head.'

She hit send and immediately wondered if she'd been too rude, when Trent was just trying to help. She would message him again in the morning, to make sure he wasn't offended. For now, the stress of the day was finally catching up with her and all she wanted to do was crawl into bed.

The word 'injunction' lodged in her head all night, chasing her through an extended dream sequence that started on Joey Talavera's Silicon Valley estate. The billionaire had the face of her old geography teacher, Mr Hutton, reborn as a flat-earther, and Krystal was Tiffany from *EastEnders*. Ginny was on a mission to put rat poison in Hutton/Talavera's tea, but it turned out he only drank mineral water from a particular spring. That presented a serious problem as the water changed colour every time she tried to add the poison. Exposed as an assassin, she escaped the estate, which had somehow shifted into the middle of a vast desert while she was there. She managed to flag down a car, which turned into a London bus as soon as she got into it, full of passengers waving bits of paper at her and telling her she'd been injuncted. It was a relief to banish the pursuers by opening her eyes and find it was morning already.

She stared at the ceiling, thinking through her plans for the day. She'd promised to call Mel, and perhaps they could meet for lunch, although it would have to be Pret, because she was broke. Maybe Mel could think of some way of turning Craig's trip to California to their advantage. It was a shame Lorraine had been so negative on that score.

Part of her problem, she realised, was that she had so much flying around in her head. Once upon a time, she'd have blogged about it, just to get it all down, but she'd mothballed her blogsite after the horrors of the Cambridge Union.

She sat up in bed. If there was one thing she'd learned in the past five years, it was that the bullies only won if you let them. She'd been prepared to put her own name to a major Orange Peel exposé in the *Chronicle*. That was no longer going to happen, because Talavera had injuncted the publishers of the *Chronicle*, but he hadn't injuncted Ginny.

She swung her legs out of bed, suddenly energised. She knew what she must do. Maybe Talavera would end up setting his lawyers on her, too. But, for the moment, she was free to write whatever she wanted.

PART THREE

Sadie @sadie93ozumvjfs
Hello @HipstersRuin. Can I ask why you follow @GlobyDick? He's an outspoken globularist. I'm a big fan of artisan gin so I love your product, but endorsing Terg racism is not acceptable
RT 52 L 151

Hipster's Ruin ✓ @HipstersRuin
Hello Sadie. We've unfollowed that account now. Thanks a lot for drawing the mistake to our attention. We hope you continue to enjoy Hipster's Ruin artisan gin
RT 276 L 463

GlobyDick @GlobyDick
Er, hello? I had no idea you were following me @HipstersRuin, and I'm not bothered if you unfollow. But you just called me a racist on the say-so of @sadie93ozumvjfs who has 10 followers. Believing the world is round is not racist
RT 34 L 118

GarrettWalsh ✓ @Garrett_Walsh
The makers of an alcoholic drink have defamed someone – whom I know personally to be a humane and caring individual – on the basis of a baseless tweet from an anonymous account. I'll be writing about this in my column in The Bystander
RT 67 L 239

Nægling @Sword_of_Beowulf
What a time to be alive!
RT 2 L 50

Copper Knickers @NicolausCopernicusLives
Hey @HipstersRuin. Will @sadie93ozumvjfs buy all the gin
you won't sell to the people you pissed off with this?
RT 0 L 6

Mekell King @pointymekell
Thanks @HipstersRuin for demonstrating why companies
that entrust their reputation to social media teams are
taking big, silly risks. Any sign of a grown-up yet?
RT 1 L 11

Hipster's Ruin √ @HipstersRuin
A statement from us

> We work hard to make Hipster's Ruin as socially sensitive
> as possible.
> Over the years we've followed a lot of people on here. From
> time to time we've unfollowed some too. The other day
> we unfollowed a Twitter account because content on their
> feed about the shape of the earth wasn't in line with
> our values of sensitivity and respect.
> This has upset some people.
> We've still got work to do, but we believe everyone should
> be protected from offence, which includes minorities who are
> understandably offended by a strident belief in hemispheres.
> We will continue to make sure our social media channels
> remain fair, sensitive and free from racism. It's on all of us to
> create the conditions where everyone can live happy lives free
> from offensive ideas.

RT 4.2K L 27.5K

HolbyFan @holbyfanhatestergs
A million times thank you. You're brilliant. Best artisan gin
maker ever
RT 3 L 306

Sadie @sadie93ozumvjfs
Thanks so much @HipstersRuin. You're the best. I'm going out to buy a bottle to celebrate
RT 6 L 59

Nægling @Sword_of_Beowulf
[face-palm emoji]
RT 0 L 241

GlobyDick @GlobyDick
Artisan gin maker, my arse. @HipstersRuin is a subsidiary of the UK's biggest drinks manufacturer, which doesn't actually pay any tax in the UK. I didn't want the bastards following me anyway
RT 28 L 76

Hipster's Ruin √ blocked **Globy Dick**

1

For all his reservations about this trip, Craig couldn't fail to be impressed by the British Airways business lounge at Terminal Five.

'Told you, didn't I?' said Shane. On the basis of one previous visit, he was talking like he owned the place. 'Go and check out the bar. They've got everything you could possibly want. All free, obviously.'

'Shall I get you something?'

'A G&T? Thanks. Oh, and if they've got it, can you make sure the gin is Hipster's Ruin?'

'Since when did you get so fussy?'

'I'm not bothered about the taste. I just want to support them. They've been brilliant lately on Twitter.'

Craig did as he was told. Sure enough, the bar did stock Hipster's Ruin, along with some equally fancy artisan tonic.

Since it was self-service, he mixed two G&Ts.

'How can a gin company be brilliant on Twitter?' he said, bringing the clinking glasses back to the sofa that Shane had commandeered. 'Isn't there only so much you can say about gin?'

'They weren't tweeting about gin. They've turned out to be awesome allies. Someone pointed out they were following this outspoken Terg – God knows why – and they immediately apologised and unfollowed the guy. That led to a massive pile-on, as the rest of the Tergs tried to kick up a fuss, saying they'd never buy Hipster's Ruin again. As if they ever did. But the company stood firm. They put out this amazing statement saying everyone should be protected from offence, including minorities offended by globularism. It was stunning, and they got about 30,000 likes for it.'

You've drunk your own Kool-Aid and you're now a total crackpot, thought Craig. 'Right. I see,' he said. He raised his glass. 'Anyway, cheers.'

'Cheers. Here's to a great trip.'

In my dreams, thought Craig.

They had nearly an hour before they were due to board. They both flicked through magazines: *Vanity Fair* for Shane, *Hello!* for Craig. It wasn't his normal publication of choice, but there was something so surreal about this island of luxury and pampering in the middle of a busy airport terminal, so far removed from the ramshackle Victorian buildings in which he usually spent his day, that a lurch into the unfamiliar seemed appropriate.

They read in silence, sipping their drinks and grazing on savoury snacks from the buffet. Suddenly Shane cried: 'Ha! It's Joey and Krystal!'

'Where?' Craig looked up, alarmed to think the Talaveras might be in the lounge. He wasn't yet ready for his introduction to celebrity royalty.

Shane tilted his copy of *Vanity Fair* and pointed. There, posed in full Annie Leibovitz splendour amid their desert acres, were their hosts-to-be.

It was a relief that they weren't in the airport, but Craig's eyes widened nonetheless. 'That's not where we're going, is it?' The house was a series of modernist white cubes, all set low to the ground, in a harsh wilderness studded only with cactuses and rocks.

'No, this is the other place. Where we're going is much more civilised. The pied à terre mansion, remember?'

'Phew.' All Craig's fears about walking into a trap had flooded back. The isolated setting looked just the location for a visitor to have an unfortunate accident.

'Honestly, the Palo Alto house is beautiful. You're going to love it.'

Craig nodded, wishing that were true, as they went back to their magazines. 'Can I ask one thing?' he said after a moment.

'What's that?'

'Why precisely are you and Joey having this meeting? You said there were potential hiccups. Is there some kind of crisis?'

Shane took a precautionary look around him and dropped his voice.

'I haven't mentioned any of this, but you may as well know. Yes, actually, we've had some major stuff to deal with.' He dropped his voice even further, so Craig had to strain to hear. 'Mel has broken her confidentiality agreement. She's been telling people all sorts of things she shouldn't.'

Craig remembered to feign surprise. 'No! Really? Aren't

there massive penalties if she does that?'

'You bet there are. She'll have to give back every penny we gave her, plus interest. Don't worry, we'll make sure she does.'

'Who has she been telling?'

'A bunch of leading Tergs had a secret meeting. Ginny Pugh was there, plus Lorraine Churcher from the *Daily Chronicle*, and that bloke from *The Bystander* who's always writing bigoted things about the True Earth movement. A roll-call of appalling human beings. And Mel, who made a speech about everything that happened when she left Orange Peel. Absolutely nothing left out. Of course she told them all about' – he mouthed the name *Joey* – 'and his conditions for funding us.'

'Wow. That is major. How do you know all this?'

Shane looked over his shoulder again to check there was no one within earshot. 'We had someone there.'

Ginny had shared her suspicions with Craig, and she was clearly right. 'Really?'

'Yes.' Shane smirked with undisguised pride. 'Robbie infiltrated the Terg movement ages ago, so we always find out whatever they do.'

'This is all such heavy stuff.' Craig tried to sound as casual as possible. 'So who is it, your insider?'

'I can't tell you that. Otherwise—'

'You'd have to kill me. I know.'

'Actually I don't even know myself. It's someone of Robbie's and I haven't asked him who it is. He prefers it that way.'

'So what's going to happen now? If all those journalists were there, is the whole thing going to end up in the papers?'

'No, don't worry. We've seen to that.'

'That's good to hear.' His play-acting was improving. 'How did you manage it?'

'We got Joey to take out injunctions on the *Chronicle* and *The Bystander* to prevent them writing about him. They can't even say there's an injunction in place. It's a really useful piece of law. Obviously it's not great in principle, if you believe in free speech and all that, but it's been a godsend. Otherwise they could have done all kinds of damage. I needn't remind you, if Orange Peel has to shut, or if Joey cuts the funding, we'll almost certainly lose the house.'

'Yes, I know. You don't have to tell me.'

'So it's sorted for the time being, but Joey's keen to put together a strategy to prevent future attempts. The Tergs don't have much support, but their new organisation is obviously a worry, especially as they control some quite influential parts of the media.'

A column in the *Chronicle* and an occasional page in *The Bystander* weren't Craig's idea of influential, compared with the support given by most of the rest of the press and virtually all the broadcasters to the True Earth movement. But he kept that to himself.

'What would happen if someone told Mel's story somewhere else? In a blog, say?'

'You're thinking of Ginny Pugh?'

Craig panicked. By asking too much, he'd exposed himself. 'Well, not really. It could be any—'

'No, you're right. It's a good question. We know from our source that Ginny Pugh was there when Churcher and the *Bystander* guy were debriefing Mel. We think she'll either try and run the story in another paper, in which case we'll hear about it when they approach us for a comment and we'll slap an injunction on them, or she'll do it on her own blog. I checked the other day, and she hasn't posted anything on it for a few years, but it's still there. If she tries to publish' – his eyes were shining – 'we'll be waiting for her. She won't know what's hit her.'

The evident pleasure he took in this prospect made Craig inwardly shudder, but he owed it to Ginny to find out more. 'In what way?'

'Joey'll take her to the cleaners. Bankrupt her.'

'But…if the story is basically true…?'

'Doesn't matter. He's got the world's deepest pockets, so he can string any action out for as long as he wants before it comes to court. The fees alone will destroy her. Robbie's had experience of this kind of stuff, so the pair of them know what they're doing. To be honest, Robbie can't wait. He's absolutely raring to go. It's really quite hilarious.'

Shocked on Ginny's behalf, Craig was momentarily at a loss for what to say. Fortunately he was spared the need, as the tannoy announced that boarding for the British Airways flight to San Francisco would shortly commence.

'Come on, that's us,' said Shane.

'Let me just nip in there.' Craig nodded in the direction of the toilets.

'Don't be too long.'

'I won't.'

'In that case, why are you taking your phone?'

Craig felt the blood rush to his face, certain he'd been found out this time, but Shane was smiling and had turned back to his magazine.

The gents' was fitted out with fresh flowers and soft towels like the bathroom of a smart hotel. Craig shut himself in a stall and started writing a WhatsApp message. His fingers shook as he tapped out: 'Urgent news. You're definitely right about the spy. S has just confirmed it. He won't tell me who it is, but he implied they were present when you interviewed Mel.'

He hit send, then continued in a new message: 'Also, DON'T publish anything about what Mel told you on your blog. That's what they want. They're planning on tying you up in a court case that will bankrupt you with the fees alone.'

He pressed send again. As he did so, Ginny's reply to his first message arrived. 'Thanks so much for the intelligence. Confirms what I thought re both existence and identity of mole.'

Having read it, he carried on writing. 'We're at Heathrow, just about to board. Don't write back from now on. I don't want S to see or hear the notifications. I'll let you know when it's safe to chat.'

He hit send, took the opportunity for a quick leak, then prepared to head back to the lounge.

He was washing his hands when another text pinged in. 'Yikes, that's really scary,' Ginny wrote. 'Thanks for the warning. I've nearly written the blog but I'll hold off publishing it.'

Craig frowned. What part of 'don't reply' didn't she understand? But of course their messages were crossing. Sure enough, another one now arrived. 'Sorry, just got your last about not answering. Understood loud and clear. Be safe. Message me when you can.'

He was going to reply with a 'will do' but thought better of it, because she'd only reply to that one too, and he'd never get out of the bathroom.

A business-suited guy of around his own age came in,

standing aside as Craig exited the inner and outer doors and made his way back into the lounge. As he went, he deleted the entire WhatsApp conversation with Ginny and changed her name in his contacts from 'Ginny Pugh' to 'Patient VP'. Better safe than sorry.

Shane was on his feet already. 'I knew you'd be ages if you took your phone. What were you doing?'

'Multi-tasking. I realised I'd forgotten to post a status update on Facebook to say we're on our way to San Francisco.'

That was safe: Shane wasn't on Facebook so he'd never know Craig was lying. However, as they made their way to their boarding gate, Shane said: 'I bet I know what you were really doing.'

'What?' Craig felt his heart thumping.

'You've got some man on the go, haven't you? A bit on the side?' He said it without jealousy, laughing, as if it were a great joke to find Craig out.

Craig felt himself blushing. It must look like guilt. 'I swear to you, I don't have a man on the go. When do you think I've got the time?'

'If you say so,' said Shane with a self-satisfied smile, stepping onto a downward escalator. He was clearly enjoying the tease.

If only he *were* having an affair, thought Craig. It would be a lot less complicated.

After they'd taken off in the middle of the morning and spent eleven hours in the air, it felt strange to arrive in California just after lunchtime on the day they'd set out. Craig had no idea how the flat-earthers rationalised time zones, and he decided he was happy to keep it that way. There was certainly no point snarking at Shane on the subject. Given the precariousness of his own position, he ought to focus on being a willing house guest rather than lampooning their host's worldview.

A uniformed Hispanic chauffeur awaited them in the arrivals hall with a sign marked 'Mr Foxley'. 'Welcome, gentlemen,' he said, as Shane made himself known. 'Follow me.'

A younger man hovering in the background now lunged forward to grab both their bags, wheeling them along as the driver led the way to a gleaming grey Tesla, parked right outside the airport building. Car parks were clearly for little people. The driver tossed a 'Thanks, buddy' at the airport functionary who'd been standing guard over the vehicle, and held the rear door open for his passengers to get in.

'He's a different driver to last time,' said Shane, as if it mattered.

'Do we go over Golden Gate Bridge?' Craig was excited, in spite of everything.

'No, we're going the other way.'

It was disappointing not to see anything of the city, but Craig gazed through smoked-glass windows at the Bay as they sped south on the busy freeway, following signs for Santa Clara and San Jose.

After a quarter of an hour they left the main highway and entered the grid system of a town.

'This is Palo Alto,' said Shane.

'That rings a bell. Why have I heard of it?'

'It's quite famous. Stanford University is based here, which helped spawn the whole Silicon Valley phenomenon.'

'No, there was something else. That institute of yours is here, isn't it? What's it called? Peter something? Are you going to go and see them?' This was a wind-up. The Peter Amber

Institute had been founded when Shane still took him into his confidence, so Craig knew perfectly well it was really in India.

'It's actually just a registration addr—' began Shane, before recognising the dig. 'Ha ha, very good. You won't make those kind of cracks in front of Joey, will you?'

'I promise,' said Craig. He wished he could confess this much of the truth: that an open snark about Orange Peel's activities was at least honest and made him feel less of a heel than the undercover betrayal in which he was engaged.

They'd left the town proper and were climbing gently through an affluent residential sprawl into the hills.

'Not far now,' said Shane. 'Wait till you see the place. It'll blow you away.'

Part of Craig wanted not to be blown away, to be able to sneer at the billionaire's lack of taste, but of course it was impressive: the sweeping drive, the vineyard, the manicured grounds, the perfect setting in a valley cleft, and the relatively modest scale of the house itself, which seemed to have been designed for living rather than to be admired for its opulence.

Another uniformed Hispanic guy, apparently a butler, emerged to receive them. Shane greeted him like an old friend.

'He was the chauffeur last time,' he told Craig, who was rapidly tiring of this then-and-now commentary.

Their guide escorted them to a spacious first-floor room, with a large ensuite wet-room done entirely in silver granite. The bedroom's shuttered windows overlooked the water gardens to the rear of the house.

'Do you remember me telling you? It's modelled on the Alhambra in Granada. That's where Joey's ancestors originally came from,' said Shane.

'I'm not sure the water channels are painted swimming-pool blue in Granada.'

'That's the Californian touch. Think David Hockney.'

The butler coughed politely. 'Mr Talavera left instructions for you to be served lunch in the cabana, gentlemen, whenever you're ready. Just some simple cold fare.'

'Is Mr Talavera not here?'

Craig could see that Shane was wounded.

'He's down at Menlo Park, and Mrs Talavera is resting, sir. They'll both join you later.'

'CEOs gotta CEO,' said Craig, who was more than happy to delay meeting their hosts.

The 'simple cold fare' turned out to be cauliflower tacos with beansprout slaw and coriander cashew sauce, a steak salad with kale, sweetcorn, pickled radishes and something which the butler, whose name was Jaime, identified as chimichurri dressing, followed by honey cheesecake topped with cinnamon, all of it accompanied by a pale pink Zinfandel from the Talavera estate. Craig was almost prepared to forget that this trip was an ordeal.

They were drinking coffee – decaf was the only option – when a voice hailed them from the direction of the house.

'Hey guys! I'm so sorry not to have been available to greet you when you arrived. Shane and Craig, right? You'll have to excuse me if I forget which is which at first.'

In her magazine shoots and TV appearances, Krystal Vardashian Talavera was never less than radiant. She was nipped, tucked, enhanced and spray-tanned, obviously, but none of it to excess; what really counted was the dazzling, infectious smile. In the flesh, the big surprise was her size.

She was birdlike, and not just any bird: she reminded Craig of a wren. As the guests stood to press hands and air-kiss, they both towered over her, even Shane. This lightest of physical contact felt like a transgression: her ams and wrists were like soft, slender twigs that might snap under the slightest pressure.

Craig let Shane do the introductions and the talking.

'It's wonderful to meet you. And thank you so much for inviting us to your wonderful home. It's a great privilege for us to be here.'

'It's our pleasure to have you. I've heard such a lot about you from Joey. And great to have you along too, Craig. I hope you won't be too bored when these two spend all their time talking shop. That's when the pool will be your friend. You just lay out there to your heart's content. I hope you brought your swimming costume?'

'We both did.' Craig smiled at her gratefully. He felt pale, sweaty and ungainly in her presence, but her warmth was instantly appealing.

'Good. I'm not sure when Joey's going to be back, so feel free to make good use of it this afternoon. There are plenty of fresh towels here in the cabana. Make sure you boys use a lot of sunscreen, though. You look like you'll need it.'

'We will. Thank you.'

Of course she wan't planning to sit around all afternoon making small-talk. Why would she?

'So I'll see you guys later. There's spring water in the ice-box and a buzzer on your table: just call for Jaime if you need anything.'

In the warmth of the Californian sun, beneath a near-cloudless sky, Craig struggled to remember why he'd been so reluctant to come. But he could see the telltale signs that

Shane was aggrieved: a shrug, a purse of the lips, the tension as he hunched rather than relaxed in his chair.

'Don't take it personally,' he said, as Krystal retreated to the house. 'And isn't she fabulous? I really like her.'

'Let's hope you get to see her for more than two minutes the whole time we're here,' said Shane. 'I'm not counting on it.'

Craig spent the rest of the afternoon beside the infinity pool, slathered in Factor 30, sleeping off several weeks' worth of fatigue. Shane, who had even fairer skin, disappeared indoors, sulking still, but Craig suspected his spirits would pick up as soon as Talavera arrived.

Sure enough, at around five o'clock, Shane appeared at his elbow.

'Joey's home now. You should put some clothes on and come and say hello.' He didn't wait.

Quickly pulling jeans and a t-shirt back over his trunks, Craig made his own way up to the house, following the voices. He found Shane, Krystal and Talavera sitting on the terrace, with a pitcher and three full glasses on a low table beside them.

Talavera raised an arm in greeting.

'Hey, Chris. Come and join us, dude. Can I pour you some iced tea? It's made with peaches and vanilla chai.'

Craig waited in vain for Shane to correct him, then said: 'It's Craig, actually. Great to meet you. And yes please to iced tea. It looks wonderful.'

Talavera's strong, deeply tanned hand, which he now extended as he stood up in welcome, was as meaty as Krystal's had been delicate. He was six-feet three of beaming, brawny beefcake. Craig could see how Shane had been seduced.

'How d'ya like the place?' he asked, pouring iced tea into a fourth glass.

'It's stunning. Such a beautiful spot. You've got your own piece of paradise here.' As Joey knew full well already, of course. It was weird that someone could be so rich and still so needy for compliments.

'Do you like the formal garden? I had it laid out just like the Alhambra in Granada, Spain. Do you know it?'

'No, I've never been. I'd love to, obviously.'

'Now you don't need to,' said Shane. Did he have any idea how obsequious he sounded?

'You could compare the two,' said Joey.

'My favourite part of your garden is the pool,' said Craig. 'I've spent the afternoon snoozing next to it. It's been bliss.'

'Nap away. Use it all you want.'

'Thank you. And how are things with you, er, Joey? Is all well in your world?'

'There's the odd wrinkle that your husband and I have to smooth out. That's why it's great to be able to talk in person like this. I'm so pleased you guys were able to make the trip our here.'

Krystal stood up. 'I know you're dying to get down to that talk. Why don't we leave them to it, Craig? Dinner isn't till eight. What say I take you on a tour of the vineyard? All the wine we drink in this house comes from there, and our guests often enjoy seeing where the grapes were grown. Would you like that too?'

'I'd love it,' said Craig, draining his iced tea. 'I don't really know anything about wine, but I'm always keen to learn.' And more than happy not to have to listen to flat-earth talk, however useful that might be for purposes of espionage.

'Let's go, then.'

'See you guys later,' said Craig. Joey raised his hand in another wave, but Shane barely glanced at him.

Krystal led the way along the gently crunching gravel path through the middle of the ornamental garden. 'I hope I wasn't dragging you away from a conversation you wanted to hear,' she said, when they were out of earshot.

'Very much not.'

She laughed. 'So you're not a true believer?'

Her easy manner gave him the confidence to be open with her. 'I'm afraid not.'

'Can I tell you something?'

'Go ahead.'

'Me neither.'

It was Craig's turn to laugh. 'I can't tell you how pleased I am to hear you say that.' He considered for a moment. 'I hope this isn't out of turn, but doesn't that make life awkward?'

She smiled. 'I'm good at changing the subject.' She led the way through a gate and up a rising incline. 'Come on. Let's go this way.'

She strode ahead of him. He knew from Wikipedia that she was ten years older than him, but she was much fitter. In his defence, she had much more time to spend in the gym or yoga studio than he did, but it was still embarrassing how quickly he started panting.

As the path crested a low brow, she waited for him to catch up. 'So how much do you know about wine-growing?'

'Close to nothing. Actually no, that's a lie. Literally nothing.'

She laughed again. 'So you won't know that this used to be the most important grape-growing county in the whole country? Prohibition changed all that, of course. People tore out their vineyards, planting apples, cherries and plums instead, but gradually the grapes are returning. We have a cooler climate here than Napa, but we also have large temperature swings, with warm days and cool nights. Those swings force the vines to work harder, concentrating the flavour in the fruit. We also have a lot of limestone in the soil, which helps create more elegant and structured grapes...'

Most of it went over his head, but he was content to walk beside her among the long, neat rows of vines, each plant already laden with clusters of fruit, in the gentle warmth of the evening sun. He tried to ask the occasional question to pretend he was keeping up, but she saw through that. 'Don't worry, I'm not gonna test you later,' she smiled.

She took them in a wide, circular route which brought them out on the other side of the house. They stopped to gaze down at the ornamental garden, with its turquoise canals gurgling between manicured miniature hedges.

'My husband's so proud of his Spanish roots, as you can see,' she said. 'Sometimes I just wish he could have been satisfied with this, his homage to the Alhambra, instead of taking it... well, you know where.'

Craig was mystified. 'I'm not with you. What do Joey's Spanish roots have to do with' – he wanted to say 'his crazy beliefs', but checked himself – 'the conversation he's currently having with my husband?'

She looked surprised. 'You know the Granada connection, right?'

'I know his ancestors came from there.'

'Well, sorta. You should do some googling. Before Joey made his name and fortune, there was only one famous

Talavera in history. That was Hernando de Talavera, who lived in the fourteen hundreds. He was an important man in Spain: the confessor to Queen Isabella. In return, she made him Archbishop of Granada.

'And he was Joey's ancestor?'

She pulled a *meh* face. 'Not really. For a start, he was a Catholic bishop, and those guys didn't have a lot of kids. Not the kind to bear the family name, anyway.'

'He could have had brothers.'

'Yeah, maybe. And maybe some of their descendants ended up in Mexico, which is where Joey's great-grandparents came from. It's possible, I grant you. Just not proven.'

'I see. At least I think I do. But I'm still not clear what all this has to do with...well...the other stuff.'

'Really? You don't know?'

This was getting awkward. Was he really being as stupid as she made him feel?

She broke the tension with a playful punch on his arm. 'Nah, why should you know about it? I live with it because I married the name, and I forget most other people have very little knowledge of all that history.' She resumed walking. 'Come on, let's go down to dinner. Maybe later in the week I'll fill you in on a little fifteenth-century Castilian history.'

2

Ginny had been about to publish her blog – she was giving it a final read, making the odd tweak here and there, and adding some hyperlinks – when Craig's message arrived, to warn she was falling into a trap. She could always have pulled it back, of course. Unpublishing a post was a simple job. But items deleted from the internet could be traced, and nothing was beyond the technical capability of one of the world's richest tech moguls. So it felt like she had dodged a bullet, and she was grateful to Craig.

As for the confirmation of a spy in their midst, once more it gave her no satisfaction to be proved right. To think they were being watched was unsettling, like having a peeping tom outside her flat. She wished she knew for certain who it was, but Craig had narrowed the options down: someone present during the interview with Mel at the Black Lion. That meant

Mel herself, Lorraine, Garrett Walsh, Ginny or Globy Dick Dave. It was inconceivable that Mel was working for the other side; what could she possibly gain? The same went for the two journalists. Ginny knew she could rule herself out, so yet again it looked like she'd been right. Lorraine had made her feel like a crashing snob for suspecting Dave, but sometimes the obvious answers were correct.

If Globy Dick was the mole, he could do little damage, because Ginny had made sure Dave no longer had access to confidential information. Since the Apfel meeting he'd sent her a few direct messages, clearly seeking to get closer, which she'd either ignored or answered monosyllabically. Mindful of Lorraine's rebuke, she initially felt mean about that, but now she considered herself vindicated. However, it occurred to her now that blanking him wasn't the only option. If you knew someone was a spy, and they didn't know you knew, it made sense to exploit your advantage.

She would discuss it properly with Mel and Lorraine. Until then, there was certainly no harm in stringing Dave and his paymasters along. She found his last message, from three or four days earlier, and wrote in reply: 'Sorry for the slow response. I'm not sure if you've heard, but we've hit legal obstacles at the *Chronicle* and *The Bystander*. My plan is to go ahead and publish something on my own blog, to see if anyone else in the media picks it up. I've been delayed writing it because editors keep offering me paid work' – if only that part of the lie were true – 'but I should be ready to publish next week. I'd appreciate your support in helping to spread the word, once it's out there.'

She'd just clicked send when Mel called.

'So your hunch was right,' she said, when Ginny had filled

her in. 'If the mole really is Dave, we ought to make use of him.'

'Great minds. I've started doing that already. I told him I'm definitely going ahead with my blog.'

'Hmm.' Mel, as so often, sounded underwhelmed. 'That's fine as far as it goes, but it doesn't do our opponents any damage. I was thinking of something a bit more...consequential.'

'Such as?'

'We could tell them we've got articles planned in a string of other publications. That will force Talavera to spend a lot more money on lawyers.'

'Surely he doesn't care how much money he spends? It won't bother him at all.'

'I wouldn't count on that. In my experience, seriously rich people don't enjoy parting with their money, especially if they're self-made. Where there's a tycoon, you'll usually find an appallingly paid workforce. These men don't become billionaires by having hearts of gold.'

'I guess not.'

'If he starts firing off injunctions to every media outlet, that may also focus the minds of editors and proprietors. They don't like being bossed around, especially by foreigners who don't spend any money advertising in their publications, so it may end up backfiring on Joey.'

'A case of the Streisand effect, you mean?'

'I don't know what that is.'

'It's where an attempt at censorship creates more publicity than it prevented. If I remember rightly, Barbra Streisand sued a photographer for putting an aerial shot of her house in Malibu on some online record of the Californian coast. She said it was an invasion of her privacy, even though literally three or four people had ever looked at that photograph. Her actions changed all that: hundreds of thousands of people logged on to look at her house. It went down as the most spectacularly counterproductive manoeuvre in legal history.'

'I can't promise anything so dramatic in our case. But yes, that's the sort of thing I mean.'

'Right. Leave it with me, then. I'll string Dave along some more.'

'I leave it in your capable hands. Will you also tell Lorraine and Garrett? They need to know about this too.'

'Yes, I will. I'll send them messages as soon as we're done here.'

'Well done. Oh, and Ginny?'

'Yes?'

'You really have done a wonderful job in befriending Craig. It could end up making a massive difference. Call me old-fashioned, but I feel it in my bones.'

In the evening, she watched a re-run of a witless film comedy in which a couple of goofy forty-somethings wound up doing internships at Google. It was lame stuff, but she was drawn in because it was set in Silicon Valley. She wondered how Craig was getting on.

She got her answer the next morning. Still in her dressing gown, she opened an email in which he proudly revealed his new friendship with Krystal Talavera. He was plainly giddy with celebrity awe, which made her smile, but she also took his point: who could have predicted that Joey's own wife would be a secret member of the Terghood?

'She told me Joey's obsessed with his ancestors,' he wrote. 'Not the immediate ones who came to California from

Mexico, but centuries before that, back in Spain. Although there's no proof, and Krystal made it obvious she thinks it's fantasy, he's convinced he's descended from Hernando de Talavera, the Archbishop of Granada in the time of Ferdinand and Isabella. She said that's the key to all his flat-earth beliefs. I had no idea what she meant, but she told me to google it, which I did. Now I think I know what she meant. I hope you're sitting down, because it'll blow your mind.

'Before moving to Granada, Hernando was the Bishop of Avila. He was the leader of the group of clerics who ridiculed Columbus when he described the voyage he wanted to make to the Indies. They told him he'd fall off the edge of the world. Do you see what that means? Joey thinks the Talavera family name has been besmirched. His 'ancestor' has gone down in history as the leader of a group of superstitious flat-earth buffoons. He's trying to restore the family honour and salvage Hernando's reputation in the only way he can: by proving the earth was flat all along.

'I'm going to try and confirm this with Krystal, but I'm pretty sure that must be the story. I've no idea where it leaves us. It may not make any difference. But I wanted to pass it on to you ASAP, in case you had any ideas. Let me know what you think.

'It should be OK to email me back now, by the way. Joey and Shane are having a massive bromance and neither of them pay me any attention.'

Ginny read this account quickly once, then went back and studied it again more slowly. She'd never been curious as to why Joey believed the earth was flat, but Craig's account precisely matched her Aussie friend Trent Meyer's theory. She hadn't given it a second thought at the time, but perhaps she should.

To the limited extent that she'd ever considered the matter, she'd always assumed that Talavera's flat-earth beliefs must be underpinned by some kind of conviction, however naive and ill-informed. Instead, it seemed, it was all about vanity: first, in imagining himself to be descended from an illustrious forebear simply because they shared a surname, and then in taking that namesake's discredited reputation as a personal affront. The narcissism was staggering. Talavera's own feelings had been hurt, so the entire world had to be reshaped to make him feel better. He was a tyrannical toddler in a man's body, which was perhaps not so rare, but his colossal wealth allowed him to subject billions of people to his temper tantrum.

She remembered something else about Trent's message. Hadn't he said there was more to the story than Joey realised?

She googled 'what time is it in Australia?' and found that it was 10pm. Not too late to message, and hopefully not to Zype either. 'Trent? Are you there?' she typed. 'I'm really hoping you're up for a video call. Ideally right now. It's about Hernando de Talavera, who may suddenly have become a lot more relevant. I'll explain why when we speak.'

She hit send and sat staring at her phone screen, willing a message to come back and trying to calm her nerves with a yoga breathing exercise. For five minutes there was nothing, and she was about to get up off the sofa to go and get dressed, when the reply arrived. Yes, he was up for an immediate Zype. Good man, Trent.

She realised she ought to get dressed anyway before talking to him on video. Racing to put the kettle on so she could grab a cup of coffee before setting up the call, she was back two minutes later and ready to open a Zype window. It was weird to be using this technology, Talavera's brainchild, to discuss their strategy to oppose him.

Peering down into his laptop camera, Trent didn't look quite so dreamy as he did in his profile picture. Unflatteringly lit, he was wearing heavy glasses and a ragged t-shirt, his hair badly dishevelled.

'Sorry it's so late where you are,' she said. 'I'm really grateful you responded so quickly.'

'My pleasure. You're a famous lady. It's an honour to be talking to you.'

'Oh please.' It was so strange when people said this. Obviously it was a big improvement on being barracked by an angry mob, but it was so far from how she saw herself. 'I'm just glad you could spare the time.'

'No worries. Why don't you go ahead and tell me what you need? I assume we're talking fifteenth-century Spain?'

'We are indeed. I can't go into too much detail, because I need to protect my source, but you're dead right: Joey Talavera's flat-earthery is connected to Hernando. If my source is right, Joey has a massive complex about Hernando's historical reputation. Your hunch was spot on.'

'Wow. It's amazing to hear that confirmed. Obviously I'd love to know how you know it's true, but I respect your need to protect your source.'

'Yeah, I really can't say, I'm afraid. What I can tell you is that we have access to someone extremely close to Talavera, but we only have it for a very limited time. That's why I wanted to speak to you urgently.'

'And you want to know what I meant when I said there's more to the story than Joey realises?'

'Exactly.'

'Let's get right to it, then. In a nutshell, the story Joey

believes is a pile of crap. It's a myth that originated in a piece of fiction masquerading as biography, written in the nineteenth century. Bishop Talavera did preside over an inquiry into Columbus' chances of success, and that inquiry did advise Queen Isabella to steer well clear and not to invest in the venture. Advice she ignored, obviously. However, the recommendation had nothing to do with Talavera thinking the earth was flat. No one believed that, and they hadn't done so for well over a thousand years. Bitter arguments broke out two or three decades later when Copernicus first made the case that the earth orbited the sun, and it took a long time for his theory to be accepted. But every last one of his opponents believed the earth was round.'

Ginny frowned at the screen. 'I'm thinking back to my childhood. I'm sure I was taught that Columbus' sailors were terrified of falling off the edge of the world. Or am I imagining that?'

Trent grinned. 'I don't think you are. You probably were taught that when you were small. Primary schools tend to love it. At least, they did when you and I were that age. It's all the fault of Washington Irving, the American writer who wrote a fanciful biography of Columbus in the 1820s. The United States was a young country in need of an origin story, and Irving provided it: the brave, rational, visionary explorer triumphing over ignorance and superstition to discover a wondrous new land. Never mind that Columbus didn't ever set foot on the American mainland. Nor, obviously, that there were millions of people living there already. The Columbus myth met a national need, and the posthumous reputation of Hernando de Talavera was part of the collateral damage.'

'That's fascinating. I suspect Joey has no idea of all this.'

'So you have an opportunity to put him right.'

'Maybe we do.' She tried to picture Craig relaying this new information to his new friend Krystal, and Krystal attempting to persuade Joey. 'Will he believe us, though? He's so invested in his own version. Literally. He must have spent millions of dollars so far. How are we going to convince him? I can't see him ploughing through a load of history books. From what I hear, he's not the scholarly type.'

'What if we could find proof, in Hernando's own words, that the original Talavera wasn't a flat-earther? Would that do the trick?'

'Now you're talking. Do you think you can?'

'I can't promise, but I know where to start looking. It's got to be worth a try.'

'It would be amazing if you could find something, Trent. Right now it feels like we're running out of other options.'

'Don't get your hopes up, but I'll do my best. And if I can't find anything, that's not the end of the world. We'll win this battle eventually. We can't let insanity triumph.'

'Agreed.'

'You said the window of opportunity was about to shut. How long have I got?'

'Two or three days, maximum.'

'Strewth. No pressure, then.'

'Will you have enough time?'

'I can but try. It depends whether I can do online searches or I have to go to an actual library, which will clearly take longer. Some of these old sources are digitised, but by no means all.'

'I'm sure you'll do your best.'

'We just need a little bit of luck to go with it. Cross your fingers for me.'

3

It was a couple of days before Craig had another chance to speak to Krystal in private. She was often out, either supervising the wine-making business or power-brunching; when she did join them, Joey and Shane always seemed to be present too. On their third morning, however, Craig noticed her heading towards the pool. He changed into his trunks and followed her, with his phone in the pocket of his shirt and a novel tucked under his arm, by way of cover.

'Come to catch some rays?' she said, as he arrived from the cabana, where he'd picked up a pool towel. 'Put on plenty of sun-screen.' She was lying in the full sun, celery-thin in her tiny bikini and vast Cartier shades.

He held up his factor 30 to show her, but she didn't move her head and he realised her eyes were closed. 'Don't worry, I will.' As he squirted the cool cream onto his chest and rubbed

it in, he ventured casually: 'I followed your advice and looked
into Hernando de Talavera.'

'Oh yes?'

'He was ridiculed by history for telling Columbus he'd fall
off the edge of the world, wasn't he?'

'He was.'

'So that means…Joey is drawn by ancestor loyalty to
Hernando's beliefs?'

She chuckled. 'You got there.'

Craig fell silent, keen not to rush too obviously into this
conversation. He concentrated on applying cream to his arms
and legs, then said: 'It's admirable, of course. Not everyone has
such a strong sense of their own heritage.'

'Hernando has been dead for five hundred years, so I'm
not sure he gives a crap. Pardon my French.'

Her tone was deadpan, and Craig couldn't tell if she
was serious or not. Did Joey's beliefs genuinely annoy her?
Couples sometimes moaned about each other to third parties
as a form of banter, without really meaning it.

He knew he should tread carefully, but the opportunity was
too important to pass up. 'Does Joey know it's all invented?'

'What is?'

'That story of the bishop saying the fleet would fall over
the edge.'

'Is that invented? I think it's what they tell us in school.'

'Perhaps they do, but it's not true. I've been doing some
reading. Hernando de Talavera wasn't really a flat-earther.
Nobody was, in the fifteenth century. They all knew the earth
was round by then. That part of his opposition was a myth
invented by the writer Washington Irving to make Columbus
look more heroic.'

She sat up and twisted to look at him directly. 'You're kidding?'

'No.' He opened his book and pretended to read. Let her think she had to drag it out of him.

'Wait, how can I learn more about this?'

He laid the book on his chest. 'I can find you some references, if you want. Why? Do you think it might change Joey's view?'

'Maybe. Who knows?'

She stretched out once more, and the conversation seemed to be over. Craig picked up his book, meaning to read it this time. But she was clearly reflecting on what he'd just told her. After a moment she said: 'Is there any proof?'

'Proof of what? That Washington Irving made up that part of the story?'

'That Hernando wasn't a flat-earther.'

'Search me,' said Craig. 'I'm really no expert.' He affected languor but his mind was racing. Ginny had already told him her Australian historian friend was looking for proof. Now Krystal herself had requested it, without prompting. That felt like serendipity. The question was, could he supply what she needed in the few days left before they flew back to London?

Once he was satisfied that Krystal's attention had drifted away, he pulled out his phone and tapped out an email to Ginny, flagged as urgent, summarising the conversation. He continued: 'Any joy your end? Bear in mind we're leaving here the day after tomorrow, so if Trent doesn't come up with something soon, we've missed our chance. Is there a Plan B? Even if we can't find Hernando saying the earth is round, is there some simple dossier of evidence we can put together to convince Joey?'

It was early evening in London, and Ginny replied immediately. 'I haven't forgotten when you're leaving. Believe me, Trent's doing his utmost. I'll let you know as soon as I get anything. And I'll have a think about Plan B.'

For the rest of the morning, Craig continued to check his phone whenever he got the chance, but nothing else came from Ginny. By mid-afternoon he had to accept that it was night in the UK, and he wouldn't hear anything for another eight hours or so. But it was deeply frustrating.

It didn't help that he was stir-crazy. Beautiful as the Talavera estate was, he yearned to explore the surrounding area. Even Shane agreed, when they met in their room before dinner, that it seemed a shame to have come all this way and not seen San Francisco.

'I wish we could just get a bus there or something,' said Craig. 'It's the unexpected downside of staying with a multi-billionaire: their houses are badly situated for public transport.'

'To be fair, most of America is badly situated for public transport,' said Shane.

'We should have hired a car at the airport. Then at least we could go where we wanted.'

When they joined their hosts downstairs, Shane tentatively raised the question. 'We were thinking we might take an Uber into San Francisco,' he said. 'I've only spent a few hours there, and Craig has never been.'

'An Uber? You can have a car. Luis will drive you,' said Joey. 'Why didn't you mention it before? Is this some kinda English thing? Not being able to ask?'

Craig privately conceded he was right on that point: it probably was some kind of English thing.

The next morning, Luis – their airport chauffeur – drove

them in the Tesla to the city. While Shane buried himself in his phone replying to emails, Craig risked a look in his own inbox. Still nothing from Ginny or Trent.

They mooched around Fisherman's Wharf and Ghirardelli Square, then Luis parked the car near the south side of the bridge so they could walk across, gazing towards the lonely rock of Alcatraz Island and doing couple-selfies, like any other tourists.

Over lunch in Chinatown, Craig tentatively asked about work. 'How's it been going with Joey? Have you made progress on the stuff you wanted to discuss?'

'I think so,' said Shane, managing to get a string of noodles into his mouth with chopsticks, a feat that Craig had never mastered. 'We've heard that Ginny Pugh is definitely going ahead with her blog, which is good news, because we can tie her in legal knots as soon as it goes live. Our source also tells us that other papers are planning to publish, which is a pain, because we'll need more injunctions.'

'But Joey's happy to keep funding it all?'

'Definitely. He's super-pleased with the progress we've made so far.'

'So he should be. You've changed the world in the past five years.'

Shane took it as a compliment. 'I know. Fortunately Joey thinks so too. He's very appreciative, which makes a big difference. But he's also stepping up the pressure.'

'Pressure?'

'To move from the True Earth campaigning we're doing at the moment to the...you know...full monty.'

Craig nodded, in an attempt to look sympathetic. 'And you're trying to slow him down?'

'It's got to be carefully managed. I've learned a lot about harnessing digital technology to change mass opinion, and it's amazing what's possible if you put your mind to it. But one false move could undo all our work and set us back massively.'

'I can imagine.'

'How about you? Are you having a good time? It's great you've hit it off with Krystal.'

Craig felt the blood rushing to his face. 'She's been so welcoming. It's such a shame she couldn't come today.'

Over dinner, Krystal had told them she'd have loved to show them the sights, but it was difficult for her to go out in public. For someone who'd been on as many magazine covers as she had, she explained, taking a stroll downtown – or anywhere – was a palaver. She couldn't walk ten yards along a pavement without a queue forming for selfies, which was bad enough for her, but even worse for anyone with her. They had to stand around waiting.

'That would be so weird, wouldn't it?' said Craig. 'Doing the tourist trail with Krystal Vardashian. Imagine the Facebook pictures.'

Shane yawned. 'Shall we get the cheque?' Given his keenness to reshape the world on Twitter, it was strange he had no interest in Facebook.

'Go for it.'

'Then what shall we do? Golden Gate Park or the Castro?'

The beauty of having a driver – especially one who could park wherever he wanted – was that they could do both. Maybe this was better than getting a hypothetical bus, Craig conceded.

He sneaked another look at his phone on their back to Palo Alto. Still nothing from Ginny. He wanted to message her, to tell her Joey was planning on taking out more injunctions, but he didn't have the nerve in front of Shane.

He did it when they got back to the house, and continued to slip back to their room whenever he could during the evening, to carry on checking for a reply.

'Are you OK?' asked Shane at one point, noticing how often he excused himself.

Craig feigned a grimace, wobbling his hand, and said: 'Must have been that Chinese.' He felt guilty for the casual racism – no one ever blamed their dicky tummies on the hamburger and chips – but needs must.

He finally heard from Ginny on the evening of the following day.

They were due to leave the next morning, and Joey's chef had cooked a farewell barbecue at the cabana. It was five in the morning in London, but Craig slipped away early, just to check his phone. He was losing hope of ever hearing from Ginny, but the act of checking had become a habit. And there, finally, was a message plus three picture attachments. The text read: 'Hi Craig. Trent has just sent me this. I hope it arrives in time and does the trick. It's from a book published in 1477.'

He scrolled down to the first picture, which showed the title page of a yellowing volume. The name of the book, arranged over five decks of antiquated lettering, was

CATÓLICA
IMPUGNACIÓN
DEL HERÉTICO LIBELO
MALDITO DESCOMULGADO QUE FUE

DIVULGADO EN LA CIUDAD DE SEVILLA

Below it was printed the name of the author: Hernando de Talavera.

The second picture was a page from within the book. A red circle had been added to the photograph to highlight a passage reading: '...*unido en sí mismo y hecho de ambos una Iglesia católica y un nuevo pueblo, por una fe, por un bautismo, por unos sacramentos y unas ceremonias y unos juicios de su santa ley evangélica, para crear un nuevo reino en este orbe en el centro del universo de Dios.*'

Craig was hopeless at languages, so this meant nothing. Fortunately, Trent had provided a translation in the third screenshot: '...united in itself, made from both a Catholic church and a new nation, through one faith, through one baptism, through its sacraments and ceremonies and judgments of the holy law of the gospel, to create a new kingdom on this orb at the centre of God's universe.'

On this *orb* at the centre of God's universe. These were Talavera's own words, written fifteen years before Columbus embarked across the Atlantic. This was exactly what they needed! The guy didn't believe the earth was flat, and here was the proof, in a form that even Joey would surely understand.

Shoving his phone back into the pocket of his shorts, Craig raced downstairs and out into the garden, praying that Krystal would still be there. His heart sank when he saw just Joey and Shane at the table, nursing glasses of brandy.

'Hey Chris,' said Joey. Craig had given up correcting him. 'I thought you'd gone up to bed.'

'No, no. Of course not. I'd have said goodnight. I just thought I'd give you both some space, in case you still had business to discuss. I was actually looking for Krystal. Has she gone indoors? There's something I wanted to ask her.'

'No, I'm here,' said a voice behind him. Dressed in a monogrammed robe, and shaking out her hair as she pulled off a bathing cap, she climbed the steps up to the cabana from the pool.

'Oh hi. I was actually just looking for you because… You know that thing you asked me to look out for?' He wished he were better at this. 'Well, I've found it. Maybe I can show you?'

'Sure.' By contrast, she sounded completely unruffled. 'Why don't you go on up to the house? I'll meet you on the terrace.'

'Sounds like they're plotting something,' said Joey, with a wink at Shane.

'No,' said Craig. Even as it came out, he knew he'd said it too quickly. 'It's just…for a thing.'

That was truly pathetic, but Joey had lost interest already and returned to his conversation with Shane.

Craig made his way back to the house and took a seat on the terrace, as bidden. By the time Krystal appeared, he was wired with nerves, but she remained collected and soothing.

'So what ya got?' she said quietly, sitting down beside him.

He pulled out his phone and opened the pictures.

'This is Hernando de Talavera, in his own words, talking about the earth as 'an orb in God's universe'. Here it is in the original. Does Joey read Spanish?'

Krystal shot him a look that said 'yeah right'.

'OK, well here it is in English. That's pretty conclusive, don't you think? And easy to grasp. Also, the book was published was in 1477, long before the voyage.'

She examined the photographs, scrolling back and forth between the Spanish and the English versions of the text, and then looking at the first page, reading the title under her breath. At least one of the Talaveras spoke Spanish.

She turned to him with a smile. 'Leave it with me. This is great work by whoever found it. I think it may be enough to make him reconsider.' Suddenly her face was stern. 'I have one condition, though, before I show it to him.'

'What's that?' Craig hadn't expected this.

'If I make my husband stop all the nonsense, will you give me your word that his name will never appear in connection with anything that happened in the past five years?'

Craig was thrown. 'I don't really know. I mean, it's not up to me.'

'Yes it is. You can tell whoever found this information that I'll only use it if Joey is spared any public embarrassment. If you agree to that, I think I can shut it down. But if he's to be ridiculed, I won't do it. Tell them that was the condition. If they break the deal, I'll personally come after you all.'

She was so steely, he believed she really would. It was on him to decide.

'It's a deal,' he said, because he had no choice, and she was all smiles again as he air-dropped the pictures to her phone. If Ginny, Mel and the rest of them had a problem with the arrangement, that was just tough.

'Awesome. Listen, Craig my darling, it's been wonderful working with you. I hope we'll remain friends. I'm going to give you my personal number – not to be passed on to anyone else, of course. And please give me yours, in case I need to be in touch. I won't see you tomorrow because I have a super-early start, but I hope you guys have a great flight.'

They hugged. He was still beaming inanely when he got back to his room, and not just because of the success of his operation. Celebrity might be a ridiculous charade, but it was a seductive one.

After Luis dropped them at the airport the next morning, Craig insisted on finding the check–in desk.

'We don't need it,' said Shane. 'We've checked in online and we've got our boarding passes on our phones. We just need the bag-drop.'

But Craig refused to be deflected. He'd made a decision.

'This may be an unusual request,' he told the clerk when they reached the front of the queue. 'But do you have any space in economy? Perhaps someone would like to swap?'

'What the hell are you doing?' hissed Shane.

'Don't worry. I'm just asking for me, not you.'

The clerk looked equally surprised. 'You're asking for a *down*grade?' she asked, as she scanned Craig's reservation details into her system.

'Yes, I suppose I am.'

She grimaced at her screen, then looked up. 'Sir, I've been doing this job for six years and no one has ever asked for that. I'll need to go check.'

He watched her trot away and huddle with her supervisor, gesturing in his direction. The supervisor looked over at him too, frowning. Was he wondering what stunt this crazy passenger was trying to pull?

Eventually she returned and shrugged. 'If you're quite sure, sir, we do have room in economy. But I've been asked to make clear that you won't be able to change your mind. Or use the business class lounge. Are you certain you want to go ahead?'

'That's very kind of you. Yes, please. Quite certain.'

She printed out a new boarding pass and wished him a pleasant flight. He could feel Shane fuming beside him, and he waited for the eruption that would happen once they'd moved away from the desk and were alone together.

'Are you out of your mind?' demanded Shane, on cue. 'Do you have any idea how much that seat cost? And you're just giving it away?'

Craig wondered if it was true. Had he lost his mind? No sane person chose to fly eleven hours in economy if they could travel business class instead. Perhaps he just needed to suffer. He'd passed the pictorial evidence to Krystal for the highest possible motives, yet his own betrayal of Shane weighed heavy on his conscience. Squashing himself away in a smaller airline seat might not be the greatest act of self-flagellation in history, but it was the best option available. The alternative, sitting alongside his husband for all those hours and knowing what he had done, was more than he could bear.

Not that Shane saw it like that, of course. Why should he? As far as he was concerned, his husband had turned his back on him in public. The hurt was etched on his brow. Once they cleared security, he turned away and wheeled his case in the direction of the business lounge without a backward glance. Craig couldn't blame him.

He waited in the regular lounge and took his economy seat on board. He watched films on the flight and slept fitfully, with the aid of a couple of miniature bottles of wine. Somehow the time passed but he was groggy, with a bewildered body-clock, by the time he met Shane again at the Heathrow luggage carousel.

He braced himself for anger, knowing his husband had every right to take his abandonment personally, but none came.

'How was cattle-class?' was all Shane said. He looked

relaxed and refreshed. 'I know your Christian principles make you feel guilty for spending a week with a billionaire. If it makes you feel better, that's fine. Just so long as you don't expect me to join you.'

Without waiting for a reply, he turned to his phone, which was now beeping back to life. Craig watched from the corner of his eye. Would Krystal have shown the Talavera evidence to Joey by now? If so, would he have sent some kind of apocalyptic email, telling Shane he was pulling the financial plug and the flat-earth campaign was over? Evidently not. There was nothing in Shane's face to suggest he was reading anything out of the ordinary.

Their bags came through and they emerged into the arrivals hall.

'I don't know about you, but I'm getting a cab home,' said Shane. 'Are you joining me, or would you prefer to suffer on the Piccadilly Line?'

'I'll join you,' said Craig, with as much dignity as he could muster. Tiredness was creeping up on him and, for now, at least, he'd atoned enough.

4

Ginny knew Craig was due back from California any time. Desperate to hear what had happened with Krystal, she texted him when she thought he was about to land, asking him to call as soon as he could. She couldn't settle to anything else until she heard from him.

He eventually rang just after lunchtime. 'How did it go?' she said, before he could even say hello. 'Did you manage to give Trent's evidence to Krystal?'

He filled her in, telling her everything they'd discussed, including the conditions he'd been obliged to accept. 'I hope I did the right thing. She had me on the spot, and I didn't know what else I could do.'

Agreeing to a gagging order went against the grain for Ginny, as a journalist, but she could see his point. 'In the circumstances, I'm sure you did the only thing possible. Mrs

Talavera is clearly a forceful and persuasive lady who knows her own mind, and we needed her help. While I'd dearly love the whole world to know exactly how and why all this has happened, and who paid for it, it's more important to make it stop. So that's the main question now. Do you think she's had a chance to talk to him yet? And what are the chances she'll succeed?'

'Your guess is as good as mine. She said she thought there was a decent prospect. She gave me the strong impression that she's embarrassed by Joey's flat-earth obsession, so she has a personal interest in talking him out of it.'

'Is there anything else we can do to support her?'

'I don't think so. I reckon all we can do is wait.'

That did nothing to calm Ginny's nerves. 'But how will we know?'

'What do you mean?'

'If she's managed to talk him round. Will he cut off all his funding to Orange Peel at a stroke? If that happened, you'd hear about it from Shane, wouldn't you?'

'I guess so. He's pretty secretive, but I can't imagine him keeping something like that to himself. It would be devastating for him. For us both, really. We'd lose the house.'

To her shame, she hadn't thought about the material sacrifice he was making. 'I'm sorry, Craig. I hadn't realised.'

'Don't be. It was bought with dirty money.'

'All the same...'

'I'll be fine. Honestly. Anyway, that's all hypothetical. Krystal may not be able to talk Joey round. Conspiracy theories addle your brain, so it's unrealistic to expect Talavera to roll over immediately and accept he's got it all wrong.'

She knew he was right. She ought to ratchet down her

expectations. Besides, even if Joey did recant, the True Earth movement wouldn't necessarily disappear.

She promised Craig that she'd pass the news, along with Krystal's condition, to Mel, Lorraine and Garrett, which she then proceeded to do. The three of them agreed that Craig had done his utmost with Trent's material, and they just had to keep their fingers crossed.

Having convinced herself not to hope for too much, she was surprised when, two days later, Craig called her again. He was hissing down the phone and she could barely understand at first.

'I can't really hear you. Say that again.'

'I can't talk any louder. Shane will hear.'

'OK. Just say it again.'

'It's happened,' he repeated. 'I can't quite believe it, but Joey really does seem to have pulled the plug.'

Her hand trembled as she held the phone. 'No! How do you know? Are you sure?' She realised she was whispering too, which made no sense, but it added to the drama.

'Shane's just come home from the office. He's had a terrible day. Apparently Joey sent a message to Cyrus Benjamin, his main contact on the board. He said he's had a complete change of heart and doesn't want anything to do with Orange Peel or the True Earth movement. He didn't go into any more detail, so none of them knows why it's happened. They're blaming Shane. Xandra Cloudesley, the chair of the board, wants to know what the hell we did while we were staying in California to upset Joey so badly.'

Ginny owed Shane no sympathy, but she could see that this particular blame was undeserved. 'I'm sorry he's carrying the can. What have you said to him?'

'What can I say? That I'm shocked, and it's unfair of Xandra to pin it all on him. At least that part's true, so I'm not lying. I feel so conflicted, though. On the one hand, I can't believe we really did it, and I'm proud to have played a part. On the other, I feel like a complete traitor to the person I vowed to love and honour for the rest of our lives.'

'I'm sorry we've put you in this position.'

'You didn't. I went into it with my eyes open. I just have to decide how long I can carry on living this lie.'

'You think you may split up over it?'

'I don't know. At times I think I owe it to him to leave, for the sake of honesty. But if his world is about to fall apart around him, and it's partly my fault, abandoning him would be like kicking him when he's down.'

'I've been single for years, so I'm no expert. But the way I see it, you should only stay in a marriage if you love each other. If you don't, you can't keep it going artificially. You're just storing up resentment further down the line.'

'Maybe.'

'Sorry, it's none of my business.'

'No, that's fine. It's good to be able to say it out loud to someone. But I've got to go now. I'm in the bedroom and Shane may come in at any time.'

'No problem. Call me when you've got more of a chance to talk.'

'Will do.'

'And Craig?'

'Yes?'

'Thank you. From all of us. You're a hero.'

He didn't reply, and the call was cut.

Ginny sat for a while staring at the screen. She was hoarse

from whispering. She felt bad for Craig, who sounded thoroughly miserable, but she mustn't let it obscure the more important point. *They had won.*

'YEEEEESSSSS!' she shouted to her empty flat, punching the air.

She tried to call Lorraine, whose phone went to voicemail, so she sent a text containing more exclamation marks and champagne emojis than letters of the alphabet. She sent a similar message to Trent, then danced around the kitchen and punched the air for a while, after which she got back on the phone and called the person who most deserved to hear this news.

'I'm speechless,' said Mel, when Ginny had gabbled through her tale. 'This is utterly wonderful. And what extraordinary *global* teamwork. Without you in London, Trent in Australia and Craig in California, it would never have worked.'

'And Krystal, everyone's new favourite Vardashian.'

'I never had an old favourite Vardashian, but I'll certainly raise a glass to Krystal.'

'It's a shame about her confidentiality condition. I wish we could tell the world the whole story. To stop it happening again, if nothing else.'

'In case another crazy Californian billionaire decides to convert the world by stealth to flat-earthery?'

'Maybe not in exactly the same way.'

'It's probably not an option, even if we were prepared to break the deal with Krystal. I don't imagine Talavera will lift those injunctions. He'd be stupid to do that.'

'That's true. I'd forgotten about those.'

'Treat it as a brilliant win, in fiendishly difficult circumstances. Our focus now should be on the Zest Badge members that Shane seduced. We need to persuade them to ditch the True Earth claptrap.'

'That may be easier said than done.'

'I've got an idea that may work. From what Craig said, do you think Shane or anyone else at Orange Peel knows about Krystal's publicity ban?'

'We only had a short conversation, and he doesn't know much himself. But I don't think they do. As far as I know, Joey didn't give Orange Peel any reason for his change of heart, so they're totally in the dark. They've no reason to think Krystal is involved.'

'Good. That's what I suspected.'

'What have you got in mind?'

'Leave it with me. If it works, you'll know about it soon enough.'

Their assumption turned out to be correct. Xandra and the rest of the board had no idea their Terg opponents had any kind of arrangement with Krystal, let alone that it came with conditions.

So when Mel called her former chair threatening to hold a press conference, in which she would reveal all the details of Orange Peel's arrangement with Talavera unless the board met her demands, Xandra capitulated with barely a murmur.

The first of these demands was for Shane to be sacked. Still mindful of Craig's guilt and distress, Ginny had her qualms. But this was Mel's fight too, and Ginny couldn't stand in her way.

For her part, Xandra seemed more than happy to comply. She still blamed Shane for upsetting Joey while under his roof.

The second condition was harder for Xandra to bear. Once

Shane was out, Mel herself must be rehired in his place. She knew the cupboard was bare, financially speaking, so she didn't expect the salary Shane had enjoyed. Instead, she would use the pay-off they'd given her five years earlier, which she still hadn't touched. However, she required a written assurance that no one would attempt to recover it, and that her non-disclosure agreement was null and void.

Gritting her expensive teeth, Xandra had no choice but to submit.

The final condition came later, once Mel was back at the helm. She demanded, and received, Xandra's own resignation from the board, plus those of Geena Holland, Cyrus and Miranda Zappel. That left Damon Burch, who'd discreetly remained on friendly terms with Mel after her banishment and now became chair. In consultation with Mel, he set about appointing a fresh board, starting with Diana Dorado and Cora Odell. They wanted another man for balance, and Mel was keen to ask Globy Dick Dave, as a strong working-class voice. He'd been in regular touch after Shane's departure, offering moral support, but Ginny vetoed the idea, saying she'd all but proved he was the mole in the Terghood. They ended up asking Captain Wilf Phillips instead.

Mel press-released these changes, spreading the word that Orange Peel was under new management and returning to first principles. Then she began dismantling her once-proud achievement, the Zest Badge programme.

'Have you considered keeping it going, so you can withhold the badge from any organisation still spouting True Earth woo?' said Ginny. They now met regularly for lunch at Gino's.

Mel shook her head. 'I've thought it all through. The Zest Badge scheme was what made us so desirable to Talavera in the first place, and therefore so vulnerable. Virtually every company, charity, local council, school or government department in the country had got used to Orange Peel telling them what to say and think on geographical matters. That meant it was frighteningly easy for Shane to alter the message and expand its scope. There must have been individuals within all those organisations who noticed the shift, but they were institutionally bound to Orange Peel, so no one spoke out. Cutting those institutional ties is the easiest and most efficient way to restore rationality.'

'I can see the logic of that,' said Ginny. 'But doesn't Orange Peel get income from its Zest Badge courses? Won't you need that to survive?'

'You're assuming I want Orange Peel to survive. I always wanted to shut it down. It had served its purpose.'

Ginny smiled. 'I'm in awe of you, Mel. You're so principled, even when it comes to destroying your own creation.'

'You've no need to be in awe. You sacrificed more than I did in the course of this whole nightmare. Orange Peel wasn't even your baby, so you didn't have a stake in it.'

'I guess this fight hooked a lot of us in, didn't it?'

They both ate in silence for a few moments, then Ginny said: 'You know, it still drives me crazy that we'll never be able to tell the story. If Talavera were elderly, I could patiently wait till he died and then write the history. But he's barely older than me. And he's a Californian who probably lives on egg-white omelettes, so he'll outlive me by decades.'

'There is one option.'

'What's that?'

'Fictionalise it. Dress it up as something else and turn the real players into made-up characters.'

Ginny put down her fork, allowing the idea to play in her head. 'I guess it's a possibility. When you say dress it up as something else, what do you mean?'

'Don't make it about the shape of the earth. Find some other subject where a bunch of fanatics take incontrovertible truths and rip them up for the sake of some crazy ideology. Then spin your story around that. You can still have a bank-rolling billionaire pulling all the strings. It just won't be Talavera, so you can write what you like.'

Ginny was intrigued. 'I've never tried writing fiction, so I don't know if I could do it, but it's not a bad idea. What would that other subject be, do you think?'

Mel shrugged. 'I'm not sure, off the top of my head. Something of the same standing as geography or physics. Chemistry, maybe?'

'I'm not sure about that. Chemistry's a bit specialist. It's not like there are basic laws that everyone in the world knows. I certainly don't.'

'Biology, then. There are some basic truths there. You could make your flat-earthers argue that biological sex is a false concept imposed on the world by racist imperialists. Or is that too far-fetched?'

'I think it may be.' Ginny sighed. 'Perhaps I just need to let the whole thing go.'

'There's a lot to be said for letting things go.' Mel raised her glass to sink the last mouthful of Valpolicella. 'We won, that's the main thing. Now, let's focus on the most crucial question of all,' she said, twisting in her seat in search of a waiter.

'Which is?'

'Which is…whether we've got room for some of Gino's tiramisu.'

5

Shane stared gloomily down from the window at the fairy-tale pinnacles of Tower Bridge. It was strange to be back in this bizarre council-block penthouse, where his adventure with the dark arts had first begun.

Back then, he could scarcely have imagined how successful his collaboration with the apartment's owner would be. Despite that, everything had come crashing down, and Shane had fallen hardest of all. Six months on from his sacking, he remained dazed by the experience. He still had no idea why the end had come.

He didn't see many people nowadays. To add to his misery, Craig had suggested a trial separation and had moved to a rented flat. The house would have to be sold, but Shane hadn't done anything about that yet. Depression paralysed him and he rarely even ventured outside. He'd resisted Robbie's invitation, too, but his former mentor refused to take no for an answer. Shane was grateful for his persistence. No one else had bothered.

Today, Robbie was dressed in tight jeans, a blue Fred Perry t-shirt and white braces, complete with fourteen-hole Doc Martens. His head was completely shaven and he looked like an elderly mod – albeit the kind who kissed visitors on both cheeks by way of welcome. He'd served a typical Robinson White lunch – short on carbs, long on roast meat, rich sauces and wine – and conversation focused on their triumphs rather than their humiliation.

'I still don't know why it all went pear-shaped, though,' complained Shane, refusing to be diverted from his self-pity. He sounded whiny even to himself, but he was past caring. 'I got on brilliantly with Joey all week. Why did he turn against us – against *me* – so badly? I just don't know what I did wrong. Do you?'

'I can honestly say I have no clearer idea than you,' said his host. 'I wouldn't necessarily take it personally. We were all cut loose by the same edict. Myself, Cyrus, poor Dr Rao…none of us has had any contact with Joey or any explanation from him. I have, however, taken the liberty of asking someone to join us for coffee who may be able to shed more light.'

Shane was in no mood to meet new people. 'Who?'

'Can't you guess? It's our insider.'

Shane shrugged. He was intrigued, but not enough to admit it.

'Don't get too excited, will you?' said Robbie, as the door buzzer sounded. 'There they are, right on cue. Can you let them in, while I see to the coffee? Push the button under the entry-phone handset.'

If Shane had thought about the mole at all, he'd pictured a bland man, grey in persona, who could blend into any background. But Robbie's insider turned out to be a woman of about fifty in heavy spectacles, neatly but not expensively dressed, who introduced herself on the doorstep as Tricia. Shane wondered if that was her real name

'In Terg circles, I was mainly known as Copper Knickers, which was my Twitter handle,' she added, as she shook his hand. 'Robbie's choice, not mine.'

'It's nice to meet you,' said Shane, forcing himself to make the effort. 'Thank you for everything you did for us.'

She smiled broadly. 'Don't worry, I was very well paid. It's just a shame it dried up.'

'Tell us about it,' said Robbie, appearing behind them, coffee pot in hand. 'Do come through, Tricia. We'll take coffee in the drawing room.'

'I never tire of this view,' she said, clearly a regular visitor.

'Are you still in touch with that group of…erm…?' said Shane. He found it hard to use the word 'Terg' nowadays. His opponents had proudly reclaimed it. The thought of them crowing at his downfall made him shudder.

'Not if no one's paying me, I'm afraid.'

'It took a lot of persuasion for Tricia to join us today. She's only here out of the extreme goodness of her heart,' said Robbie.

She blew him a theatrical kiss, and he started pouring coffee.

Frustrated by smalltalk, Shane wanted information. 'Do you know why Joey dropped us so suddenly? I've been over and over it, but I just can't understand what happened.'

She shook her head. 'Not really. I kept my ear to the ground for a few days after it went to pot, but they all seemed to have taken a vow of silence. They knew they had an informer, you see. Most of them seemed to think it was this bloke called Dave, so they froze him out, which was a shame. I was quite pally with him and he was one of my best sources. The one thing I did hear – and I may have got this all wrong – was that they found something in an old book. It apparently made all the difference.'

'An old book? What kind of book?'

'No idea, sorry.'

Shane looked at Robbie. 'What do you make of that?'

'What can we possibly make of it? We can beg Tricia to go back on Twitter as Copper Knickers and keep her ear to the ground. But if they're all keeping shtum, I'm not sure she'll learn anything.'

'Even if she were prepared to do it, when she isn't getting paid any longer,' added Tricia.

'You see?' said Robbie. 'Not easy. I suspect we're going to have to admit defeat. We'll never know what was in the book they found, if indeed they really found a book. Don't look so crestfallen. When I hear Tricia's story, my first thought isn't about the book.'

'Isn't it?'

'No, it jolly well isn't.'

'All right, tell me. What's your first thought?'

'Isn't it obvious? That none of this had anything to do with your stay in California. Our opponents discovered something. We don't know what it was, but it caused a sudden change of heart in Joey, who no longer thinks the earth is flat. Which, to be honest, is for the best. It's just that some of us were doing very nicely out of it. But it was entirely unrelated to your being his house-guest at the time. That's surely some comfort?'

Shane attempted a smile. 'I suppose so. Thanks, Robbie. I do really appreciate the way you're trying to cheer me up. You're a real friend. Perhaps my only friend.'

'Now then, let's not get maudlin.'

'But it doesn't help, does it? I've lost my marriage, I'm about to lose my house and I'm probably unemployable.'

'Hold it right there,' said Robbie, rising in volume, as he tended to do towards the end of his second bottle. 'You may have lost your relationship, which I'm sorry about, but there are other fish in the sea. And you may have to sell your house, but you can buy another, even if it's smaller. You'll be fine. As for being unemployable... Are you joking?'

'No, of course I'm not.'

'In that case, have a word with yourself. And if you won't, I will. You, my lad, are responsible for convincing millions of people – no, tens of millions – that it's racist to think the earth is spherical. You convinced tens of millions more not to disagree, against all their natural instincts. Everything you told them was utterly bonkers, but somehow you made it stick. And you did it virtually single-handed, with just a little help from myself. You don't think that makes you employable?'

This was undoubtedly flattering, and Shane found himself blinking back wine-soaked tears, but he wasn't convinced. 'Who's going to employ me? How often does someone like Joey Talavera come along?'

'More often than you think. Maybe not in quite such extravagant form, but you're a master manipulator, Shane. You have an extraordinary talent for using modern communications technology to make people believe things that they'd once have once considered lunatic. That's a very transferable skill. There will be other clients, believe me.'

Shane saw that he might be right. Slowly, the mist began to lift. 'I hadn't thought of it like that.'

'I know you hadn't, but it's high time you did. In fact, let's drink to it. Have you got a glass, Tricia?'

He fetched her one and topped them both up with claret. 'Everyone ready? In that case, let me propose a toast. To new clients!'

'New clients,' echoed Tricia.

Shane felt lighter than he had for months as he raised his glass. 'New clients,' he said, and he actually smiled. 'I wonder who they'll be.'

AFTERWORD

It may not come as a huge surprise, if you've got this far, that *The End of the World is Flat* owes its existence to Twitter. It might never have existed if I – along with many others – hadn't spent too much time on that site during lockdown.

Not that Twitter is full of conspiracy theorists railing against the evils of globularism; I looked, and it really isn't. So far, flat-earthery remains the niche view of a crackpot minority. You need to look hard to find bona fide advocates.

What you can find, however, is an alarming growth in other, equally unscientific beliefs, supported by a well-funded industry of pseudo-scientists whose post-hoc rationalisations are invoked as 'evidence' by angry young (and not so young) keyboard warriors. They demand unswerving obedience to their bizarre new orthodoxies. Defiance can be frightening and costly, as the six dedicatees of this novel can testify. Many people, consciously or otherwise, choose the easier path of compliance.

A familiar cry amid these online battles is 'What next? Are they going to tell us the earth is flat?' That's where I came in. I started imagining what resources – and what kind of bullying and/or subterfuge – you'd need in order to make profession of flat-earth beliefs obligatory in great swathes of public and professional life. Whether you find that idea fanciful or terrifyingly believable depends on how much you've been keeping up with those debates.

Most of my fiction contains a historical element. In my novels about Gerard Manley Hopkins, Thomas Gainsborough and St Edmund, the historical material was as accurate as I could make it. That's not the case here. As eventually becomes clear, the early scenes involving Christopher Columbus derive from the colourful imagination of his nineteenth-century US biographer Washington Irving – whose best-known creation is Rip Van Winkle – rather than genuine sources. Mine is a story about distortion to suit a narrative. This phenomenon may have been turbo-charged by social media, but it's as old as the human race.

The scenes where Columbus arrives in the Caribbean tally more closely with known history. To write them, I leaned heavily on biographies by Kirkpatrick Sale and Laurence Bergreen. Hernando de Talavera really did exist, much as described by Trent Meyer. He did write a book *Católica Impugnación*. I've taken a slight liberty with the quote I've pulled out of it – not every word is Hernando's – but I haven't distorted his beliefs, as far as I know.

Most of what I know about the history of flat-earthery comes from Christine Garwood's invaluable *Flat Earth:*

The History of an Infamous Idea. My entire knowledge of two-dimensional map-making, including the orange-peel projection (or the Goode homolosine projection, as it's more formally called), comes from YouTube, an amazing resource if you want to quickly mug up on complex subjects; I owe particular thanks to Chris at Mango Map and Dr Arun K. Saraf of the Indian Institute of Technology (neither of whom know me from Adam, of course).

Incidentally, although I haven't specified the exact date, *The End of the World is Flat* begins in the first half of the 2010s, during the Obama presidency. At that time, Google was still using the Mercator projection for all its maps. Since 2018, they have represented the earth as a globe. Good for them.

Many of my online friends – some using their real names, others an alias – have been part of this process without realising it. Others have actively helped. It's in the nature of the weird and unstable times in which we live that they may not thank me for naming them. The one person I will name is my publisher, colleague and friend Dan Hiscocks, who backed me in this project ever since I told him the idea and warned him it might be controversial. Many in our industry wouldn't have had the courage.

In the first draft of this afterword, I noted that there was one key difference between my story and the enforced imposition of bizarre ideological beliefs in the real world: namely that my version has a neat and happy-ish ending. 'If any part of *The End of the World* is far-fetched,' I wrote, 'it's the ease with which Talavera is persuaded to back down. But all story-telling needs a resolution, so I hope you'll indulge me in that.'

As I complete my final batch of edits, the battles that inspired this novel have taken a remarkable turn, with the real-world equivalent of the Zest Badge scheme apparently disintegrating in the glare of belated media attention. The story may not be over – apart from anything else, there is no Mr Big bankrolling the whole shebang in the real world – but it's beginning to look as if my wrap-up wasn't so far-fetched after all.

As you can imagine, watching these events unfold as I put the final touches to the fictional ones has been a surreal experience. But that's the twenty-first century all over.

Simon Edge
31 May 2021

By the same author

The Hopkins Conundrum

Tim Cleverley inherits a failing pub in Wales, which he plans to rescue by enlisting an American pulp novelist to concoct an entirely fabricated 'mystery' about the poet Gerard Manley Hopkins, who wrote his masterpiece *The Wreck of the Deutschland* nearby.

Blending the real stories of Hopkins and five shipwrecked nuns with a contemporary love story, while casting a wry eye on the *Da Vinci Code* industry, *The Hopkins Conundrum* is a highly original mix of fiction, literary biography and satirical commentary.

A splendid mix of literary detection, historical description and contemporary romance which will appeal equally to fans and detractors of Dan Brown
Michael Arditti

Thoroughly enjoyable hokum. Edge wears his Hopkins learning lightly, avoiding didacticism or handholding... A merry page-turner
The Spectator

A deft fusion of genuinely funny writing and deeply poignant drama
Daily Express

A funny, genre-fusing page-turner
Attitude

A witty satire... By turns gripping and laugh-out-loud funny
Press Association

The Hurtle of Hell

Gay, pleasure-seeking Stefano Cartwright is almost killed by a wave on a holiday beach. His journey up a tunnel of light convinces him that God exists after all, and he may need to change his ways if he is not to end up in hell.

When God happens to look down his celestial telescope and see Stefano, he is obliged to pay unprecedented attention to an obscure planet in a distant galaxy, and ends up on the greatest adventure of his multi-aeon existence.

The Hurtle of Hell combines a tender, human story of rejection and reconnection with an utterly original and often very funny theological thought-experiment. It is an entrancing fable that is both mischievous and big-hearted.

A clever and enchanting fable
The Lady

Simon Edge has given us a creator for our times, hilariously at the mercy of forces beyond even his control
Tony Peake

An interesting and funny theological thought-experiment
Attitude

Edge delivers a warm-hearted narrative of redemption that's never judgemental but is inclusive, funny and undoubtedly heretical. Read it or burn it, depending on your sense of humour
Gscene

Wonderful… frequently hilarious… this thought-provoking exploration of homosexuality, atheism and God with a telescope is a delight
NB magazine

A Right Royal Face-Off

It is 1777, and England's second-greatest portrait artist, Thomas Gainsborough, is locked in rivalry with Sir Joshua Reynolds, the top dog of British portraiture.

Gainsborough loathes pandering to grand sitters, but he changes his tune when he is commissioned to paint King George III and his family. So who will be chosen as court painter, Tom or Sir Joshua?

Two and a half centuries later, a badly damaged painting turns up on a downmarket TV antiques show being filmed in Suffolk. Could the monstrosity really be, as its owner claims, a Gainsborough? If so, who is the sitter? And why does he have donkey's ears?

Mixing ancient and modern as he did in his acclaimed debut *The Hopkins Conundrum*, Simon Edge takes aim at fakery and pretension in this highly original celebration of one of our greatest artists.

One part mystery, one part history, one part satire, and wholly entertaining. A glorious comedy of painting and pretension
Ryan O'Neill

A laugh-out-loud contemporary satire skewering today's tired reality TV formats married with a tale of vicious rivalry
Liz Trenow

I enjoyed this beguiling book very much. Beautifully managed and brilliantly resolved
Hugh Belsey

The more of Simon Edge you read, the more you realise that every element of his stories is hand-selected and glued to the bigger picture – it's whimsical, farce-like…scrapbooky, in the best possible way
Buzz Magazine

Anyone for Edmund?

Under tennis courts in the ruins of a great abbey, archaeologists find the remains of St Edmund, once venerated as England's patron saint, but lost for half a millennium.

Culture Secretary Marina Spencer, adored by those who have never met her, scents an opportunity. She promotes Edmund as a new patron saint for the UK, playing up his Scottish, Welsh and Irish credentials. Unfortunately these are pure fiction, invented by Mark Price, her downtrodden aide, in a moment of panic.

The only person who can see through the deception is Mark's cousin Hannah, a member of the dig team. Will she blow the whistle or help him out? And what of St Edmund himself, watching through the prism of a very different age?

Simon Edge pokes fun at Westminster culture and celebrates the cult of a medieval saint in another beguiling and utterly original comedy.

I loved this smart and divinely wry book. What a terrific eye and ear is at work here!
Elinor Lipman

A sharp-edged political comedy guaranteed to make you laugh out loud
The i Paper

Hilarious and painfully believable
The Lady

A dose of history with flawless comedic timing and pacing
Foreword Reviews

The perfect pick-me-up. Funny and uplifting
Waitrose Weekend

If you have enjoyed *The End of the World is Flat*, do please help us spread the word – by putting a review on Amazon (you don't need to have bought the book there) or Goodreads; by posting something on social media; or in the old-fashioned way by simply telling your friends or family about it.

Book publishing is a very competitive business these days, in a saturated market, and small independent publishers such as ourselves are often crowded out by the big houses. Support from readers like you can make all the difference to a book's success.

Many thanks.
Dan Hiscocks
Publisher
Lightning Books